Also by Joe Corso

Engine 24 Fire Stories series
The Time Traveler Series
The Old Man and the King
The Starlight Club Series
The Revenge of John W
Lone Jack Kid Series
Shootout in Cheyenne
Gunfight in Abilene
The Time Portal
Lafitte's Treasure
The Comeback
Tommy Topper and the Pixie Princess

The Revenge of John W

By Joe Corso

The Revenge of John W

Joe Corso

Published by
Black Horse Publishing
Cover Art by Marina Shipova

Black Horse Publishing
www.blackhorsepublishing.com

Acknowledgements

I would like to thank my cover designer, Marina Shipova; beautiful job, as always!

Thank you also, to Jason Sweeney, for allowing me to use his name for a like-minded and fitting character.

*"How did I escape? With difficulty.
How did I plan this moment? With pleasure."*

Alexandre Dumas, *The Count of Monte Cristo*

TABLE OF CONTENTS

PROLOGUE

Wikieup is a small, unincorporated community on U.S. Route 93 in Mohave County, Arizona. It is located approximately 37 miles south of Interstate 40 and approximately 124 miles northwest of Phoenix, Arizona. In 2000, the population of Wikieup was 305.

When Abigail married her husband, John, she was a beautiful woman, twenty years old, with a shapely figure. She was forty-seven years old now, and she looked sixty. Three days short of her thirtieth birthday, she had her only child. They named him John Wesley Hardin after her husband. Her husband told her - and she believed him, because she wanted to believe him - that the famous gunfighter John Wesley Hardin was a distant relative of theirs. He told her that a cousin on her husband's side was married to Hardin's attorney brother, Joe. At least that was the story that was handed down from father to son and it was what her husband told her - and he was an honest man who never told a lie - so she believed him. She hesitated at first to name her son after the gunfighter because she didn't want the taint of his name and reputation associated with her son, but in her life, she could be proud of very few things. She loved her son and deep down inside her, the one thing she could be proud of with certainty was they were related to a famous man.

When her husband died suddenly of a heart attack, they lost their sixty acres of land because she had no way of keeping up with the mortgage on the property. William Hayes was the man who held their mortgage, and it tortured him to have to evict the mother and son from their home. Hayes was an upstanding Christian man who felt genuinely sorry for her and the boy. He spent sleepless nights thinking of a way for them to keep their home and property, but it was to no avail. Hayes was fifty-seven years old, with thinning hair and the beginning of a paunch. He made the tough decisions in his business, and this one was the toughest decision of all. His sleepless nights continued as he tried to find a solution. But none came. Then, after a night of tossing and turning, he awoke in a sweat with a solution to their problem. It came to him clearly in a dream. He looked through his red-rimmed, sleepless eyes at the alarm clock on his night table: 5:10 a.m. Hayes wanted to call Abigail right now, but he knew he'd have to wait. He made a feeble attempt at falling back to sleep again, but he was too excited. He got up and showered and shaved. After he dressed, he went down to the kitchen, made himself a breakfast of bacon and eggs, and chased them down with hot black coffee. With time to kill, he read his papers. Time passed slowly, but finally, the clock on the kitchen wall signaled 8 a.m. He put aside the newspapers, picked up the phone on the kitchen counter, and called Abigail Hardin. When she picked up, he asked her to come to his office at her earliest convenience.

Mrs. Hardin parked her husband's old Ford F-150 pickup truck by the curb in front of Hayes' office. They entered the store and Mr. Hayes greeted them as if they were royalty. Hayes knew the Hardins were poor but proud people, so he was careful not to embarrass them by reminding them of their misfortune. Mrs. Hardin wore the one decent dress she owned. She wore her pretty blue dress at funerals and weddings, not that they invited her to many weddings these days. Nor was she invited to any in the last twenty years. The last time she wore this dress was last year, at her husband's funeral.

After they sat, Mr. Hayes asked if they'd like coffee, or if, because of the heat, they'd prefer a refreshing cool soft drink. The Hardins politely refused his offer, not wanting to spend any more time in his office than necessary. Hayes could see that they were uncomfortable, so he decided it would be better for all concerned if they got this over with as quickly as possible. Hayes knew he couldn't keep skating around the issue. He had to get to the point, and that's what he did. He was quiet for a moment, trying to build up his nerve. Finally, he nodded to himself and he confessed to Mrs. Hardin that he hated taking their property from them and that it ate away at him just thinking about it. Especially when John Sr. came into his office as proud as a peacock, and with sad eyes, he paid the loan every month with his last dollar. All of his hard work took its toll and one day, John Sr.'s body finally gave out on him and he died with a shovel in his hands. Mrs. Hardin could tell by Mr. Hayes's expression how he felt about her situation. What she didn't know was that Hayes was trying to recall the dream he had, which was now fading from his consciousness, and then work it out. But he had to figure a way to do it for them. He had to do something that would ease their pain and the pressure they were feeling. Hayes knew from his dream that he had the answer, but he couldn't see it clear enough to recall exactly how to make it happen, but he knew he would do something for them. After all, he saw it all in his dream.

Mrs. Hardin gave him a sad, tired look, knowing that he was suffering from having to take their land from them. She also knew that he told her the truth when he said he was trying to work something out, but for the life of her, she couldn't figure out what he could do for her and her son.

Hayes stroked his chin, lost in thought for a moment, trying to recall his dream. Then it came to him, and he punched his right fist into the palm of his left hand. It was clear now. It had solidified, and he marveled at its simplicity. The solution was obvious. It had been staring him in the face all the while, and he wondered why he hadn't thought of it before. He shook his head, feeling stupid for not thinking of it sooner.

"Look," he said. "You lost your property. We get that. But what I neglected to take into consideration was you had equity in that property."

This revelation surprised her because most men would just gloss over that fact, reclaim the property, and then sell it again. Profit was profit - and wasn't that was what business was all about? She lost her property legitimately, and now it was his to sell again. However, William Hayes was not that type of man. He could never do that to someone. He waited for her to absorb what he just told her.

She understood what he said, but she looked questioningly at him. "We're not looking for charity, Mr. Hayes." She took a deep breath. "It is impossible with one income to keep up with the notes. I have no recourse but to give the property back to you. My son and I will just have to figure out a way to get by. But make no mistake about it, Mr. Hayes, we will get by."

She had grit, and he looked at her with admiration. Then he looked at her young son sitting there. He noticed for the first time that the boy had tears in his eyes. He had been concentrating solely on Mrs. Hardin, and he hadn't realized until now how hard this was on the boy. Hayes looked at the boy and when the boy turned his face from him to wipe a tear from his eye, Hayes felt terrible for the embarrassed, hurting boy. The Hardins were sitting in front of him like two beggars, wondering where their next meal was coming from and pretending they knew.

"Look, I just thought of something," Hayes said. "So please be patient for a moment while I search my files for something." He opened the top drawer of his filing cabinet and began searching through his files. Nothing. He opened the second drawer and searched rapidly through those folders until he exclaimed happily, "Aha! Here it is. Here's what I was looking for!" He opened the file, took a sheet from it, and waved it in front of them. "This paper might just be the answer to your problems!" he said excitedly.

Mrs. Hardin's eyes lit up. "What is that paper you're holding in your hand, Mr. Hayes? And what do you mean, it might be the answer to our problems?"

"It's simple," he said. "I'm going to use the remaining equity in your sixty-acre property and swap you out for a piece of land that, to be honest with you, is not worth much, and it will never be worth anything. But it's forty acres of desert land and the good part is, it has a small miner's shack on it where you can live. It will give you a roof over your head, and with no mortgage to worry about. You will own the property free with no mortgage. Let me find the deed to this property and draw up the papers for you to sign." The mother and son looked at each other hopefully, praying that Mr. Hayes might have thought of a way to help them after all.

Hayes spent the next fifteen minutes typing out an agreement. When it he completed it, she signed it and handed it back to him. He checked her signature to make sure she signed in the right places. Satisfied, he smiled. "There's no running water or electricity in the house, but there is a well. There's no bathroom, but again, there's an outhouse. The beautiful part is this property is now yours, clear with no mortgage. You don't have to worry about another monthly mortgage payment. It's not the prime sixty acres of land like you lost, but this land is desert property at the foot of a mountain. Your property is quite a way off the beaten path with only a dirt road to get you there. But I can't stress it enough: it's all yours." He looked up at them with sad, sympathetic, red eyes. "I want you to know that I never meant for this to happen to you folks. On Christmas Eve, I threw you out of your home. I know how hard you, your husband, and your son worked to eke out a small living on that land and how hard it was for you to come up with the mortgage payment each month." He hung his head down and said softly, "The last thing I wanted to do was to throw you off of your land. It was the hardest chore I've ever had to do, and it made me real sad doing it, Mrs. Hardin. I hope you can find it in your heart to forgive me."

Mrs. Hardin saw the same pain and sadness in his eyes that she saw before. "Don't fret, Mr. Hayes. You did us a right kindness, one that John and I will never forget. I know we aren't in any position to return your kindness right now, but maybe someday we'll be able to help you. If that time ever comes, we will be there for you and you have my word on that." She turned and looked at her son. "Now, John, you remember Mr. Hayes's kindness to us and what he did for us today. Never forget it, John. And when you grow older, if Mr. Hayes is ever in trouble and he needs you for anything, I would be obliged if you honored my wishes and helped him with whatever difficulty he may be in. You hear me, boy?"

It surprised John at the depth of his mother's conviction, but he knew how proud she was. "Yes, momma, I understand."

"Understanding isn't enough, son. Promise me you will honor my promise to Mr. Hayes."

"Now, now, Mrs. Hardin. There's no need to put that burden on the boy."

"No, you don't understand, Mr. Hayes. You saved us. You gave us hope when there was no hope, and we Hardins never forget a kindness when it's given to us. Since there are no men folk left but John here, he has to be the man in the family and keep his promise."

She waited expectantly, with a tinge of impatience for her son to acknowledge her request. Finally, to her relief, he said, "Yes, Momma, I promise." He turned to Mr. Hayes and put out his hand. "Mr. Hayes. From this moment on, we are in your debt. I want you to know that I will be there to help you in your time of need, if it is in my power to do so." That was a lot of words for a young man to say, and it impressed Mr. Hayes.

The meeting ended and Abigail Harden took Mr. Hayes's hand in hers and shook it, and then she impulsively kissed him on the cheek. Embarrassed by her unintended act, she demurely bowed her head and whispered, "Thank you for your kindness, Mr. Hayes, and may the good lord look over you and yours for all the days to come."

Abigail and her son, John, opened the door and were about to leave when Mr. Hayes called out to them, "Hold on a minute, folks. Don't leave yet. I have something I want to ask you. Do you have any way to make a living? Do you have any kind of income? Can you support the property? I know it's yours and you paid for it, but you still have to eat and dress yourselves. Can you do that?"

Mrs. Hardin thought for a moment before answering. "Well, we have a milking cow and some chickens. We have some seed and John's old Ford pickup. We'll make do somehow."

Mr. Hayes shook his head. "That's not good enough, Mrs. Hardin. You can't survive on one milking cow and some chickens." Hayes walked over to John and looked him over without saying a word to him. Finally, he walked back to his desk, sat down, and asked them to close the door and take a seat. "I told you I have something I want to ask you."

Abigail couldn't imagine what he wanted to ask her now that they concluded their business, but she came back in and dutifully took a seat.

"My business is growing, Mrs. Hardin, and I was thinking of hiring someone to help me. I keep putting off hiring a man, but now that you're here, I was wondering if maybe John would like to come and work for me. He knows the desert like the back of his hand. He's personable, and I think he would make a good sales associate if he put his mind to it. What do you say, John? Would you like to work here in this office with me?"

John looked to his mother for support, but her face showed nothing. No reaction, no emotion, and no support.

"It's up to you, son," she finally said. "Mr. Hayes is giving you the opportunity that I could never give you. But it's up to you. You must decide if you want to work here, or work on our property."

John scratched his head, and then unconsciously he rubbed his chin while thinking of Hayes's offer. Then he smiled for the first time that day. "Sure, Mr. Hayes. I think it would be swell working here with you. But only if you think it can work out well for you. If I don't do good, if you tell me I'm not cutting the mustard, and you have to let me go, you won't be hurting my feeling's at all."

Mr. Hayes smiled. He liked this boy. He was sincere and he could tell that he didn't have a nasty bone in his body. "Tell you what. You come in tomorrow morning at nine and we'll start you off by having you answer the phone. Then when you're comfortable working here, I'll have you show some properties and we'll ease you into the sales end of the business. I think you'll enjoy working here. All you have to remember is to be yourself. If you can sell yourself to a customer, then you'll sell them the property they want. If they get the idea that you're trying to put something over on them, then we'll not only lose the sale, we'll also lose a customer. I make it a point to be upfront and honest with all of my customers. That's why my business is growing. People know when you're trying to fool them. But they also can tell when you're being honest with them. As long as you are honest and tell the truth, we'll get along just fine."

"Now come over here and look at the map of the county." He pointed to a spot on the map and circled it in red. "Here is your property." He pointed to the door. "You go right when you leave this office. Drive down along Rt. 93 until you get to the Wikieup Post Office. The trading post is near the motel. You make a left on Huenga Drive and follow the dirt road for about ten miles. You'll take that road toward the mountains until you come to a fork in the road. Make a right turn at the fork and keep on that road until you come to an old abandoned mine. That mine is part of your property. Continue past the mine for one quarter of a mile. Look for a tree split by lightning; it'll be on your right. Beside the tree is a 'for sale' sign alongside a dirt road. Make a right, and take the dirt road for about a half-mile, until you come to the mine workman's shack.

"The shack is in pretty good shape, and you're lucky, because when I inspected the place, I checked the roof and it doesn't leak. The inside was dry, which was always a good sign. Here's the key to the front door. After you make money, you can convert that shack into a right decent house. It'll take a lot of weekends of hard work, but it can be done. If you decide to go all out, you could even bring water from the well into the house and put in a proper bathroom. The outhouse is in decent shape, but it could use a new door. You can use it until you build a cesspool and install modern plumbing in the house. Questions? No? Okay, John, I'll see you in the morning." He smiled, feeling better now than he had for quite a while.

He took Mrs. Hardin by the hand and said, "Mrs. Hardin, I wish you all the luck in the world with your new home, such as it is. If you need anything, anything at all, you just call me and if I can help you, I will. You can't imagine how glad I am that it worked out like it did. After seeing you lose your home and property, I was concerned that I would be at a loss to help you."

Mrs. Hardin looked up at him with fire in her eyes, and steel in her bones, and she meant with all of her heart every word she said to him. "Don't you worry none about us, Mr. Hayes. I had the same depressing concerns you did when I first walked into this office. But now that you gave us the property, and a roof over our heads, and you gave John a job, we have a new lease on life. And it's all due to you. God bless you, Mr. Hayes."

CHAPTER ONE

John W. Hardin Jr. never worked at any other job, except for using his strong back to help his father toil their land. These thoughts were on his mind as he walked tentatively into the Hayes Real Estate Office at 9 a.m. sharp, wearing his father's cowboy hat, which his mother gave him when his father passed away. John hoped he would like this job, because now that his father was no longer here, he hated the thought of working like a mule again. But if this job didn't work out, he'd have to go back to toil the land, because that was all he knew. He was a bright lad, but he had no schooling, so what else could he do but toil the land if he and his mother were to survive? But that was yesterday. Today he was going to a different type of job, and if he was diligent and tried hard, he just might have a future. So, he wore his father's shirt and bolo tie under his clean dark brown leather vest, which he loved and was the better of the two that he owned. When he put the shirt on, he pictured his father wearing it at Sunday church services.

Mr. Hayes knew John had to be nervous, so when he arrived at work, Hayes shook John's hand. To make him feel comfortable, he said, "Welcome to your new job, John." Hayes flashed John W a sincere smile. "You're on time and I like that. I take notice of things like that." Hayes studied John for a moment, and then said to him, "Before you start your new job, do you know Harvey's Men's Store on Main Street?"

"Yes, sir. I passed it on my way here. Why?"

"Before you get started work, I want you to go to Harvey's and buy yourself a nice sport jacket that's suitable for office work. You need something to wear over your shirt other than that nice vest you're wearing. Then get yourself two other shirts and a good pair of comfortable walking shoes. Oh, and get three pairs of socks to wear with your new shoes."

John was crestfallen. He looked down at his boots, then at

Mr. Hayes. He said, in a soft voice, "I don't have any money to buy clothes with, Mr. Hayes."

"I know that, boy. Here, take my business card and hand it to Harvey. Tell him to call me after you buy your clothes and don't worry about paying for them. I'll take care of it. Consider it a 'starting bonus.'"

An hour later, John returned to the real estate office, beaming and looking real spiffy.

"Now that's more like it," Mr. Hayes said, grinning. "It's not that you didn't look nice before, John, because you surely did. It's just that it wasn't the right look for our office. A jacket signifies professionalism. When you're showing properties way out in the desert and it's real hot, of course, you can take off your jacket and show the property in your shirt. Remember, first impressions are the most important ones, and to someone coming into this office and seeing two men wearing nice jackets and nice shirts - well, it puts them at ease. They know that they've come to a reputable place. It's 'thought transference,' John. They associate the package - us - with the product - with the property they are looking to buy. It's like buying cereal. If the box is really attractive, they assume the product will be the same, when in fact it may be terribly inferior. It's perception, John. If the customer perceives us favorably, then they'll perceive our business in the same light.

"Consider this. Let's assume that we have the exact property the customer is looking for, but we dress slovenly. That will give the customer the wrong impression of our business and us. It wouldn't sit right with the customer and it wouldn't be fair to us because we *are* offering the customer a superior product. That's why at work we have to dress professionally. We must give a good impression at all times. Understand?"

John thought about what Mr. Hayes had just told him. When he put himself in his customer's shoes, it made complete sense to him. "Yes, sir. I understand. And thank you for the swell jacket and clothes. I never had clothes as nice as these."

That pleased Hayes. He noticed the cut of the jacket. It fit his new employee nicely. "It's a good choice, and it gives you a professional appearance, John. The western cut gives you a cowboy look that fits in with the western land that we're offering our customers." Mr. Hayes pointed to one of the three empty desks in his office. "John, I think the desk would be perfect for you because it faces the door, and it's closest to my desk. But you're free to choose any of the three desks you think you'd feel comfortable in."

"No, Mr. Hayes, I'll use this desk. It's perfect."

John was a natural salesperson, but didn't realize it. Within six months, the real estate sales at Hayes's office doubled, and a year and a half later, sales doubled again. The additional business caused expansion, so Mr. Hayes contacted the owners of the strip mall and told them he wanted to rent the empty store next to his office, but with a small modification. The proviso was they remove the wall between the two stores to allow Mr. Hayes to expand his office space to accommodate the sales people he needed in order to handle the business John W. Hardin was bringing in.

The owners of the stores in the strip mall where Hayes had his office, as well as some other businesses in the town, used Jake, a local maintenance worker. The moment Hayes signed the lease for the new store, Jake removed the wall separating the two stores, doubling the office space. Within two weeks, they completed the renovation and the Hayes Real Estate Company had a new grander, more professional look. They replaced the small faded store sign with a larger hand-painted sign that lit up at night. Jake constructed a stone fascia that made the store look like an adobe building, which fit in with the Wikieup area western look. Hayes's real estate business had grown, and it was no longer a small hometown enterprise. His new office kept pace with the growing needs of people looking to migrate from the frigid winds and heavy snows of the northern states and move to the warmth of the Arizona sun. The Hayes Real Estate Company was prepared to meet their needs. Hayes had expanded with three offices spread out strategically in prime areas of Mohave County.

John W supervised the sales team at the two branch offices. When they became stand-alone offices, Hayes and John investigated, expanding into other counties. They performed a market survey that showed where the growing migratory trends in the real estate market would likely be. Their research showed Flagstaff in the Coconino County area was where they projected serious growth to occur. Since Flagstaff was the targeted growth area, Hayes opened a branch office there before his competitors got wind of what he was doing. Now that he had a working office set up in Coconino County, he needed a man to supervise that office. So he advertised for a man with the right qualifications in the local Flagstaff papers.

During the two years John worked for Hayes, he had become a substitute for the son Hayes never had. Conversely, John found in Hayes the father he lost when his dad passed away. The years changed John. He was no longer the insecure seventeen-year-old boy who walked into the Hayes Real Estate office with his mother two years ago. He had grown into a tall, dark-haired, handsome, muscular young man who for two years had been a steady visitor to the Hayes household, and had fallen in love with Hayes's daughter Victoria - and she with him.

Victoria - and she with him.

CHAPTER TWO

McCormack Mining Company Headquarters in Phoenix

"Are you sure about this?"

"Yes, sir," Josh Peterson said. "After we purchased the 'Good Hope' mine, we did as you requested. We kept the mines still producing gold and silver and we sold all the mines that were draining our resources. Some mines we sold still had gold or silver in them, but it cost too much to get the ore out, so those mines were closed and the property sold. But now, with the price of gold and silver skyrocketing, it would be profitable to re-open some of those old mines."

McCormack interrupted. "What are you doing about getting those old mines back, Peterson?"

"Well, we've contacted everyone whose properties would, at present, be profitable and they've all agreed to sell their property back to us except one - the most important one. It belongs to a Mrs. Abigail Hardin. She gained the property two years ago from a Mr. William Hayes, and she and her son have been living in the mining shack on the property since they took possession of the property. We contacted her and told her we were interested in buying her property for more than she paid for it."

"And?" McCormack asked.

"She said she was happy living there, and she wasn't interested in selling."

McCormack sat there, scratching his chin. "And she does not know what she's sitting on?"

"No, sir. She does not know that the played out old mine on her property is hiding the mother lode the original miners searched for, but never found."

McCormack shook his head. "This makes little sense to me. The mine is played out. I'm holding the report in my hand. What makes you think there's still gold in that old mine?"

Peterson had expected that question. He reached over and picked up a large poster-sized board leaning against the side of his chair. It showed a pencil sketch of a mountain on it. "Look here, sir," he said, pointing to a spot on the side of the mountain. "This is where the Lucky Ben mine is located." He took his fountain pen and pointed to Hardin's mine. "It's opposite of our mine. Our geologists have performed an analysis on the Lucky Ben mine and according to their analysis, they're certain that a huge vein of gold - the 'mother lode,' if you will - still exists in the old mine on Hardin's property. The original owners of the mine took enough trace gold out of that old mine to make them rich. Our thinking is that if they would have continued digging into the mountain another twenty or thirty feet, they would have struck gold worth billions today."

"You're sure about this?"

"Yes, sir. I have the reports confirming it here in this file. I'll leave the file in the folder for you to read."

Being the shrewd, calculating man that he was, McCormack asked Peterson, "Why not continue digging further into the mountain from our mine? Wouldn't we meet up with the Hardin's mine if we did that?"

Peterson shook his head. "Do you have any idea how large that mountain is? That would take years and cost you a fortune to get to the gold in the Hardin mine. It's more cost efficient to buy the Hardin property and dig 20 or 30 feet to get to the gold than spend a fortune trying to get to it from the other side of the mountain. It's all here in my report," he said, placing the folder on McCormack's desk.

"Good, Peterson. That will be all for now. Good job."

After Peterson left the room, McCormack turned to the other man in the room. The man sat in the corner and listened with interest to everything that they said, but never uttered a word. Rutgar Kleinst was a German mercenary who McCormack hired when he first took control of the mining conglomerate. Kleinst took care of some very troublesome people problems for him. Rutgar was very effective in eliminating those problems. Through the years, Rutgar had become useful to McCormack. He recognized a golden calf when he saw one and he made it his business to become indispensable to McCormack. Soon, he got what he wanted, and he became Jack McCormack's right-hand man, the man in whom McCormack confided, and on whom he depended to take care of his troublesome problems.

Rutgar sat and listened, and he hadn't said a word during the entire dialogue that took place between the two men. He was a quiet man who followed a workout regimen to keep himself in top condition. At five feet eleven inches, he wasn't a tall man, but he was all muscle with a blonde military buzz cut, set atop a square face that never smiled. He appeared out of place in McCormack's corporate world. But he listened to every word exchanged between the two men.

"So, Rutgar," McCormack asked. "Give me your thoughts on this bit of unfinished business?"

Rutgar, who spoke perfect English with a slight but still noticeable German accent, smiled, flashing a perfect set of white teeth. "I'll need a few days to assess the situation, and I'll give you my opinion on Monday."

"Good. Do that. But, Rutgar, don't take too long. I want this last piece of property and I'm an impatient man."

McCormack's threats never bothered the dangerous Kleinst. In fact, it was McCormack who should have been worried, not Kleinst. Rutgar loved physical confrontations. It gave him the opportunity to prove his proficiency with his fists and feet. But he understood McCormack and besides, McCormack paid him handsomely. So, he let it pass and smiled.

More to placate McCormack than anything else, Rutgar said, "Don't worry, Jack, this won't take long. I'll get right on it." By the end of the week, Kleinst had enough information to formulate the plan he'd present to McCormack at their scheduled meeting on Monday morning.

"With that smug look on your face, Rutgar, I assume you found a solution to the Hardin mine problem."

The older man, who assessed him with his dead eyes, did not intimidate Rutgar, as he sat behind his desk, waiting to hear his report. McCormack reminded Rutgar of a little boy waiting for a treat that his mother had promised him. Only McCormack wasn't anyone's mother. He was a ruthless tyrant who would destroy anyone who got in his way. McCormack stood six feet two inches tall. He was fifty-five years of age, with thinning black hair that was showing signs of grey. In a few short years, his thinning hair would lead to male pattern baldness, which at present he tried to hide by combing his hair to the side. As a young man, McCormack had a powerful physique. Over the years, good living and an overindulgence in food and drink turned his body to fat. His face had gained a W. C. Fields Drinker's nose. His blotchy complexion gave people the impression of standing before Nero or Caligula, the Emperors of Excess.

"Yes! I did my research, and I have the answer to your problem. The woman's son has been working for the Hayes Real Estate Company for the past two years. In fact, he built the company single-handedly into what it is today. They have three offices in Mohave County and they're planning to open an office in Flagstaff, in Coconino County."

"So what does his expansion have to do with my gaining his property?" McCormack barked.

"Relax a minute, Jack. I'll get to that in a moment." That mollified McCormack and he sat back in his large comfortable plush leather desk chair, waiting for Rutgar to finish explaining his plan to him. "Hayes is looking for someone to run the Flagstaff office and I have a man, Tom Jenkins, who I worked with a few years ago. He's a smooth talking con man from Amarillo and he's between gigs right now. I contacted him and explained what I want him to do and he's agreed to work with us. He's already applied for the Office Manager's position. Once he's hired, he'll run that office. Then I'll see to it he becomes the go-to guy for Old Man Hayes."

"What about the kid who's working there now?" McCormack asked.

"That's the best part. We'll kill two birds with one stone."

McCormack reached for a cigar. He always did that when he was nervous or excited, and it excited him at the prospect of owning another lucrative gold mine. "I don't understand what you're getting at. Maybe I'm a little dense, but I don't get it. I'm a simple man, Rutgar, so explain it to me, but a little slower this time."

McCormack was far from being the simple man he liked

people to think he was. In fact, he was quite the opposite.

"It's quite simple, boss. Are you still friendly with the Governor?"

"Of course I am. Who do you think put him in the Governor's seat?"

Rutgar rubbed his hands. "Good, because I intend to frame the kid. Once that's done, we'll sabotage the old man's business and then we'll take it over. Once the kid is out of the way, it'll be a simple matter to take the land away from the old lady. The best part is, I'll make it look as if we're doing her a favor by taking it from her. We'll put our man Jenkins in the Flagstaff office as the first step in our getting the mine. That'll be the first thing we do."

McCormack nodded. He liked the direction this conversation was heading in. "You said we'd kill two birds with one stone. What's the second bird?"

"We take over the real estate company. Hayes has the largest real estate company in Mohave County and now he's expanding into Coconino County. He must bring in millions of dollars a year. Of course, if you don't want to bother with his real estate business, we can forget about that part, and just go after the boy and his mother."

"No. No. I like the real estate business. I never thought of owning one. I think it's a great idea… Go ahead. Keep talking." McCormack's fertile mind was firing on all eight cylinders now. By taking over Hayes Real Estate Company, he could bypass paying real estate commissions because he'd own the properties. And he could then negotiate the price of the property with any mine his company discovered or represented, because he'd control the real estate company that was offering it to the buyer. "I like it. It's brilliant. But how do you intend to get rid of the kid? I prefer we don't harm him if we can help it."

"Don't worry. Nothing like that is going to happen. That's why I asked you if you still have the Governor in your pocket. I'll tip the police that there are drugs stashed in his car and in his home, or better yet, in the old mine. Once they discover the drugs and he's arrested, the papers will eat it up. They love when they catch a drug kingpin and put him behind bars. I'll make sure we convince everyone the boy is dealing drugs big time, and I'll let them know his specialty is selling drugs to kids. Once the kid's put away, the old lady won't be able to hold on to the property without her son's income. And if we take over Hayes's business, then he won't be able to help her either. She'll have no choice but to sell to us."

McCormack nodded as he took a puff on his cigar and then let the smoke out. "How much do you think we can get her property for when this is all said and done?"

"Look - we can get it for nothing, but I think it's a good idea if you acted the part of the benevolent buyer who was saddened by the old lady's misfortune, and you've decided that someone should help the poor woman. I know a place high in the Grand Canyon Subdivision, between Flagstaff and the Grand Canyon, where she'll live in the mobile home you're going to buy her, and she'll be far enough away from here that she'll trouble no one. I'll see that the papers make a big deal out of your generosity. The home will cost you nothing, and to sweeten the deal, I suggest you give her a cash settlement as well. Think of how that will look in the papers - and what you'll spend on her will be nothing compared to the gold you'll take out of her old mine. When the story breaks in the papers of how you helped an old widowed woman… in the eyes of the rest of the country, you'll be a hero."

McCormack brushed ashes from his cigar into the ashtray. "I like it. It's perfect and you're right. We will kill two birds with one stone. Get right on it. Hire that friend of yours and make sure he gets the job. I don't know how you're going to do it, but make sure it gets done just the way you explained it to me."

CHAPTER THREE

John was showing a property in a recent development in Mohave County. The property abutted Yavapai County in the little triangular part that's between the three adjacent counties. It was so close to the three counties, you could put your foot on both Coconino and Yavapai Counties and still be in Mohave County. At the same time that John W. was showing the customer the property, Mr. Hayes had just finished interviewing all but the applicant for the Flagstaff manager's position. His last applicant, Ronald Johnson, presented Hayes with a letter of recommendation from a Mr. Wicks, his last employer and the owner of a large real estate office in Albuquerque, New Mexico. Johnson had managed that office and he just moved to Flagstaff. He was looking for work, in another real estate office. Johnson was Hayes's choice for the position except for one other applicant, which he still had to interview. He told Johnson that he would be in touch.

"Hi. My name is Tom Jenkins and I'm applying for the manager's job. I'm experienced in running a large office. Did it in Pennsylvania and New Orleans and if you give me a chance, I'll build this office into the largest office in the Flagstaff area?" The way Jenkins was spewing out words, Hayes didn't get a word in. "Tell you what," Jenkins said. "I want this job so bad don't pay me a dime. I'll work on commission only. If I do well, then you can pay me what you feel I'm worth. If you're not satisfied, then I'll leave. Now, what do you have to lose?"

Hayes looked at Jenkins differently and studied him a little closer. He wore a fine suit, plenty expensive; you could tell that right off. He wore an expensive Rolex and had on nice Italian shoes, polished to a spit shine. He had plenty of personality, that was for sure, and he was very confident in his ability to do the job. This was something Hayes hadn't counted on. The last man he interviewed, he all but hired, and now he was having second thoughts. This man seemed perfect for the job, but so did the other man. Hayes compared the two men for a moment, and not paying Jenkins a salary made him decide to hire him over the other applicant. He gave Jenkins the job and if the other applicant were still available when he opened his next office, he'd offer him the manager's position.

Hayes looked at Jenkins and said, "I like your background, Mr. Jenkins, but I can't hire you until my manager interviews you."

Jenkins's temper flared briefly, but he brought it quickly under control. He faced Hayes with a questioning look on his face. "I thought you were the one who made the hiring and firing decisions, Mr. Hayes, and not your manager."

Hayes didn't like anyone questioning his hiring practices, and the question took him by surprise. "That's the way it is, Mr. Jenkins. If you find it hard to accept, then I suggest you look elsewhere for a job."

Jenkins realized his mistake and babbled to Hayes in a conciliatory manner. "I'm sorry for questioning you, Mr. Hayes. It's just that I know I can do the job for you. All day, I was the best qualified man you interviewed. I just know I am. I wanted the job so badly that I got a little out of line, and I apologize for it."

His apology calmed Hayes down. "There's no need for you to feel bad, Mr. Jenkins. I know how it is to want a job and maybe not get it. Just wait until my manager gets here. It's just a formality, a part of our hiring policy. Come back tomorrow morning after 10:00 a.m., and we'll have that final interview. Then we'll talk about filling the position. Okay?"

Tom Jenkins rose from his chair and smiled. It was a con man's smile, meant to disarm a potential mark, and that was exactly what Mr. William Hayes was to him; just another mark. "Sure. It sounds great. I look forward to tomorrow morning's interview with your manager. Until then, I bid you a good day, Mr. Hayes."

"Good day to you too, Mr. Jenkins."

The following morning, Tom Jenkins sauntered into the office for his 10 a.m. interview, wearing a different suit, but the same spit-shined shoes he wore yesterday.

John W sized up the overdressed man immediately, and he didn't like what he saw. But, out of courtesy to Mr. Hayes, he continued with the interview. "I see you waived the salary we will pay you and instead agreed to work on commission, Mr. Jenkins. Why is that, I wonder?"

Jenkins just smiled that confident con man smile of his and said, "I have confidence in myself, John." He purposely used John's first name instead of his last. "Give me a chance to manage that office and I'll bring in sales like you've never seen before. I'm not bragging; I'm speaking from experience."

The interview wrapped up at 10:40 a.m. and Jenkins stood. "When can I expect your call to let me know when I can start work?"

"Easy there, Mr. Jenkins. No one said you had the job yet. We'll call you if we're interested."

Jenkins smiled, showing a set of perfect white teeth that must have cost a fortune, and gave John his hand to shake. "I hope I see you soon, partner. Take care now."

When the door closed behind him, John turned as Hayes, who had been listening to the interview, stepped out of his office to get John's opinion of Jenkins.

"What did you think of him?" he asked.

"I thought he was over the top. He's an overdressed con man and he wouldn't be good for your company, Mr. Hayes."

This wasn't what Hayes was expecting to hear from his young manager. "It couldn't be that you're intimidated by him, John. Or maybe a little jealous of him?"

John shook his head, disappointed that Hayes would think such a thing. John's only interest was in seeing Mr. Hayes's business grow, and jealousy didn't enter the picture. "Be careful, Mr. Hayes. That one is trouble with a capital T."

Hayes thought a while, and then he said, "John, I always respected your opinion, but this time I have to disagree with your assessment of the man. I'm going to hire him on a trial basis. If he proves to be the man I think he is, then we'll keep him. If you are right, then I'll fire him." The old man came over to John and put his arm around his shoulders. "Look, John. I respect your opinion more than any man I've ever known. But my goal is to have the largest real estate business in the state. I never wanted that before, but since you started working for me, I know now that *I* can do it. No, let me re-phrase that. I know *we* can do it. I can see that you love my daughter, and I know she feels the same about you. Before I leave this Earth, I want to leave the two of you something valuable, and this business is the only thing of value I own - and someday it will be yours and Virginia's, John. But, we can't do it by ourselves. We need men like Jenkins. I intend to hire him as manager for the Flagstaff office and I'll hire Mr. Johnson for the next office we open after Flagstaff."

John was clearly disappointed. He had a gut feeling that Jenkins would bring trouble with him. He just nodded while looking at the floor. "You know I'll never go against your wishes, Mr. Hayes. If you want, Tom Jenkins for the Flagstaff office, then I won't object. But, I want it understood that I don't trust that man and I don't like him. Just so you know where I'm coming from, Mr. Hayes."

Hayes nodded his head in agreement. "I hope you're wrong about him, John, but if you're not, then it's on the record and I won't hold it against you if you prove me wrong."

"Thank you for that, Mr. Hayes."

CHAPTER FOUR

Mr. Hayes hired Tom Jenkins, and he immediately started hiring a staff that was loyal to him. He wasn't worried about being paid a salary by Mr. Hayes. He was getting a substantial weekly stipend from the McCormack conglomerate. In effect, he was building the Flagstaff office for them, rather than for the Hayes Real Estate Company, Inc. Six months later, Mr. Hayes opened another office, this time in La Paz County, which is south of and borders on Mohave County.

What neither John W. Hardin nor Mr. William Hayes could know was that shortly after the world as they knew it was about to come crashing down on them. McCormack was about to unleash Kleinst on them. They would show no mercy to them. John W. Hardin would go to prison forever, and everyone would forget him, except for his mother. Mr. Hayes would have everything he held dear to him stripped away in one fell swoop. It would be like shooting ducks in a barrel to McCormack. He would gain possession of the mine and he would have Jenkins run the real estate business he was about to steal from Hayes. It was delicious. Nothing could stop them, and nothing could go wrong with their plan. It was foolproof.

John woke to a loud knocking at the front door of his home. He looked at his alarm clock. 2:30 a.m. He thought, *who the heck could bang on my door at this hour of the morning?* "Okay, okay. Hold your horses. I'm coming." He opened the door to see a dozen men in uniform with guns pointed at him. "Wha'... What's this all about?"

"Shut up and turn around."

Just then, his mother came to the door in her bathrobe. She turned to the cop, who was placing cuffs on her son. "What's this about, young man?"

"Go inside, ma'am. This is official police business."

Mrs. Hardin wouldn't budge. "You still haven't told me

what this is about, officer."

Clearly annoyed at the old lady standing before him in her bathrobe, questioning him, he simply said, "Drugs. That's what this is about."

"But that's impossible," she said.

The cop laughed. "Tim, bring over one of those bales."

The police officer dutifully did as he was told and brought a large bale with a rope wrapped around it. He laid it down on the ground in front of Mrs. Abigail Hardin. "This is just one bale of hashish. We found another 5 bales of the stuff, along with three large bales of pot and another 4 large cartons of crack cocaine envelopes ready for distribution. It looks like we've busted a major drug laundering operation and your son is the kingpin."

"What?" John W said, before being dragged to a police cruiser and shoved roughly in the back seat. The police didn't condone anyone selling drugs to children. "Mom, call Mr. Hayes and tell him what happened. This has to be a big mistake."

The steel in Abigail resurfaced. "Where did you find these things, officer?" she said, pointing to the bale the police had dragged in front of her.

"We received a tip this morning and when we checked it out, we found it was true. We found drugs in that old mine back there. It looks like that's where your son kept it. Good plan, if I say so myself. Who'd ever look in an old abandoned mine for drugs?"

"But my son had nothing to do with any of that. He's a hard-working boy. You can ask Mr. Hayes. He'll tell you. He'll vouch for my son."

The cop had no thoughts either way. He was there to do a job, and he was doing it. Now it was up to the courts to decide if her son was innocent or guilty.

As the police car pulled away, John was truly frightened. John always tried to be a good boy. He always tried to do the right thing for everyone. He was honest with his customers and with Mr. Hayes, his employer. John wondered what would happen to Virginia if he were to go to jail. Would she wait for him? Wait a minute. What was he thinking? How could he go to jail? He did nothing wrong and the court system would prove his innocence. He believed in the American system of justice, because it was fair, and it would prove him innocent of these ridiculous charges. Mr. Hayes would find him an excellent lawyer and he would prove that he had nothing to do with drugs. During the drive to the police station, he thought. Could anyone be behind this? If that were true, then who could it be? The Hardins had nothing of value. Except, of course, his property. But Mr. Hayes told them it was worthless and would always be worthless. So, this had to be a mistake because he had nothing anyone would want bad enough for them to frame him and have him arrested.

CHAPTER FIVE

The trial over the arrest of the drug-dealing kingpin made headlines around the country. Mr. Hayes hired the best lawyer in the state, but the evidence against John was overwhelming. There was nothing Hayes or any other lawyer could do to help John. All the evidence was circumstantial, but the District Attorney himself tried the case. Even the government got involved when they attempted to find out if they transported drugs across state lines. Evidence showed that it was, in fact, what happened. Poor John didn't stand a chance. When the trial ended, they sentenced John to fifty years in jail at hard labor in the Arizona State Prison system. What little money John had saved he spent on his trial. Mr. Hayes sold two of his offices to help defray the cost of the trial, but it was to no avail.

John W knew from the hostile environment in that cold courtroom and the malevolent stares he was getting from the jurors that he didn't stand a chance. The evidence supplied by an unidentified source to the prosecution was overwhelming and John W himself had to admire whoever framed him. The disdainful looks he was getting from both jurors and spectators alike told him that the verdict was a foregone conclusion. He was right. The prosecutor brought the trial to a speedy conclusion, and it didn't take long for the jurors to reach a guilty verdict. Once they announced the verdict, he could tell by the jurors' body language that they couldn't wait to leave the courtroom. The good citizens of Mohave County didn't tolerate drug dealers - especially one as high on the totem pole as John W. Hardin was. He supplied drugs to their children, and that was a fact. All the evidence presented at the trial was true, because the newspapers and television news reporters said it was true. Who in that courtroom would ever doubt the veracity of the media? The boy took a quick glance at his mother, who had always been his security. When their eyes met, it was as if a current had passed between them and their eyes locked in silent communication. He knew her pain and frustration were from her inability to help him when he needed her most. She looked at him, envisioning him frittering his youth away in a prison, and that caused her more pain. Her suffering saddened him even more than his arrest - and he held back tears that were on the verge of pouring from him like an open faucet. He dared not look at her as he hung his head in shame determined, not to cry in front of her. He would not to show any emotion for his mother's sake. When the jury pronounced him guilty, as he was sure they would, the tears could come later.

The judge scanned a section of law pertaining to sentencing guidelines as the jury returned to the courtroom and took their seats. He kept his book open but put it aside. "Ladies and gentlemen of the jury, have you reached a verdict?"

The jury foreman stood. "We have, Your Honor. We find the defendant guilty of all charges."

The judge nodded in agreement. He expected nothing less. The judge rested his hand on the open journal and looked around the crowded courtroom. He off took his glasses and cleared his throat. Without realizing it, he tapped his glasses on his desk as he spoke. All eyes were on him as he went into a long tirade about John W, which lasted for fifteen minutes about the evils of selling drugs to children. In the heat of that tirade, he tapped his glasses harder to emphasize the point he was making. When everyone was sure the judge had finished, he then read John the riot act for getting involved in the drug trade. When he finally worked himself into frothing at the mouth, he stood and pointed his finger at John, telling him, "Look at your mother. Look at her! You should be ashamed of yourself for causing your mother so much misery and grief." The judge got so carried away with his brim and firestone lambasting of John W, you could hear a pin drop in the courtroom. Suddenly, there was an audible sound bouncing around the courtroom walls like a window breaking, only much quieter.

The sound stopped the judge in his tracks and he looked around the room for the source of the noise, but he couldn't find it. When he put his glasses on, he was embarrassed to find that a cracked lens, which everyone in the room noticed, had caused the noise, causing snickers and guffaws in the courtroom. The judge placed his glasses back on his desk, hoping no one noticed, even though everyone had. He glanced down at the open book, trying to focus his eyes on the words, which were difficult without his glasses. The judge strained to read the statute, knowing he had a problem now that he had no reading glasses. He squinted and with difficulty made out the intent of the paragraph. Satisfied that he read it correctly, he closed the book and ordered John W. Hardin to stand. Then, without further discussion, he sentenced him to fifty years at hard labor in the Florence, Arizona Territorial Prison, the same prison that the prisoners of Yuma built back in 1909.

CHAPTER SIX

One day, a man knocked on Mrs. Abigail Hardin's door. He asked if he could come in, as he had something to discuss with her that would help her son's appeal case. She welcomed him into her home, wondering what he had that would help her son.

"Mrs. Hardin, I represent a very rich man. He owns an enormous company, and he's been following your son's case with interest. He feels they unjustly accused your son and he would like to help you in your time of need. So he sent me here with an offer that should help you out of your predicament."

Mrs. Hardin interrupted the man. "Can I get you a glass of cold water or tea? It's very hot today."

"Why, yes? A glass of water would be fine. Thank you."

She returned a few minutes later with a tray with a pitcher of water and a glass on it. She sat it on the end table. "Now tell me how you can help my son when no one else could."

"Well, I don't know if I can help him directly, but I can help him indirectly."

"Please, say what's on your mind, Mr.? Mr.? What did you say your name was?"

"It's Mr. Winters, ma'am."

"Tell me, Mr. Winters, how can you help my son indirectly if you can't help him directly? You know, Mr. Winters. I'm getting a bad feeling about this meeting."

"Please don't feel that way until you hear me out."

Abigail let out a sigh. "Go ahead. I'm listening."

"My employer wants to purchase your land as an excuse to give you money. It's worth nothing, but it would justify his giving you the money you need to pay your lawyers. He also has a home on a tract of land near the Grand Canyon, all paid for and furnished, that he would like to give you. I checked with the Mohave County Land office and I found out what you paid for this property. I did it only to make sure we gave you far more than it is worth. This property is worth two thousand dollars. We will give you seventy-five thousand dollars and the home, but we can only do it in exchange for this worthless piece of property you own. We need it to justify this transaction with our shareholders. Since we own a corporation, we just can't be giving money away for nothing. No, we have to show some sort of exchange and this is the only way we can justify the monies we will give you. Do you understand what I'm saying to you, Mrs. Hardin? Once we complete this transaction, you'll have enough money for a retrial."

Mr. Winters didn't convince Abigail he was telling her was the truth. "Why would your boss want to help us when the entire world is against us?"

"That's just it. The entire world's against you and he feels it's unfair. If you would let him, he would like to help you."

"Seventy-five thousand, you say?" She took the bait. She was hooked. "Why yes? Seventy-five thousand. And the home?"

"Yes, and the home."

"Make it one hundred twenty-five thousand and you have a deal."

Winters smiled. They allowed him to go to two million. "That's quite a lot of money, Mrs. Hardin, but I'll talk my principal into taking the deal. A lot rests on my say so. But I'd like to see you be able to help your son with his legal problems. Just sign here, Mrs. Hardin, on the dotted line below your name."

"Just hold on a minute, sonny. I don't see any check being given to me."

"You're right, ma'am. I have it right here in my attaché case." He opened his case. He pulled out a blank check, and he made it out for one hundred twenty-five thousand dollars and handed it to her. "Here you are, Mrs. Hardin."

"Where are the papers for my house?"

Winters once again reached into his attaché case and pulled out another document. "Here is the deed to your new home and the property it sits on, along with the bank statement stating that we paid the home and property in full." Winter's document stated that the home and property they gave her were as a gift rather than as an exchange of properties.

"Give me your pen, Mr. Winters, and I'll sign this document."

CHAPTER SEVEN

Hardin thanked God for small favors that the old Yuma territorial prison was no longer used. His father had taken him there once, and he remembered from the tour they took, it opened its doors on July 1, 1876 to accept its first seven prisoners and it closed on September 15, 1909. John was thankful that they sent him to the newer prison, which the bailiff told him was now the oldest functioning prison complex in Arizona.

Back in the early 1900s, the prisoners that were transported to Yuma Territorial prison tried hard not to touch the iron bars with their bare skin, but they had little success as their rig jostled along barren desert roads. They knew second and third-degree burns would be the result if their flesh touched iron, because it was as hot as an oven in the transportation conveyance in which they were riding. Unlike the metal cages on wheels pulled by horses, and sometimes burros, over a hundred years ago in the stifling 120 degree Arizona heat, They transported John Hardin to prison in an air-conditioned police cruiser and not in a prison bus like other criminals. It seemed odd that they gave him preferential treatment, and he felt a foreboding. But, young John W had no time to ponder his dilemma because when the cruiser arrived at the prison, a prison guard took him to a holding cell and ordered him to disrobe. After removing his clothes, he led him naked to a shower, and they gave him a prison uniform. They logged him into the prison rolls as a prisoner of the state of Arizona.

Although he didn't know it, he would get no introduction into the prison system nor would the Warden give him a talking to. Instead, they took John W. Hardin down three levels and placed him in a cell that was rarely, if ever, used these days. Once inside the cell, the guard manacled his hands and feet. The sneering guard laughed as he told John W that he would remain in this cell until they moved him to a very special facility, an old forgotten prison, which was being dug out of the desert and was being prepared just for him.

The guard alluded to a very special facility once known across Arizona as the Gila Bend Arizona State Prison. It opened in 1908, and it was another fine example of a prison built by the inmates of the Yuma Territorial Prison. The prisoners worked in the scorching hot 120-degree summer heat, so they only worked until twelve noon. The desert site was their home and they wouldn't leave it until they completed the prison. They modeled the tents in which the men lived after a Roman military camp. They spaced the tents equally and positioned them in a semi-circle around the perimeter of the prison. The tents remained that way during the entire time they removed the sand, and laid the cinder block foundation for the new prison. Soon, the prison emerged from the desert like a sleeping dragon.

A few months passed, and one day the prisoner in charge of construction entered the Captain's tent and reported the good news to him. They cleared the prison and the foundation, walls, roofs, cells, and the guards' living quarters were now ready for use. They finally completed their new prison. The Captain smiled and left with the prisoner to inspect the completed prison. They walked the perimeter and the supervising prisoner pointed out certain areas that required special attention during construction.

After the inspection, the Captain smiled and surprised the prisoner by saying. "Good job, Willard. Come on, let's go back to my tent and we'll have a drink to celebrate. I've been saving a bottle for this occasion." Willard Smith accepted the Captain's offer. After the two men finished their drink, the prisoner left. The Captain cranked up his Model T Ford and left the prison for the long ride to Tucson. He couldn't wait to send the Governor a telegram, giving him the good news that they completed the Gila prison and it was ready for use. When he sent the telegram, he hoped the Governor would wire him back telling him to take a well-earned vacation and leave his sergeant in charge of the prison. Then, when his vacation ended, he hoped the Governor would then instruct him to return to his home in Tucson. As he read through the telegram, to his surprise and utter delight, the Governor told him to leave for a well-earned two-week vacation. Then, he said that when his vacation ended, he was to go home for another two weeks. But, as the Captain read the rest of the telegram, it shook him to his core because, to his disappointment, he got the very thing he didn't want. The Gila Bend prison would now be his prison as well, because he was now the new warden.

They didn't select the prison's location in the middle of the Gila desert arbitrarily. They built it in that exact location to deter prisoners from escaping. If they escaped, there was nowhere for them to go. It was 286 miles of nothing to San Diego and 126.9 miles to Tucson in another direction. That made the Gila Desert Prison the most isolated place in Arizona. In 1942, when its last prisoner died from natural causes, the State of Arizona, rather than closing the prison, turned it over to the United States Army. The old prison was perfect for army use because of the hot desert climate. It was the perfect terrain in which to train soldiers to get them accustomed to desert warfare. General Erwin Rommel was successful fighting a strategic war in the Tunisian Desert in North Africa from June 10, 1940 to May 13, 1943. They trained men at the old prison site to stop Rommel once and for all. General George Patton led the men sent to fight General Rommel, and he defeated him. Soon after his defeat, the momentum shifted to the Allies. When Rommel returned home to Germany, Hitler, with the threat of killing his family, forced him to commit suicide. The Japanese surrendered on September 2, 1945, ending the war. Two months later, the Gila prison was closed.

Governor Holland Wilson decided the Gila prison would be perfect for what he had in mind and he issued an order for it to be re-opened. No one other than he knew it would only house two prisoners, and if a nosy journalist discovered his secret, he would tell him the prison was being used as a pilot program for incorrigible prisoners. His real motive was to confine the two men permanently in the dungeon. Three years ago, when the Governor visited the prison site, it surprised to see that very little of it remained above ground. The shifting sands of the desert had reclaimed most of the prison, burying it under the Gila sands. His face grimaced into a malicious smile, which he was careful to hide from his pilot. *Oh yes,* he thought to himself. *Dutch Henry will sing like a canary when he realizes that this will be his home from now on. He'll tell me everything, and if he doesn't talk, he'll spend the rest of his life here.*

When Jack McCormack heard the story, he giggled like a child. "How long do you think the kid will last out there in the desert, confined to a cell with all that heat and no one to talk to?"

The Governor returned the smile. "Hell, we have some tough old buzzards in this state. The old man is in that prison three years now, and he is still as belligerent as ever."

"What's his story?" McCormack asked.

"He's just a crazy old prospector who doesn't know when to give up. He's trekked up and down the Superstition Mountains, digging for gold most of his life. The old man never had a pot to piss in - then one day he comes into my store in Payson and he wants to trade some gold nuggets for an outfit."

McCormack squinted his eyes in confusion. "What in hell's an outfit?"

Wilson looked at McCormack sideways, surprised that a man in the mining business didn't know what an outfit was. So, he explained to McCormack what an outfit was, as if he were a child. "He bought all the things a prospector uses. You know, desert clothes, a pick and shovel, a weapon, a canteen, a horse, a burro, and a host of other items that every prospector needs."

"Why the hell didn't you say he wanted to buy some prospector's *gear*? If you would've said 'gear' instead of 'outfit,' then I would have known what the hell you were talking about."

The Governor shook his head and continued. He didn't want to get into a pissing contest with the man who nominated him for governor at the Democrat State Convention, backed him with his money, and to whom he owed his governorship, so he ignored the barb and continued telling his story. "Of course, this was long before I became governor of this great state."

"So what happened?"

"Nothing - then. But it piqued my curiosity. I asked him where he found the gold nuggets. He just smiled and said he found them in a stream way up in the Superstition Mountains, but I could tell he was lying. He got the gold somewhere up in the mountains all right, but he didn't get them by panning for the gold in a stream. I asked him if he was going to file a claim and he gave me a tight-lipped smile, and he said 'no,' 'cause he didn't want the government putting their hands in his pocket. I asked him if he had a run of luck and struck it rich. He just laughed. 'Could be,' he said."

Talking about gold always interested McCormack and he was eager to hear how the story turned out. "What happened then?"

"Well, I didn't see him for a few years until one day, out of nowhere, the front door opens, and he comes sauntering into the store. I was in my office going over my books when I spotted the old geezer on my surveillance system. I stopped what I was doing and ran out to greet him. I had to find out if he hit it big. It excited me, but I acted casual as I approached him. I asked him how he was doing. 'Pretty good,' he said.

'The way he said it, I knew it was more than 'pretty good, but I asked him anyway.' 'Did you find any more gold?' 'Some,' he answered. I just knew in my gut that he hit it big. I had that feeling and I guess he must have sensed it, because he became more evasive. I figured if he struck it rich, then it made sense that he wouldn't want anyone to know about it. One thing was for sure, he had money, and plenty of it, and the thought crossed my mind that he may have stumbled onto a lost gold mine. I damned sure didn't want another Lost Dutchman Gold Mine found without being a part of it, so I asked him again. 'How much gold did you take out of that mountain?' When he heard the question, he became suspicious. He gave me a look of disapproval and he said, 'Oh, enough to get by on.' That was all he said, and then he turned to my clerk, paid for his gear and then he walked out of the store.

"But, after he left, Dutch Henry, that was the old man's name, lingered in my thoughts and for a long time and I just couldn't get him off of my mind. I just knew he struck it rich. I had tried to get him to tell me where he was getting his gold for twelve years, and as the weeks, months and years passed by, it became an obsession. But I was powerless to do anything about it. It was a different story, though, when I became governor, because after they swore me in, I came into a lot of power. So, after things settled down, and I was comfortable in the Governor's seat, I tracked down Dutch Henry.

"My troopers found him in Tucson, living high, staying in a fancy hotel, and spending money like it was water. I ordered my men to bring him in for questioning. When they brought him before me, I told him that this doesn't have to be painful; all he had to do was to tell me about his gold. I tried reasoning with him. I told him that as governor, I could take much more of the gold out of the mountain than he ever could by himself. No matter how rich you are. I said to him. If I were your partner, I would make you ten times richer than you could ever be on your own. But it was no use. The old man was stupid because no matter how hard I tried to reason with him to get him to tell me where his gold mine was, he wouldn't budge. He just looked at me as if I were crazy, then he put his head back and laughed. 'I don't need you, sonny. I got it all under control.' He told me, 'the gold I found was because I scratched holes in the Superstition Mountains for the last forty years. I guess the mountain felt a mite sorry for me because it led me to what I had been searching for all of my life. And what I found I ain't sharing with nobody. It's mine, and it's going to stay mine, and when I die, it's gonna die with me. So put that in your pipe and smoke it.'

"I let it drop for the moment. Then later, quite by accident, I found out about the old abandoned Gila Bend prison in the desert. I was poring over reports of prisons we were considering closing when I came across a folder misplaced among a lot of other folders. This folder contained a handwritten list of prisons that were shut down in the 1900s. That's when I discovered that one of those old closed-down prisons was the Gila Bend prison. According to the report buried in that folder, the prisoners from Yuma Territorial Prison built it in 1909. After the Second World War, they ordered the prison closed by the state of Arizona. After I read about it, it had the same effect on me as Dutch Henry's gold. It, too became an obsession with me, and I was determined to see it for myself. Knowing about this prison lit a fire under me and I just had to see it. So one morning, I had my pilot fly me to the site by chopper. Man, was I surprised when I saw it, because the desert had almost completely reclaimed it. I hollered over the roar of the rotor blades, motioning at the ground, telling the pilot that I wanted him to land near the site. After we landed, I took my time walking amongst the ruins, trying to figure out how much of the prison was still hiding under the sand. Well, there was only one way to find out, so as soon as I got back to my office, I issued an order for the prison to be reopened. What was surprising was, when I contacted the department of prisons, no one had ever heard of this prison - and *they're* in the prison business.

"I hired a firm from the Arizona list of verified vendors to remove the sand covering the prison. I decided that as soon as I received the call telling me the prison was once again completely habitable - if you can call living in that environment habitable - I was going to take the old man to see it. A few months later, I received that call. I was told the prison was once again ready to accept prisoners. The morning prior to flying out to see the prison, I showed the old man pictures of the hellhole in the middle of the Gila desert where he would spend the rest of his life if he didn't tell me what I wanted to know. But he was a selfish bastard, and he still refused to tell me anything. I couldn't believe how unreasonable he was. I knew then that there was only one thing left to do. He had to see the prison for himself."

"What happened then?"

Wilson smiled a knowing smile and then continued telling his story. "I thought I finally got into the old man's thick head because he seemed to soften a bit when he asked me to give him a month to think about it. I met with him a month later and I asked him if he was ready to tell me the location of his mine. He just laughed and said, 'I'll never tell you where my mine is, so do your worst. I'm not telling you jack shit.'

"That's when I had him arrested on a trumped up charge and had him put in that hellhole. It's been three years now, and whenever I visit him he still won't tell me where his mine is located. I'm convinced the man is nuts, because whenever I ask him about his mine - he just laughs at me."

McCormack listened with interest and, with a mirthless grin, he asked, "And that's where you're putting this Hardin kid?"

"Yep. No one will eve see or hear from him again. He's lost to the ages now. He'll die in that prison. I have a skeleton crew working there. It's hot as hell but the work is easy, because they have two prisoners to take care of, and they only work until twelve noon, so they don't mind putting up with the heat. They'll see to the kid's needs just like they do with the old man. You know, make sure he gets his three meals a day, water, a shower once a week, and a new prison outfit every six months."

All this talk of gold mines reminded Holland of something and before the thought flitted from his mind, he asked McCormack, "How did the gold mine you traded the old lady for work out for you?"

"It worked out great, better than I thought it would. We hit the mother lode, and with today's gold prices, we'll take a billion dollars out of that mine, so just make sure that boy remains in that prison."

CHAPTER EIGHT

William Hayes sat at his desk and read, and then re-read the local papers with disbelief. The major gold strike in Mohave County near the mountains in an old reactivated gold mine was headline news all over the country. He put the paper down, thinking of what he had just read. Gold found in that old abandoned mine on the property he gave to the Hardins? Who would have known there'd be any gold left in that played out mine? Not him, that was for sure. So, he thought about the question he just asked himself. *Who could have known there was gold in the mine other than the person who bought the property from Mrs. Hardin?* Only one man, he concluded, would gain the most if John W was out of the picture, because then it would be a simple matter to negotiate a deal with his unsuspecting mother, and that person was Jack McCormack. Hayes hastily opened his bottom desk drawer, took out a leather business card folder, and searched for a particular card. He found it on the second page.

Hayes read the name above the gold embossed badge on the business card to make sure he had the right card. *Jason Sweeney, Private Detective*. He picked up the phone and dialed the New York City number. After a brief conversation with Sweeney, he hired him.

Jason's father, Horace Sweeney, was a private detective. He was a good one during the 1960s. During those tumultuous years, he opened his own detective agency. When Jason was old enough, he went to work for his father. On the day that he reported to work, it surprised him to see the name in large gold leafed lettering on the door: Sweeney and Son. Jason discovered he had a natural aptitude for investigative work. Over the years, he and his father built the business into a major detective agency. Then the day came when his father announced he was retiring and Jason would assume control of the company.

Hayes logged on to the agency's website and read Sweeney's references, then he made a few discreet inquiries and was pleased to find Sweeney's past customers highly recommended him. He was told Sweeney was honest, and he was like a bulldog with his assignments, because he was always successful. Hayes spoke to Jason briefly, then he wired him the deposit Jason required to search for the information Hayes requested on Jack McCormack and McCormack Industries.

McCormack was a self-made millionaire many times over. Hayes wanted to know how he made his fortune. He instructed Sweeney to locate the whereabouts of John W. Hardin, who they sentenced to prison three years ago in Arizona. Hayes told Sweeney they sent Hardin originally to Florence Territorial Prison to start his sentence, but since then, he'd vanished without a trace. Hayes overnighted Sweeney all of his accumulated trial information, including copies of all the newspaper articles he collected over the three years that John was in prison. Three weeks later, Hayes received a phone call from Sweeney. Sweeney told him he was flying in tomorrow to see him. He asked Hayes to meet him at the Phoenix Sky Harbor International Airport at the Delta terminal at 11:30 a.m. Without hesitation, Hayes said he'd be there.

Business was terrible at the Hayes Real Estate Office. What was once a growing business was now experiencing a dramatic downturn. The business slowdown occurred after they sentenced John to prison. Letters had poured into the office from concerned customers who were used to the smiling, affable young man who advised them about what properties to look at, and which properties to stay away from. Young Hardin satisfied his customers with the service he provided them. His customers could not - would not - believe he was guilty of the horrible crimes with which they charged him with. He was no drug lord, and everyone knew it. God knows he couldn't tell one drug from another if you handed them to him and his customers knew it. It was a horrible miscarriage of justice and they were positive that when the truth came out, they would release him. But, over time, the letters slowed down until they trickled to a stop. It was as if John W. Hardin, distant relative of the famous shootist, never existed, because no one asked about the young man any longer.

A year passed, then another, and then John's mother took sick and died; some said of a broken heart. She had kept in touch with Mr. Hayes, always wanting to know if there was anything new about her son. The answer was always the same. "Sorry, Mrs. Hardin, no one will tell me anything concerning your son. I don't even know what prison they took him to. I've checked every prison in the state and I'm told he is not in any of them. They must have taken him to a Federal prison because he is not in any Arizona prison, at least none that I know of."

She thanked him and told him she'd check back in a month. A month passed, and she hadn't called. Then two more months passed and still no word from her. Hayes was concerned about her, so he drove out to her home to see if she was all right.

Abigail Hardin lived in a remote section of the Grand Canyon Subdivision facing the Pennsylvania Peaks. Her property was between the Grand Canyon and Flagstaff. She had no neighbors around her. All she had was the manufactured mobile home she lived in, which sat directly under the power lines that passed overhead, and that was the reason she had electricity. The power company agreed to drop a line straight down, but they wouldn't supply electricity anywhere else. She got used to the water she had trucked in. If she had extra money, she would have a well dug. But it cost a small fortune and meant drilling down five thousand feet to reach water. So instead, she just rationed her water carefully and lived frugally.

Hayes tapped on the front door. There was no answer. He spotted her old pickup truck sitting behind the house, so he knocked again - this time harder. Still no answer. He rang the doorbell. Nothing. He knew she was home because her truck was still here. It was a ten-mile walk to town, and he knew she wouldn't do that, not when she had her truck sitting here. He walked over to the truck, saw the key in the ignition, stepped in, and turned the ignition on. The truck started right up. So it wasn't dead. His thoughts turned to the woman in the house and a dreadful feeling washed over him. Hayes knew what he had to do but hated doing it because he was certain of what he would find when he entered the house. He walked back to the front door and turned the door handle, but she locked it from the inside. He took out his cell phone and dialed 9-11. When the operator answered, he told her what he suspected. He asked her to send help and said he didn't want to break into her house without having a police presence with him. The dispatcher told him to remain where he was and not do anything. A cruiser would be there in twenty minutes. The sheriff pulled alongside Hayes's car a half hour later. A young police officer got out of his cruiser and walked over to Hayes.

"I'm Officer DeLong. You must be Mr. Hayes?"

"That's correct, officer. I hope I'm wrong, but I believe something terrible has happened to my friend, Mrs. Hardin. I wanted to break into her house, but I didn't want to do it without a police presence, you understand?"

"Yes, I do. You did the right thing. Now let's see if we can get into the house damaging nothing."

The officer tried the door again, but it remained locked. They walked around the house, looking for an open window. Because the house was five thousand feet above sea level, the windows were almost always open, unlike the homes at a lower sea level like in Phoenix or Scottsdale. Delong found an open window and pushed the screen in.

"Look, young fella," Hayes said. "I'm kinda old to be climbing in windows. That's for a much younger man than me and one who's in better shape, like you, to do."

The deputy smiled, seeing the logic in what he said. "Okay, I guess I'm elected. Give me a boost up to the window." The officer put his foot into Hayes's cupped hands and Hayes pushed him up to the window. The young officer pulled himself through the window and into the mobile home. He stuck his head back out the window. "Go to the front door. I'll open it for you." When the deputy opened the door, he shook his head sadly and said, "You better stay outside. I don't think you want to see this. She's been dead for quite a while now. She's bloated, and the stench of death is overwhelming. Let's go out to my car and I'll radio for an ambulance."

CHAPTER NINE

They descended two levels down a spiral staircase. At the bottom of the stairs, they faced another metal door similar to the one above. A guard chained John's hands behind his back. Then he took his arm and led him down a long walkway lined on either side with empty cells until they came to a cold, hard metal door in the rear of the dreary cell area. The guard took a key from his key ring and opened the heavy metal door. He led John along a dark passageway until they got to the cell marked "11A." John couldn't figure out why they marked the cell "11A" when there were only eight cells on the floor.

While the guard struggled to open the cell door because of the rusty hinges, John looked at the miserable cell in which he was being housed. It looked very old, almost like it was built in the late eighteen hundreds or early nineteen hundreds. He was thankful for the new cot placed in the cell, but he still couldn't understand why he was being locked up in this terrible place. The hinges of the door to the cell apparently hadn't been oiled for at least a century, because the door squeaked and groaned, fighting hard to stay closed as the guard struggled to open it. He guessed that the men who dug the prison out of the desert must have forgotten to check the cell doors, never thinking that some sand might still be in the lodged in the hinges. The guard was breathing heavily from the exertion of opening the cell door when he told John to get in.

After he stepped into his cell, he turned to the guard. "Can I ask you a few questions?"

The guard frowned. "The Captain ordered us not to talk to you, but since we're alone, go ahead and ask your questions and I'll try to answer them."

"Do you know why they put me in this place?"

"No! Next question."

"Will I be fed and clothed and can I take a shower once in a while?”

“You’ll be fed three meals a day.” The guard leaned close and whispered, “The meals may not be very tasty, but if you eat, you’ll stay healthy and staying healthy is important down here.” Then in case anyone was listening, he said in a commanding voice, “You’ll get clothes twice a year. And with the new rules, you’ll get a shower once a week. Any more questions?”

“Yes. Will I be able to get some exercise?”

“Probably not,” he said, but then he leaned close and again whispered, “But I’ll see what I can do for you. I’m as much a prisoner here as you are, so I’ll do what I can for you.”

“Thanks. I appreciate it.”

“Look, I don’t know what you did, but it must have been something terrible to get put in here.”

“What if I told you that I didn’t do anything wrong. That I was framed.” John W looked at the guard’s face and could tell that he didn’t believe him. “Yeah, I know. You’re thinking that’s what all prisoners say. But it’s true. I don’t know what I did to get put in here.”

The young guard heard stories like this from just about every prisoner he came in contact with. He turned to leave but John stopped him.

“One last thing. Can you find out how my mother is doing?”

The guard nodded his head and said in a low voice, “Well, I don’t think I’ll ever get a chance, but if I do, I’ll see what I can find out. It’s the least I can do. It just ain’t right for a man not to know how his mother is doing.”

“Thank you. I didn’t expect to find any kindness in this place. I see I was wrong. There still are people with a heart left in the world and it appears I may have found one.”

The guard looked sympathetically at John and said in a low voice, “There’s not hardly any kindness in this place, but since you will be here for a long time, I don’t see the harm in helping you a little if I can. Just don’t expect me to do anything against my orders because I won’t do it. I’ll see you die first. Do you understand me?”

“Yes. I understand.”

“Good. Just so we understand one another. Now I have to

go, so make yourself comfortable. You'll be here a long time."

"Wait!"

"What now?"

"I don't know your name?"

"Lee. My name is Lee."

"Lee what? What's your last name and where do you live?"

"It's Lee Flowers and I live in Tucson." The guard smiled and said, "Now don't plan on coming to see me anytime soon. You hear." As he turned to go, he said, "See you tomorrow morning before I go off duty."

"Good night Lee. See you tomorrow."

Lee never showed up the next morning or the morning after. In fact, Lee never showed up again. One morning, as his food tray was being passed through the opening in the solid steel door, John crouched down and asked the guard, "Where's Lee, what happened to him?"

"He was fired because he asked about your mother. Now don't ever talk to me again and don't ask me any more fool questions because I won't answer you. I'm no jerk and I'm not going to get myself fired because of your stupid questions. Now eat your food and be quiet." The food tray door slammed shut, cutting off all the light in the little cell. The only light in the cell came from a shaft extending from the upper floors. John figured it was a design flaw but in the middle of the day, the light was welcomed when it lit up the cell for a little while.

John thought to himself, *whoever was brought to this cell never returned to the upper level.* This was just a feeling, but it felt real enough to him. John had no illusions of escaping from this place. Even if he did escape, how would he ever get back to civilization? He'd die in the desert without water or food or he would die from the sun. No, he had to place his hope in Mr. Hayes and his mother to get him out of this terrible place.

Day, weeks, months, and years passed by slowly. John kept his hopes up for the first few weeks but as the months turned into years, he lost all hope of ever getting out. He marked the days with a fork that a guard had forgotten to take. As best he could figure, he had been in this cell for almost five years. He had given up trying to exercise and was lying with his back to the wall when he heard a scraping sound. He thought it was a rat, but the scraping continued, so he got up from his cot and went to the section of wall where the scraping was coming from and tapped the wall - and he received a tap in return. When he was a kid, his father took him to see the movie *The Count of Monte Cristo.* He thought how ironic it would be if the prisoner tapping back was an old monk with a fount of knowledge to impart and a fortune to leave him. He laughed at the thought. That only happens in the movies. But friendship and companionship - well that happens in real life - so he started scraping the grout from around the stone with his fork along the spot where the scraping noise was coming from.

Two days passed before he noticed the point of a knife protruding from a portion of the grout between the stones. The prisoner on the other side of the stone pushed with his feet while John pulled the part of the stone he could grab with his fingers. Suddenly, the effort of one man pulling and the other pushing caused the stone to break free of the wall, landing unceremoniously between John's legs. If the stone had landed a little further above his knees instead of between them, he would never become a father if the opportunity ever presented itself.

A man's head popped out of the empty space. "Here take this from me." John took the small oil lamp and put it on the one chair in the room, welcoming the light it gave off. "Now give me a hand, lad." John grabbed the old man's hands and pulled him free from the space behind the wall. The man wiped his brow, then dusted himself off. "Hi, I'm Dutch Henry," he said with a warm smile on his face. "What's a nice boy like you doing in a rotten place like this?" That was his way of greeting John W. He said it with a smile and John marveled at the fact that even in a place like this, the man could still have a sense of humor. The old man immediately lifted John W's spirits. "John Wesley Hardin at your service, but my friends call me John W. It's a genuine pleasure to meet you, Mr. Henry."

"Same here, John W. But call me Dutch or Dutch Henry. Either name will do. Couldn't be that the famous gunfighter was a kin of yours, could it?"

"That's what my daddy told us. He said he was a distant cousin of Barnett Hardin on my father's side. Barnett was brother to Judge Will Hardin. My daddy told us that if you looked at the Texas Constitution you'd see another uncle, Augustine Hardin's name signed on it. At least that's what my daddy told Ma and me. But if you don't mind me asking, why were you digging your way into this cell?"

"Well, that's a long story, young fella, but seein' as we have nothing but time, I'll sit on your cot if you don't mind and catch my breath and rest a little while and I'll tell you about it.

"There's this fella who's now the Governor of this great state and me and him done some business back a few years when I needed a grub stake." John grew up in the desert and he met a few prospectors so he knew what a grub stake was. The old man continued with his story. "This man owned a large hardware store and I traded him some gold nuggets for equipment I needed, like a pick and shovel, a new canteen, and all the other items an old fool like me needed to hunt for gold up in those mountains. As the years passed, this man grew his business to where he had a lot of these hardware stores all over the state. He became so popular that he ran for Governor and won by telling a bunch of lies over the television. Well, that man tracked me down and he wanted me to tell him where I found my gold. To tell you the truth, son, I found a ton of gold. I set my mind when I was a young man to find the lost Four Peaks Gold Mine and I spent a good part of my life searching for it. The area I concentrated my search on comprised the southern portion of the Mazatzal Mountains. It was a big job trying to find what no one else ever dreamed of finding. The Four Peaks which are nearly 8000 feet high have always been an important landmark in this part of Arizona and as a kid, I always dreamt that I would be the one to find the legendary mine. So where does one start when he wants to find a lost gold mine?" He had John's absolute attention now and the young man was hanging on every word the old man said.

"Where *does* one start, Dutch Henry?"

The old man laughed, showing some brown stained teeth along with a few missing ones. "Got your attention - don't I? Well, you can't see the old fort because the intervening peaks hide it. Old Fort Reno lies about 14 miles north of the Four Peaks area. Forgive an old man's rambling, son, but I am getting to my point. Old Fort Reno was constructed on the eastern flanks of the Mazatzal Mountains, overlooking Tonto Creek to the east. The Mazatzal peak known as Mount Ord rises only four miles to the northwest of the old fort. Beyond Mount Ord, the mountains swing around to the northwest.

"During the 1800's, the Mazatzal Mountains were in the middle of Apache country. The Tonto Apaches wandered these mountains in search of game, but they had something else, something everyone wanted. Rumors circulated for years of a hidden Apache gold mine in or near the Mazatzals. Tonto Apaches, the local Indians, always seemed to have plenty of gold nuggets for trading. It was said that during the 1850's, the friendly Tontos took the famous Dr. Abraham Thorne to an Apache gold mine. Although he was blindfolded, Thorne insisted till the end of his days that the mine was in the Salt River country. I even read where in 1853, Francis X. Aubry saw local Apaches making bullets out of gold! So, I set my sights and began digging in the Mazatzal mountain area. I spent forty years searching for that lost gold mine. Through the years, I picked up traces, bits and pieces, nuggets of gold brought down the mountains by the rains but I never found the mine itself, until 11 years ago. After decades of searching I hit the jackpot. I found the lost mine, and that greedy bastard Governor Wilson wants what I've spent a lifetime searching for. I broke my ass digging the gold out of that mine, then, just when I started enjoying the fruits of my labor, Governor Wilson arrested me on some trumped up charges and threw me in this hellhole six years ago. I near starved, was almost killed a few times, nearly froze to death and this baby-assed Governor thinks he can steal my gold.

I'd rather die first than see him get it." John W. Hardin let out the breath he hadn't realized he was holding.

"Whew. That's some story. Man, what you must have gone through. Yet you endured and in the end, you did find the pot of gold at the end of the rainbow."

"You got that right, John W. I surely did find that pot of gold."

"But that doesn't explain why you were digging a tunnel to the 11A cell."

"That's not 11A, son. It's Roman numerals meaning '2A.' You can't see it but the cell across from this one is 1A. Look. When Holland Wilson, our illustrious Governor, threatened me with prison, he took me out here and showed me where he said I'd be spending the rest of my life if I didn't tell him the whereabouts of the mine he was certain I found. That was his first mistake. I may be old but I didn't get to live this long by being stupid. I told him to give me a month to think about it. As soon as he left, I went to the library and paid a young man with computer knowledge fifty dollars for an hour of his time. I wanted him to do an Internet search for me. You see, I knew inmates from the Yuma Territorial Prison built this prison. I needed to track down relatives of the men who built this place and see if they left a record or diary of their time here. The young man I gave the fifty bucks to did a hellova job. He found out that the Yuma prisoner who was in charge of building this prison was one Willard Smith doing twenty years to life.

"The boy discovered that Smith had a granddaughter, name of Priscilla Bluestone, and she was living in Amarillo, Texas. I tracked her down and told her that I was writing a book on the Yuma Territorial Prison and I wanted to speak to her about her grandfather. She agreed to see me. When I met her, I told her that I did some research and found that her grandfather was in charge of building the Gila prison. I asked her if he left a record of the work he performed on that site. She told me that she had two large boxes of her grandfather's papers and books in the attic and she agreed to let me look through them, but she didn't want the boxes brought downstairs because it would mess up her tidy house. She said if I wanted to look at her grandfather's information, I'd have to climb up into the attic, put the light on, and look through the boxes up there. When I got the first box opened and I rummaged through his papers, I found a lot of interesting information on Yuma but very little on the Gila prison except a small paperback book on the history of the place. After emptying the first box and looking through his papers, I came up empty, so I put everything back and started on the second box. I didn't hold much hope of finding anything. But I was wrong, because when I opened the second box, I found his diary right on top. I scanned through the diary, hoping to find something that would help me and I was right. This diary was the ticket. I looked through the rest of his papers and books but found nothing more that would help me, so I closed the box and took the diary downstairs. I was sweating like I was in a sauna as I showed it to Smith's granddaughter.

"I said to her, 'I hope you don't mind me bringing this diary down here, I found it in one of the boxes. It was kind of hot sitting on my haunches trying to read it upstairs in the dim light and the heat so I brought it downstairs where it's cooler.'

"'No of course not. Here sit at the table. You look very hot. I'll bring you a cool glass of iced tea to refresh you a bit.' I opened the diary and started reading from the first page and I made notes as I read through it. Her grandfather wrote important details of each step of construction and the renovations he made while toiling in the hot sun in the Gila desert. When I finished reading the diary, I had what I was looking for. Priscilla said that he kept it because he was a very thorough man and besides he didn't want to forget any of the details in case he became forgetful. I knew that she listened to what he said but she never read the diary. He didn't keep this record for fear of becoming forgetful. This was his insurance policy in case he was ever transferred there. If she had read the diary, she would have known that. She told me that her grandfather was a civil engineer before he killed his partner in a heated dispute over money and because of it, he was sent to Yuma prison. The warden approached Smith one day and told him he'd be getting out of Yuma for a while. He was making him the foreman and putting him in charge of prisoners he picked to build the Gila Prison and Smith jumped at the chance.

"Now here's how he pulled it off. Put yourself in the guard's place. Imagine their mindset. Here they are in the middle of the desert where the temperature rarely gets below 120 degrees, working in the sun without shade. What man in his right mind wants to stand outside in the sun when he could be in a tent sipping a cool beer? It was just them. There weren't any supervisors around and they weren't worried about prisoners escaping because where would they go? There was no place for them to escape to - so there was no need to watch them while they worked. The guards spent the day in the shade of a tent and they came out at noon to inspect the work the prisoners did that day. Then at noon, the prisoners would return to their tents and play cards or read a book until the following day. Then the routine would start all over again. Remember now, the cells they were constructing were designed to hold the one or two prisoners that did something really bad. One or two cells would have done the trick but Willard Smith suggested putting eight cells with an eight foot area filled with stones and dirt separating one cell from another. He laid the blueprints on the kitchen table and explained to the guards how this design was better than the original plan and it served two purposes. The first was it was a simple way to stop prisoners from talking or passing things to one another and the second was with the eight cells spread out along the length of the floor it fit the aesthetic design of the prison. The guards liked Smith's suggestion, so they approached the Captain for his approval and received it. Even the eight-foot spaces between cells were agreed to. Smith was told to build it just the way he described to it them but they added a condition he wasn't happy with. 'Make sure the space between the cells is filled with eight feet of solid rock with dirt added as a fill instead of just filling it with dirt.' But that wouldn't work for Smith. What the guards didn't know was Smith intended to build a back door out of the prison in case he was ever incarcerated there. 'Look,' Smith said to the guard. 'I can fill the space between cells with dirt and add sand instead of stone, but I don't have enough time to haul those rocks down from the mountains. The work detail doing that work would be the same as a chain gang chipping away at a mountain. Let me use sand with the dirt as a filler instead of rock. The sand will work just as well and more importantly; it will cut six months off the time needed to build this prison. But you fellas have to make that decision so I'll leave it to you. But think about it for a minute and tell me if what I'm suggesting doesn't make sense to you. If you think it doesn't, and if you still want stone, then it's no problem to get a gang together and march them out into the desert and cut it out of the mountain. But if we do that, then figure on adding another six months to complete the job.'" That got the guards attention.

"The guard liked the idea of cutting the time down by six

months and said he'd talk it over with the Captain. He told him he'd get back to him in a little while, and then he left to have a talk with the Captain. Smith watched him walk away and he chuckled to himself. Moron. I could walk to the base of the mountain and pick up all the rocks I want without chipping away at any mountain. He knew the Captain would approve sand instead of rock, because everyone knew that all the man dreamed about was to get the hell away from this god forsaken prison. It wasn't long before he heard the tap, tap, tap of the guard's steps as he walked back down the stairs. 'Forget about using stone, go ahead and build it with dirt and sand.' He said, 'The Captain said we don't need rocks, they won't serve any purpose down here.' Smith had the Captain's approval, as he knew he would."

"Are you telling me you found a way out of this place?"

"That's exactly what I'm telling you. Now, with your help we can do it in half the time. Might take us another year or two and if we're not released by then, and I don't expect we will. We can break out of here ourselves."

"Wait a minute," John W said. "We can't ever get out of here because we don't have a means to cross the desert, besides, the moment we're gone they'll know we're missing."

"That's not exactly true, John W. You see, Smith was ahead of you. He foresaw the problems you just mentioned and he found a way to work around them. Just behind that wall is a room, which isn't filled with dirt. Remember all the prisoners and the guards all slept in canvas tents."

"Yeah. But so what?"

"Smith was smart. He knew good canvas wouldn't rot in the short term and maybe not for the next two hundred years. He made sure the canvass he requisitioned was heavy-duty, long-lasting canvas. He justified it with the guards by telling them that if they had one of those torrential seasonal downpours while they were in their tents made of a thin canvas and that canvass was all that stood between them and the rain, they'd be soaked in no time at all. And remember this, when Carter found King Tut's mummy, the linen Tut was wrapped in was still serviceable. Heavy canvas will work for us just like Tut's linen. No, the canvas Smith chose for his tents will work just fine for us."

"Wait a minute. What do we need canvas for? I don't understand any of this. Please, Dutch Henry, get to the point and explain all of this to me."

The old man was getting a kick bantering with John W. Hardin. "It's simple, John. We need the canvas to inflate our hot air balloon because the air needs something to inflate. Don't you understand, the air balloon is made out of the canvas Smith bought for his tents? When he ordered the canvas, he ordered a lot more than he needed. You see old Willard Smith, Civil Engineer prisoner in charge of building this prison, had to figure a way of escaping if he was ever put in one of these cells here. The only thing he could think of to escape was a hot air balloon. In that room, behind the wall that you're leaning on." He pointed his finger at it. "There's a hot air balloon made by the prisoners out of canvas, and it's waiting to take us out of here."

"How would we inflate it, Dutch Henry?"

"Smith left the means to inflate it in that room. Once we dig our way into that room, we'll assemble the balloon and then we'll wait until we have the opportunity to inflate it without alerting the guards."

"But won't they miss us when they check on us in the morning?"

"Smith planned for that as well. You see, John. In that room, besides the hot air balloon, there's also dynamite. It's rigged and ready to blow, and it has a slow burning fuse. About twenty minutes after we're in the air, this place will go up like it was bombed. When they check in the morning, they'll find a few of our things but nothing more. They'll assume that we were killed in the explosion."

John W thought about that for a moment. "But what would they attribute the explosion to?"

The old man just smiled. "Did you know that old dynamite has some very peculiar characteristics and is very tetchy? Smith left the dynamite in the hidden room under the foundation. They'll figure it began to sweat through the years, causing it to release nitroglycerin, causing the dynamite to become unstable. Finally, after all these years of laying here in the heat, it just blew up. There is no other explanation that will make sense to anyone. The explosion will give the state the reason it finally needs to close Gila Prison. Or at the very least make it a ghost town like Yuma Prison."

John nodded. "Yeah, I guess that would explain it. This could work, Dutch Henry."

"Son, it has to work. Listen, when we get out of here, I'm going to set you up for life. I'm an old man now and I'm reaching the end of my rope. I have no relatives to leave my fortune to, so I've decided I'm going to leave everything to you." The old man paused a moment and reached up and took hold of John W's shoulders, deciding whether to continue. "Now, if for some reason I don't make it out of here, I want you to promise me that you'll get even with that lying scoundrel of a Governor for me."

"Don't worry, Dutch Henry. I'll put the governor on top of my list. I have a few people I intend to take care of too - but I promise you - the Governor will be on top of my list."

Dutch Henry slapped John W on his shoulder. "Good, that's settled then. Now let's get to diggin'."

CHAPTER TEN

They descended two levels down a spiral staircase. At the bottom of the stairs, they faced another metal door similar to the one above. A guard chained John's hands behind his back. Then he took his arm and led him down a long walkway lined on either side with empty cells until they came to a cold, hard metal door in the rear of the dreary cell area. The guard took a key from his key ring and opened the heavy metal door. He led John along a dark passageway until they got to the cell marked "11A." John couldn't figure out why they marked the cell "11A" when there were only eight cells on the floor.

While the guard struggled to open the cell door because of the rusty hinges, John looked at the miserable cell in which he was being housed. It looked ancient, almost like they built it in the late eighteen hundreds or early nineteen hundreds. He was thankful for the new cot placed in the cell, but he still couldn't understand why he was being locked up in this terrible place. They hadn't oiled the hinges of the door of the cell for at least a century, because the door squeaked and groaned, fighting hard to stay closed as the guard struggled to open it. He guessed that the men who dug the prison out of the desert must have forgotten to check the cell doors, never thinking that might be some sand still lodged in the hinges. The guard was wheezing from the exertion of opening the cell door when he told John to get in.

After he stepped into his cell, he turned to the guard. "Can I ask you a few questions?"

The guard frowned. "The Captain ordered us not to talk to you, but since we're alone, ask your questions and I'll try to answer them."

"Do you know why they put me in this place?"

"No! Next question."

"Will they feed and clothe me, and can I take a shower once

in a while?"

"We'll feed you three meals a day." The guard leaned close and whispered, "The meals may not be tasty, but if you eat, you'll stay healthy, and staying healthy is important down here." Then, in case anyone was listening, he said in a commanding voice, "You'll get clothes twice a year. And with the new rules, you'll get a shower once a week. Any more questions?"

"Yes. Will I be able to get some exercise?"

"Probably not," he said, but then he leaned close and again whispered, "But I'll see what I can do for you. I'm as much a prisoner here as you are, so I'll do what I can for you."

"Thanks. I appreciate it."

"Look, I don't know what you did, but it must have been something terrible to get put in here."

"What if I told you I did nothing wrong? That they framed me." John W looked at the guard's face and could tell that he didn't believe him. "Yeah, I know. You're thinking that's what all prisoners say. But it's true. I don't know what I did to get put in here."

The young guard heard stories like this from just about every prisoner he came in contact with. He turned to leave, but John stopped him.

"One last thing. Can you find out how my mother is doing?"

The guard nodded his head and said in a low voice, "Well, I don't think I'll ever get a chance, but if I do, I'll see what I can find out. It's the least I can do. It just ain't right for a man not to know how his mother is doing."

"Thank you. I didn't expect to find any kindness in this place. I see I was wrong. There still are people with a heart left in the world, and it appears I may have found one."

The guard looked at John and said in a low voice, "There's not hardly any kindness in this place, but since you will be here for a long time, I don't see the harm in helping you a little if I can. Just don't expect me to do anything against my orders because I won't do it. I'll see you die first. Do you understand me?"

"Yes. I understand."

"Good. Just so we understand one another. Now I have to

go, so make yourself comfortable. You'll be here a long time."

"Wait!"

"What now?"

"I don't know your name?"

"Lee. My name is Lee."

"Lee what? What's your last name and where do you live?"

"It's Lee Flowers and I live in Tucson." The guard smiled and said, "Now don't plan on coming to see me soon. You hear." As he turned to go, he said, "See you tomorrow morning before I go off duty."

"Good night Lee. See you tomorrow."

Lee never showed up the next morning or the morning after. In fact, Lee never showed up again. One morning, as his food tray was being passed through the opening in the solid steel door, John crouched down and asked the guard, "Where's Lee? What happened to him?"

"They fired him because he asked about your mother. Now never talk to me again and don't ask me any more fool questions because I won't answer you. I'm no jerk and I will not get myself fired because of your stupid questions. Now eat your food and be quiet." The food tray door slammed shut, cutting off all the light in the little cell. The only light in the cell came from a shaft extending from the upper floors. John figured it was a design flaw, but in the middle of the day, he welcomed the light when it lit up the cell for a little while.

John thought to himself, *whoever they brought to this cell never returned to the upper level*. This was just a feeling, but it felt genuine enough to him. John had no illusions of escaping from this place. Even if he escaped, how would he ever get back to civilization? He'd die in the desert without water or food or he would die from the sun. No, he had to place his hope in Mr. Hayes and his mother to get him out of this terrible place.

Day, weeks, months, and years passed by. John kept his hopes up for the first few weeks, but as the months turned into years, he lost all hope of ever getting out. He marked the days with a fork that a guard had forgotten to take. As best he could figure, he had been in this cell for almost five years. He had given up trying to exercise and was lying with his back to the wall when he heard a scraping sound. He thought it was a rat, but the scraping continued, so he got up from his cot and went to the section of wall where the scraping was coming from and tapped the wall - and he received a tap. When he was a kid, his father took him to see the movie *The Count of Monte Cristo.* He thought how ironic it would be if the prisoner tapping back was an old monk with a fount of knowledge to impart and a fortune to leave him. He laughed at the thought. That only happens in the movies. But friendship and companionship - well, that happens in real life - so he started scraping the grout from around the stone with his fork along the spot where the scraping noise was coming from.

Two days passed before he noticed the point of a knife protruding from the grout between the stones. The prisoner on the other side of the stone pushed with his feet while John pulled the part of the stone he could grab with his fingers. The effort of one man pulling and the other pushing caused the stone to break free of the wall, landing between John's legs. If the stone had landed a little further above his knees instead of between them, he would never become a father if the opportunity ever presented itself.

A man's head popped out of the space. "Here, take this from me." John took the small oil lamp and put it on the one chair in the room, welcoming the light it gave off. "Now give me a hand, lad." John grabbed the old man's hands and pulled him free from the space behind the wall. The man wiped his brow, then dusted himself off. "Hi, I'm Dutch Henry," he said with a warm smile on his face. "What's a nice boy like you doing in a rotten place like this?" That was his way of greeting John W. He said it with a smile and John marveled at the fact that even in a place like this, the man could still have a sense of humor. The old man lifted John W's spirits. "John Wesley Hardin at your service, but my friends call me John W. It's a genuine pleasure to meet you, Mr. Henry."

"Same here, John W. But call me Dutch or Dutch Henry. Either name will do. Couldn't be that the famous gunfighter was a kin of yours, could it?"

"That's what my daddy told us. He said he was a distant cousin of Barnett Hardin on my father's side. Barnett was a brother to Judge Will Hardin. My daddy told us that if you looked at the Texas Constitution, you'd see another uncle, Augustine Hardin's name, signed on it. At least that's what my daddy told Ma and me. But if you don't mind me asking, why were you digging your way into this cell?"

"Well, that's a long story, young fella, but seein' as we have nothing but time, I'll sit on your cot if you don't mind and catch my breath and rest a little while and I'll tell you about it.

"There's this fella who's now the Governor of this great state and me and him done some business back a few years when I needed a grubstake." John grew up in the desert and he met a few prospectors, so he knew what a grub stake was. The old man continued with his story. "This man owned a large hardware store, and I traded him some gold nuggets for equipment I needed, like a pick and shovel, a new canteen, and all the other items an old fool like me needed to hunt for gold up in those mountains. As the years passed, this man grew his business to where he had a lot of these hardware stores all over the state. He became so popular that he ran for governor and won by telling a bunch of lies over the television. Well, that man tracked me down and he wanted me to tell him where I found my gold. To tell you the truth, son, I found a ton of gold. I set my mind when I was a young man to find the lost Four Peaks Gold Mine and I spent a good part of my life searching for it. The area I concentrated my search on the southern portion of the Mazatzal Mountains. It was a big job trying to find what no one else ever dreamed of finding. The Four Peaks, which are nearly 8000 feet high, have always been an important landmark in this part of Arizona and as a kid, I always dreamt that I would be the one to find the legendary mine. So where does one start when he wants to find a lost gold mine?" He had John's absolute attention now and the young man was hanging on every word the old man said.

"Where *does* one start, Dutch Henry?"

The old man laughed, showing some brown stained teeth along with a few missing ones. "Got your attention - don't I? Well, you can't see the old fort because the intervening peaks hide it. Old Fort Reno lies about 14 miles north of the Four Peaks area. Forgive an old man's rambling, son, but I am getting to my point. They constructed old Fort Reno on the eastern flanks of the Mazatzal Mountains overlooking Tonto Creek to the east. The Mazatzal peak known as Mount Ord rises only four miles to the northwest of the old fort. Beyond Mount Ord, the mountains swing around to the northwest.

"During the 1800s, the Mazatzal Mountains were in the middle of Apache country. The Tonto Apaches wandered these mountains in search of game, but they had something else, something everyone wanted. Rumors circulated for years of a hidden Apache gold mine in or near the Mazatzals. Tonto Apaches, the local Indians, always seemed to have plenty of gold nuggets for trading. They said that during the 1850s, the friendly Tontos took the famous Dr. Abraham Thorne to an Apache gold mine. Although they blindfolded him, Thorne insisted till the end of his days that the mine was in the Salt River country. I even read where in 1853, Francis X. Aubry saw local Apaches making bullets out of gold! So, I set my sights and began digging in the Mazatzal mountain area. I spent forty years searching for that lost gold mine. Through the years, I picked up traces, bits and pieces, nuggets of gold brought down the mountains by the rains, but I never found the mine itself, until 11 years ago. After decades of searching, I hit the jackpot. The greedy bastard Governor Wilson wants what I have spent a lifetime searching for, after I found the lost mine. I broke my ass digging the gold out of that mine just when I started enjoying the fruits of my labor. Governor Wilson arrested me on some trumped-up charges and threw me into this hellhole six years ago. I near starved, was almost killed a few times, nearly froze to death and this baby-assed governor thinks he can steal my gold.

I'd rather die first than see him get it." John W. Hardin let out the breath he hadn't realized he was holding.

"Whew. That's some story. Man, what you must have gone through. Yet you endured and you found the pot of gold at the end of the rainbow."

"You got that right, John W. I surely found that pot of gold."

"But that doesn't explain why you were digging a tunnel to the 11A cell."

"That's not 11A, son. It's Roman numerals meaning '2A.' You can't see it, but the cell across from this one is 1A. Look.

When Holland Wilson, our illustrious Governor, threatened me with prison, he took me out here and showed me where he said I'd be spending the rest of my life if I didn't tell him the whereabouts of the mine he was certain I found. That was his first mistake. I may be old, but I didn't get to live this long by being stupid. I told him to give me a month to think about it. As soon as he left, I went to the library and paid a young man with computer knowledge fifty dollars for an hour of his time. The job I wanted him to do was to search the Internet for me. I knew inmates from the Yuma Territorial Prison built this prison. I needed to track down relatives of the men who built this place and see if they left a record or diary of their time here. The young man I gave the fifty bucks to did a helluva job. He found out that the Yuma prisoner who was to build this prison was one Willard Smith, doing twenty years to life."

"The boy discovered Smith had a granddaughter, name of Priscilla Bluestone, and she was living in Amarillo, Texas. I tracked her down and told her I was writing a book on the Yuma Territorial Prison and I wanted to speak to her about her grandfather. She agreed to see me. When I met her, I told her I did some research and found that her grandfather was to build the Gila prison. I asked her if he left a record of the work he performed on that site. She told me she had two large boxes of her grandfather's papers and books in the attic and she agreed to let me look through them, but she didn't want the boxes brought downstairs because it would mess up her tidy house. She said if I wanted to look at her grandfather's information, I'd have to climb up into the attic, put the light on, and look through the boxes up there. When I got the first box opened and I rummaged through his papers, I found a lot of interesting information on Yuma but very little on the Gila prison except a small paperback book on the history of the place. After emptying the first box and looking through his papers, I came up empty, so I put everything back and started on the second box. I held little hope of finding anything. But I was wrong, because when I opened the second box, I found his diary right on top. I scanned through the diary, hoping to find something that would help me, and I was right. This diary was the ticket. I looked through the rest of his papers and books but found nothing more that would help me, so I closed the box and took the diary downstairs. I was sweating like I was in a sauna as I showed it to Smith's granddaughter."

"I said to her, 'I hope you don't mind me bringing this diary down here. I found it in one box. It was kind of hot sitting on my haunches trying to read it upstairs in the dim light and the heat, so I brought it downstairs where it's cooler."

"'No, of course not. Here, sit at the table. You look boiling. I'll bring you a cool glass of iced tea to refresh you a bit.' I opened the diary and started reading from the first page and I made notes as I read through it. Her grandfather wrote important details of each step of construction and the renovations he made while toiling in the scorching sun in the Gila desert. When I finished reading the diary, I had what I was looking for. Priscilla said that he kept it because he was a very thorough man and besides, he didn't want to forget any of the details in case he became forgetful. I knew she listened to what he said, but she never read the diary. He didn't keep this record for fear of becoming forgetful. This was his insurance policy in case they ever transferred him there. If she had read the diary, she would have known that. She told me that her grandfather was a civil engineer before he killed his partner in a heated dispute over money and because of it, they sent him to Yuma prison. The warden approached Smith one day and told him he'd be getting out of Yuma for a while. He was making him the foreman and putting him in charge of prisoners he picked to build the Gila Prison and Smith jumped at the chance.

"Now here's how he pulled it off. Put yourself in the guard's place. Imagine their mindset. Here they are in the middle of the desert where the temperature gets below 120 degrees, working in the sun without shade. What man in his right mind wants to stand outside in the sun when he could be in a tent sipping a cool beer? It was just them. There weren't any supervisors around and they weren't worried about prisoners escaping because where would they go? There was no place for them to escape to, so there was no need to watch them while they worked. The guards spent the day in the shade of a tent and they came out at noon to inspect the work the prisoners did that day. Then, at noon, the prisoners would return to their tents and play cards or read a book until the following day. Then the routine would start all over again. Remember now, the cells they were constructing held the one or two prisoners that did something terrible. One or two cells would have done the trick, but Willard Smith suggested putting eight cells in an eight-foot area filled with stones and dirt separating one cell from another. He laid the blueprints on the kitchen table and explained to the guards how this design was better than the original plan, and it served two purposes. The first was it was a simple way to stop prisoners from talking or passing things to one another, and the second was with the eight cells spread out along the length of the floor. It fit the aesthetic design of the prison. The guards liked Smith's suggestion, so they approached the Captain for his approval and received it. Even the eight-foot spaces between cells and he agreed to Smith's suggestion. Smith was told to build it just the way he described to it them, but they added a condition he wasn't happy with. 'Make sure you filled the space between the cells with eight feet of solid rock with dirt added as a fill instead of just filling it with dirt.' But that wouldn't work for Smith. What the guards didn't know was Smith intended to build a back door out of the prison in case they ever incarcerated him there. 'Look,' Smith said to the guard. 'I can fill the space between cells with dirt and add sand instead of stone, but I don't have enough time to haul those rocks down from the mountains. The work detail doing that work would be the same as a chain gang chipping away at a mountain. Let me use sand with the dirt as a filler instead of rock. The sand will work just as well and it will cut six months off the time needed to build this prison. But you fellas have to make that decision, so I'll leave it to you. But think about it for a minute and tell me if what I'm suggesting makes little sense to you. If you think it doesn't, and if you still want stone, then it's no problem to get a gang together and march them out into the desert and cut it out of the mountain. But if we do that, then figure on adding another six months to complete the job.'" That got the guard's attention.

"The guard liked the idea of cutting the time down by six months and said he'd talk it over with the Captain. He told him he'd get back to him in a little while, and then he left to have a talk with the Captain. Smith watched him walk away, and he chuckled to himself. Moron. I could walk to the base of the mountain and pick up all the rocks I want without chipping away at any mountain. He knew the Captain would approve sand instead of rock, because everyone knew that all the man dreamed about was to get the hell away from this godforsaken prison. It wasn't long before he heard the tap, tap, tap of the guard's steps as he walked back down the stairs. 'Forget about using stone. Build it with dirt and sand.' He said, 'The Captain said we don't need rocks. They won't serve any purpose down here.' Smith had the Captain's approval, as he knew he would."

"Are you telling me you found a way out of this place?"

"That's exactly what I'm telling you. Now, with your help, we can do it in half the time. Might take us another year or two and if we're not released by then, and I don't expect we will. We can break out of here ourselves."

"Wait a minute," John W said. "We can't ever get out of here because we don't have a means to cross the desert. Besides, the moment we're gone, they'll know we're missing."

"That's not exactly true. John W. Smith was ahead of you. He foresaw the problems you just mentioned, and he worked around them. Just behind that wall is a room, which isn't filled with dirt. Remember, all the prisoners and the guards all slept in canvas tents."

"Yeah. But so what?"

"Smith was smart. The man knew good canvas wouldn't rot in the short term and maybe not for the next two hundred years. He made sure the canvass he requisitioned was heavy-duty, long-lasting canvas. He justified it with the guards by telling them that if they had one of those torrential seasonal downpours while they were in their tents made of a thin canvas and that canvass was all that stood between them and the rain, they'd be soaked in no time at all. And remember this: when Carter found King Tut's mummy, the linen they wrapped Tutt in was still serviceable. Heavy canvas will work for us just like Tut's linen. No, the canvas Smith chose for his tents will work just fine for us."

"Wait, a minute. What do we need canvas for? I don't understand any of this. Please, Dutch Henry, get to the point and explain all of this to me."

The old man was getting a kick bantering with John W. Hardin. "It's simple, John. We need the canvas to inflate our hot-air balloon because the air needs something to inflate. Don't you understand? He made the air balloon from the canvas Smith bought for his tents? When he ordered the canvas, he ordered a lot more than he needed. Old Willard Smith, Civil Engineer prisoner in charge of building this prison, had to figure a way of escaping if they ever put him in one of these cells here. The only thing he could think of to escape was a hot-air balloon. In that room, behind the wall that you're leaning on." He pointed his finger at it. "There's a hot-air balloon made by the prisoners out of canvas, and it's waiting to take us out of here."

"How would we inflate it, Dutch Henry?"

"Smith left the means to inflate it in that room. Once we dig our way into that room, we'll assemble the balloon and then we'll wait until we inflate it without alerting the guards."

"But won't they miss us when they check on us in the morning?"

"Smith planned for that as well. John. In that room, besides the hot-air balloon, there's also dynamite. It's rigged and ready to blow, and it has a slow-burning fuse. About twenty minutes after we're in the air, this place will go up like they bombed it. When they check in the morning, they'll find a few of our things, but nothing more. They'll assume that the explosion killed us."

John W thought about that for a moment. "But what would they attribute the explosion to?"

The old man just smiled. "Did you know that old dynamite has some very peculiar characteristics and is very tetchy? Smith left the dynamite in the hidden room under the foundation. They'll figure it sweated through the years, causing it to release nitroglycerin, causing the dynamite to become unstable, after all these years of laying here in the heat, it just blew up. There is no other explanation that will make sense to anyone. The explosion will give the state the reason it needs to close Gila Prison. Or at the very least, make it a ghost town like Yuma Prison."

John nodded. "Yeah, I guess that would explain it. This

could work, Dutch Henry."

"Son, it has to work. Listen, when we get out of here, I'm going to set you up for life. I'm an old man now and I'm reaching the end of my rope. I have no relatives to leave my fortune to, so I've decided I'm going to leave everything to you." The old man paused a moment and reached up and took hold of John W's shoulders, deciding whether to continue. "Now, if I don't make it out of here, I want you to promise me you'll get even with that lying scoundrel of a governor for me."

"Don't worry, Dutch Henry. I'll put the governor on top of my list. I have a few people I intend to take care of too - but I promise you - the Governor will be on top of my list."

Dutch Henry slapped John W on his shoulder. "Good, that's settled then. Now let's get to diggin'."

CHAPTER ELEVEN

William Hayes and Jason Sweeney walked into the Flagstaff office at ten a.m. I surprised the employees to see the owner walk in with a stranger. Hayes kept a somber face on and acknowledged no one as he walked straight back to Jenkins's office with Sweeney at his side. He opened the door without knocking, surprising Jenkins, who was having an animated conversation with someone on the other end of the phone. Hayes could tell it was not a client, but someone with whom he was very familiar with.

"Hang up the phone, Mr. Jenkins. Do it now."

Jenkins cupped the phone. "Hang on a moment. What do you want, Hayes? I'm kind of busy right now."

"It's *Mr.* Hayes to you, Jenkins."

Jenkins smiled until Sweeney pressed the receiver on the phone, cutting off the conversation.

"Who do you think you are? Who is this guy?" he asked Hayes.

"He's my friend, and I fired you. Get your things and get out of this office."

Jenkins's face turned crimson. "You can't fire me."

"And why can't I? Am I not still your boss? And do I not still own this establishment? Get your things and get out. *Now!*"

Jenkins was beat red. He was livid with rage. "You'll be sorry for this. I'll be back and I'll make sure you'll be the one fired."

"Maybe so. But right now I'm still the owner, and I want you out of here in the next two minutes."

"I have powerful friends in high places. They want me here. I'll be back. You don't know who you're dealing with."

Hayes replied, "You mean like Jack McCormack, who stole poor John Hardin's land, or Holland Wilson, our esteemed governor? Are those the people you're referring to?"

"Yes, that exactly who I'm referring to. I'll be back and make no mistake about that."

Sweeney had been observing the interaction between the two men and, unknown to Jenkins, he recorded everything that was said. If Jenkins had gotten out of line and tried some rough stuff, then he would have intervened, but Hayes handled the situation with intelligent, subdued anger. Anger because he now realized he had been so wrong in hiring Jenkins and John W had been so right that it had landed him in jail.

As soon as Jenkins left the office, Hayes walked up front to the sales area. "Everyone in my office… Now!"

When they seated the six employees around Jenkins's desk, Hayes looked them over. This was the first time he had met most of them. There was one woman who transferred out of the original office in Mohave County to this office. "What's your name, dear?" he said, pointing to the one familiar face he recognized.

"Margaret Nolan, sir."

"Margaret, you are now the office manager. You will assume Mr. Jenkins's position. I no longer employ Mr. Jenkins. I've just fired him. Sales in this office are so low that it has almost bankrupted me." Hayes questioned each salesperson on the amount of sales he or she brought in month by month. Hayes knew what the average sales per person should be, within a certain range. All the people he interviewed were far below average. "Were your weekly salaries supplemented by outside income?" Everyone's head looked down or away, with none of them making eye contact with him. They were nervous; he could see that. "What about you, Margaret? How were your sales?"

"They were very good at first, but Mr. Jenkins kept turning down my deals. He said it wasn't good enough. Not enough money coming in."

"I see. And what about you?" he asked, pointing to a young man.

"It's the same with me, sir. Except that Mr. Jenkins said not to worry about the sales. He would make it up by giving us an advance in sales. Whatever deals we brought to him,, he turned down. He let some go through, but not enough for us to make a living on. The advance he gave us allowed us to pay our bills."

"I see. And how about the rest of you? Was it like that for all of you?" Everyone nodded their heads.

One older man in the back spoke up. "When I came to work this morning, I was going to quit. There was something shady going on in this place. I didn't enjoy working my butt off bringing in a deal, only to have it turned down by Jenkins."

"Okay, I've heard enough. When I came in, I had intended to fire all of you after I got rid of Jenkins, but after hearing what you just told me, I'm going to give you another chance to make sales pick up again. If you produce for me, I'll see that I compensated you for your efforts. I'll give you a bonus above your salary if you exceed the quota Mrs. Nolan and I give you. I expect to receive a daily report from this office, Margaret. Heads will roll if I do not get that report. Now get to work and get me sales."

When everyone left the office, Hayes motioned for Sweeney to come closer. He didn't want the employees to hear them talking. "What's your opinion about what you observed this morning, Jason?"

"I liked the way you handled Jenkins. You surprised him by mentioning the two aces he was hiding from you. I almost laughed when I saw the look on his face when you mentioned them. As for the employees, I thought you would fire everyone, but I'm glad you didn't. They were bringing in sales, but Jenkins kept rejecting them and supplementing their salaries to make up for the sales he turned down. I think you handled it very well, Mr. Hayes."

"Jason. You don't mind me calling you 'Jason,' do you?"

"Not at all, Mr. Hayes."

"I want to keep you on a retainer. See if you can find out where they're keeping John W."

"I'll do that, Mr. Hayes, but if you'll excuse me for a little while, I have something rather urgent I need to attend to."

Sweeney left the office and rushed out onto the street, looking to see where Jenkins was heading. He spotted him crossing the street and entering a bar. It was too early for a drink. Sweeney smiled. I bet he went in for a drink and he used his cell phone to make a call to his pal, Rutgar. It didn't matter.

He had him now. He'd just follow him and see what he was up to.

CHAPTER TWELVE

Jenkins tried to seduce Virginia several times while he was the manager of the Flagstaff office, but she saw through him and remained true to her imprisoned sweetheart. Jenkins was persistent, though. He kept calling her even after her father fired him until one day her father surprised him by picking up the phone instead of her. He told Jenkins to stop calling this number, and if he continued stalking his daughter, he'd have him arrested. The phone calls stopped, but Jenkins followed Virginia, hoping to get a moment alone with her to convince her to go out with him.

McCormack got what he wanted, which was the Hardin's property, but it frustrated the Governor. It disappointed him at not getting Dutch Henry's gold. Governor Wilson was sure the old man found the lost Four Peaks Gold Mine, and he wanted it for himself. Every month, he had his pilot fly him to the Gila Bend Prison to see if the old man was ready to talk to him, but the answer was always 'no.' When Wilson realized Dutch Henry would never tell him where the mine was, he cut his visits to one every few months. Then, finally, he decided. He would let the old man rot in that hellhole of a prison for the rest of his life and if he wanted out, he would just have to call him. Wilson couldn't understand why Dutch Henry was so unreasonable. Didn't he offer him his freedom? All he had to do was to share his gold with him. Well, that wasn't true, he admitted to himself. He wanted all the old man's gold. Could he be the unreasonable one? No. How could he be when he offered the old man his freedom?

At dinner one evening, Virginia asked her father if he was making any progress in finding the prison in which John was being kept. Her father replied by saying, "We're trying, honey. But don't give up hope, because we're working hard on it. I have Sweeney looking into it and that boy gets results. He was the one who discovered that Jenkins was purposely ruining the Flagstaff office. He discovered how McCormack swindled Abigail out of her land and made millions with the gold he took out of the old mine on their property. So don't go giving up on John W, not yet." Hayes could see she was fighting back tears.

"It's so unfair, Dad. John's the most decent man in the world. He wouldn't harm anyone. How could they put him in jail with those trumped-up charges? I'm surprised anyone believed them."

Mr. Hayes looked at his daughter as if for the first time. She was no longer his little girl, and six years had passed since they sent John to prison. Hayes admired his daughter. Somehow, when he wasn't looking, she had morphed into a beautiful woman. She was pining for the man she thought she may never see again. Hayes had no way of knowing if John would ever get out of prison, so he advised Virginia to find herself another decent young man, but she refused. She said that she still loved John. She was twenty-four years old now, and she had grown into a full-figured woman with a dazzling smile and long, strawberry blond hair.

"You asked me how people could believe the trumped-up charges brought against John. Remember this: people will believe anything if it's presented logically. It all goes back to Dr. Joseph Goebbels, Hitler's minister of propaganda, who said, *'tell a lie often enough and people will believe it.'* Maybe it would be better if you went and stayed with your Aunt Harriet in upstate New York for a little while. The cool air would be good for you and, who knows, it might clear your mind. It's painful for me to see you hurting like this. I'll call her and tell her you're going to stay with her for a while."

"You're right, Dad. Maybe a change of scenery will do me some good. Call Aunt Harriet and if it's all right with her. Then I'll stay with her for a while. Maybe a change of scenery will make me feel better."

"Don't worry, dear. I'll arrange it with Aunt Harriet. You better pack now because I'll feel better knowing you're on tomorrow's flight to New York."

Tom Jenkins removed the earphones and put them beside him on the passenger seat. He'd heard enough. Hayes booked a flight for tomorrow morning on Delta to New York for his daughter. The phone tap the Governor had allowed on the Hayes residence telephone had paid off. *It was nice to have friends in high places*; he thought to himself. He took the same flight and when he got the chance, he would try to convince her to see him, maybe even go out with him. If that didn't work, he would kidnap her. Jenkins wouldn't hurt her; he just wanted to reason with her. The man looked in the mirror. He knew he was a striking man. Most women threw themselves at him. Why was she different? Why couldn't she see he had feelings for her, and he hated not being near her? She was frustrating him because she was still pining for that loser boyfriend of hers, who she would never see again. Well, Jenkins was glad that they locked him up in that rat hole of a dungeon. That was too bad for old Johnny-boy, but what was bad for John Hardin could be good for him. He knew that since they locked John in jail, this might be the only opportunity he'd have to convince Virginia to go out with him.

Sweeney was good at his job. He had unfailing instincts, which he always followed. He didn't trust Jenkins. The man was no good, and Sweeney knew it. Jenkins's record proved it. He was a swindler who was used to getting his own way. So, when he left Hayes's office, Sweeney followed him. It did not surprise him to see him parked in the street in front of the Hayes home and was wearing headphones. Sweeney watched as Jenkins pulled away from the curb and drove away. When Jenkins turned the corner and disappeared from sight, Sweeney got out of his car and rang the doorbell.

It surprised Hayes to see Sweeney standing there, but he welcomed him in. "What are you doing here, Jason?"

Jason didn't mince words. "You made a phone call a few minutes ago. I need to know who you called. It's important." The seriousness on Jason's face said it all.

"I called the airlines and booked a flight for my daughter. I'm sending her to New York to stay with her aunt. Why?" Hayes asked.

Jason walked over to the phone and unscrewed the earpiece. He found nothing. Then he turned the phone upside down, took a small tool from his pocket, and unscrewed the bottom. When he removed the bottom plate, there it was. A small transmitter attached to wires inside the base of the phone. "Did anyone from the telephone company work on your phone lines?"

"Why, yes? Two days ago, my phone line went dead. I called the phone company, and they said I had a break in the line, and they'd send someone to repair it. A telephone repairman came shortly after and worked on the line outside my home and then he came in to check my phone to see if it was serviceable. Then he left."

"I see," Jason said. He showed Hayes the little transmitter and said, "This is what they did. There was nothing wrong with your phone line. They needed an excuse to bug your phone, so they disconnected the outside phone line leading into your home. I've been watching Jenkins. He's heard every word you've been saying on this phone for the past two days. He was outside, listening, when you called for reservations. My guess is, tomorrow he'll be on the same flight as your daughter. I suggest you call the airline and change her flight. Tomorrow morning, I'll pick up your daughter and take her to the airport and if I see anything suspicious, I'll get on the plane with her. I'm not taking any chances. I'm calling my office and having one of my agents meet Virginia at the airport. He'll take her to her aunt's home. Meanwhile, call the airline and change her flight."

"I'll do that right now. Thanks, Jason. I feel much better knowing someone responsible will meet my daughter at the airport. At least I know she'll arrive at my sister's house."

CHAPTER THIRTEEN

Dutch Henry crawled through the tunnel leading to John's cell every day. The two men shared stories and kept each other company while they dug. But, more than that, they saved each other's sanity. Dutch Henry made sure he returned to his cell before meals were served, so he would be there when the slot opened and they passed his meal through. It wouldn't do for a suspicious guard to open the cell door and find the cell empty because they didn't take their meal tray. For months, the two dug, scraped, and pulled on the very large stone they had been working on for days, until it finally broke free of the rocks on either side of it. The stone they pulled out had to be large enough to allow the men to fit into through the opening, but not that large where they would have trouble maneuvering it. It had to be at floor level, so when it broke free, it wouldn't have to be picked up. When they examined the stone, Dutch Henry noticed Smith had put mortar only on the outer surface of the stone that faced the cell. He wanted to make it as easy as possible to get the stone out of the wall. Dutch Henry nodded and smiled. "Smart fella, that Smith," he murmured.

Maybe it was the knowledge he was leaving this prison tonight, or maybe the stress of maneuvering the large stone that caused Dutch Henry to clutch his chest for a moment.

"What is it Dutch? Are you all right? Don't you scare me now... you hear?"

"Don't worry about me, son. It's this old ticker of mine. It acts up every once in a while. I guess I've been overdoing it a bit with all this diggin' I've been doing." The pain went away. "I feel better now. Hand me the candle, son, and let's see what ole Willard Smith left us." Dutch Henry took the candle and lit it. Then he got on his hands and knees and, with anticipation, crawled into the space left by the stone. He held the candle in front of him, letting it light the way into Willard Smith's hidden room.

"What do you see, Dutch?"

"Come on in here and see for yourself. Pretty amazing man, that Willard Smith. I can feel him looking over my shoulder, looking at all the stuff he left us. He also left us a guest wearing a prison guard's uniform."

"Wha-what did you say?"

"I said he left us a guest in a prison guard's uniform. Come on in here and see for yourself."

John wiggled his way through the opening and into the room that had waited for over one hundred years for someone to discover it. When John finally stood and brushed himself off, he looked over at Dutch Henry who, with a tilt of his head, motioned to his left. John turned to look at where he pointed and backed away in shock, banging his head against the wall. Facing them in the corner was a skeleton in a guard's uniform, sitting in a chair. The flickering light of the candle caused the illusion that the skull was grinning at them, as if it knew some macabre secret.

"Good God. What is he doing here? And how in the world did he get here? And who put him here?"

"Hold on there, son. I expected this guy to be here. It was all explained in Willard Smith's diary. This guard heard a noise one day and came to investigate it. When Willard and the boys working in this room heard him as he was about to enter this room, he had his gun out ready to plug them. One prisoner hid by the entrance and waited for him to come in. When he stepped into the room, the guy hit him with his shovel, causing him to fall. He accidentally hit his head on the corner of a stone over there, killing him instantly. That saved them the trouble of killing him. They would have killed him anyway because he discovered their secret room and they couldn't afford to let anyone know about it. They all knew that if they put them in this hellhole, any of them could use this back door to escape. So, they killed him and kept it a secret. When he didn't report for work in the morning, the guards searched for him, but he was nowhere to be found. The assumption was that he wandered off into the desert and died there. When there was no trace of him, an inquiry showed it was the only story that made sense.

Because there was no other explanation that would account for his disappearance, the theory that he wandered into the desert and died became the official story."

The room was a fair-sized room. It was eight feet by eight feet square. Smith proved to be a fine engineer because he completed the back door escape in the hidden room without the guards knowing about it. Dutch Henry collected his thoughts and tried to remember where the trip mechanism to the door was located. He had committed his notes from the diary to memory. Now he was trying to recall the salient points that would help him escape this place. When Dutch Henry asked Smith's granddaughter if he could have the diary, she refused to part with it. He offered her a large sum of money for it and still she refused him. Smith's granddaughter Priscilla wanted the diary to remain in the family, so Dutch Henry had to settle for the notes he took. When he opened the front door to leave, he handed her an envelope. She asked what the envelope was for. He said that it was to repay her for the kindness that she had showed him by allowing him to read Smith's diary. At first, she refused to take it, but the old man reasoned with her.

"Ma'am, you don't know how much you have helped me. I will be eternally grateful to you, so please make an old man happy, and take this envelope."

She looked at him and she could see how much it meant to him if she took the envelope. She took it from him but didn't open it. "Thank you, Mr. Henry, for whatever is in this envelope. I will open it after you have left."

"That's right, considerate of you, ma'am. Thank you again for helping me with my story. I'll be leaving you now and I don't reckon we'll see each other again, at least not in this lifetime. Goodbye, now." Dutch Henry left Smith's granddaughter's house, but he left with the notes he had copied from Smith's diary.

"Let's check the air balloon's canvas. Smith researched hot air balloons. He mentioned in his diary that several one-man balloons hold 30,000 cubic feet of air. The largest holds over 800,000 cubic feet. The most popular size holds about 77,000 cubic feet and is about 70 feet high. Older balloons have 'gondolas' made of aluminum and fiberglass, but since they did not invent fiberglass in Smith's time, and he didn't have any aluminum, he made the cage out of canvas secured to half-inch steel rods.

"How long do you think it'll take us to inflate this thing?"

"If we're lucky, we might do it in about 30 minutes. It's good that we're doing this at night, because Smith wrote in his diary that a balloon lifts better in cold air rather than hot air. Did you know they used balloons in the Civil War?"

"You're kidding me, right?"

"No. I'm dead serious. They used balloons and filled them with hydrogen. Wish I had me some of that hydrogen now. It would make getting out of here a lot easier. Come on. Let's look around for that old butane burner Smith said he stored in here."

The two men scoured the room and John found it sitting on a chest they hadn't searched yet. "Here it is."

"Good. Now look for the fuel he said he stored here. I hope it's still good. He was using a primitive outfit. I just hope it works well enough to get us the hell out of here. Open that chest up. See if it's in there."

They didn't lock the chest. John just unsnapped the fasteners and opened the chest. "Dutch Henry. Come over here and see what I found."

The old man ambled to where John stood and looked into the old chest. "Well, lookee what we have here. Open those packages up and let's see what Willard Smith left for us."

John cut the cord with the sharp end of his shovel and pulled the wrapping from the packages. To their surprise, they found it contained cold weather clothes. Smith knew it would get cold at night and even colder when they climbed high into the chilly night air. The first package contained three pullover sweaters. The second contained three pairs of pants made of the same canvas as the balloon.

"God bless Smith. He thought of everything. There's where he put the butane containers." Dutch Henry said, pointing at the chest. "He put them under the packages of clothes. He knew that if he escaped, he'd need to wear something besides his prison duds. Smart man, that one."

Dutch Henry walked over to the makeshift cage and tugged on the canvas nestled inside of it. The canvas folds fought him for a moment, and then came free. “The right way of doing this is to fill the balloon two-thirds of the way with cold air, then the rest with hot air. But we can’t get cold air into it, so we’ll have to use hot air. If this gas is still good. Well, we won’t know about that until we try filling it. If that doesn’t work, I’m still leaving here. I’ll walk out on foot if I have to and I don’t care if I die out there. It’ll be better than remaining here.”

“Well then, let’s hope that this gas is still good.”

The old man thought for a minute, and then he said, “I think we should try filling the balloon with hot air from the forge. Smith rigged a fan, which we’ll have to turn to force the air through the hose in order to fill the balloon. Once it’s about two-thirds full, we’ll use the burner he left us to keep the balloon afloat. I guess that will have to be our plan, unless you can think of some other way to put air into this contraption.” The two men pulled the canvas from the balloon’s cage and set it by the wall, where Smith showed the hidden door. They hadn’t tried the door yet, nor would they. Not until tonight. A lot of things had to go right in order for them to make it out of there. The big thing was inflating the balloon.

“Look. I’m dying with curiosity,” Dutch Henry said. “Let’s see if the gas is any good. I’d like to ignite it for a moment. If it doesn’t light up, then we might as well throw in the towel and forget about it. We can save the back door for a time when our guards might get careless and leave a vehicle outside that we might borrow for a little while.” To their delight and utter surprise, they let out their collected breath as the gas ignited. With that accomplished, they shut off the gas and did a thorough check of the room to see if there was anything else that Smith had left that they might use.

Smith had secured the guard’s gun and gun belt to a piece of board that was bolted to the wall near the door opening. “Smith thought of everything,” the old man said. “Look, he even left us the dynamite strung out and inserted in all the walls with a fuse leading to the front door, so when we’re ready to skedaddle, all we have to do is to light the fuse and get out of Dodge in a hurry. Smith wrote in large letters in his diary that he left a slow-burning fuse timed to go off when we were in the air, a long way from here.” Dutch pointed to the gun. “Strap that gun on you. We might need it."

"Look, Dutch, I never killed anybody and I don't intend to start now."

"I know that. But we might need it if we land somewhere and meet up with a pack of wolves or a mountain lion or some such critter. Hell, we don't know where this balloon will take us. We don't control it, or where we want it to go. We can only go where it takes us, and to be honest with you, anywhere it takes us is just fine with me, as long as it's far away from this hellhole of a prison."

John W. Hardin strapped on the gun. He swore he felt his namesake's hand on his, as the gun fit in the palm of his hand. It was as if it belonged there. John checked the old police 38 Special for rust, but because of the dry heat of the desert, it was like new. He pulled the cartridges out and checked them, but they too were still like new. He turned each cartridge around in his fingers to see if there was corrosion or a sign they might be dangerous to fire. But the bullets were as dry as the day he loaded them into the guns' chambers.

"Come on over here and help me get the balloon out of the cage. I want to stretch it out and get it ready so that all we have to do tonight is fire up the forge and open the hidden door and bring the hose line to the balloon. When that's done, we'll inflate it. When we're ready to go, since you are younger than me, you will bring the hose back into the room, set the fuse and then you'll get your skinny ass out of that room. The last thing you'll do before getting into this here balloon will be to close the hidden door. But make sure the fuse is lit and burning properly before you do that. You hear now?"

"Yeah. I hear now, so don't worry. I know exactly what I have to do."

"Okay, we're all set for tonight. Once we start, things will happen fast. I'm hoping that the guards will play cards tonight like they always do. We don't want one of them sauntering out here and seeing our balloon filling up with hot air. I'd hate to do what those old prisoners did to that guard that stumbled upon them, but if I have to, I will."

CHAPTER FOURTEEN

Jenkins waited patiently until all the boarding passengers got on line. Then he boarded the plane. He was careful to walk around the partition on the other side of the aircraft, opposite from where Virginia's seat was. He walked to the rear of the plane to his seat, where she wouldn't be able to see him. When they exited the plane, he would catch up to her at the luggage carousel. Then he would act as if it were a coincidence that he was there at the same time that she was. Jenkins was as giddy as a teenager on his first date. He was sure this would work. He couldn't wait for the flight to end so he could talk to her. But what he didn't know was that Virginia had left on an earlier flight.

A private detective by the name of Daniel Harlbager would wait for Virginia by the luggage carousel, holding a sign with the name "Hayes" on it. He had instructions to keep her safe and to escort her to her aunt's home in upstate New York. He would remain there and watch for any suspicious persons or activity. If a telephone repairman or a utility man came to their house, he was to instruct Virginia to call him immediately or, if he were on site, to inform him immediately of the visit and then show him exactly what the man touched or repaired. Sweeney knew McCormack's influence didn't reach as far as New York. This was Sweeney's turf and they would be playing by his rules and not McCormack's or Holland Wilson's.

Virginia spotted her name on the card the man was holding and she walked over to him. "You must be Mr. Harlbager."

"And you are Virginia."

"That's me," she said with a smile.

On the drive upstate, Harlbager gave her a small button. "Please keep this on you at all times. If a stranger comes to your door, press this button. It will activate a transmitter and I will hear it. Please don't be offended, but I don't care if it's a police officer, a firefighter, mailman, utility guy, or a telephone man. Push the button and it will enable me to listen to what's being said. I will take a room in town, but I'll spend most of my time in my car near your aunt's home. Remember what I'm telling you. It's very important that you do exactly as I tell you. Most likely, nothing will happen. The people that threatened your father and framed your fiancé don't have power in this state, but it never hurts to be prepared. Questions?"

"No!"

"Tell me again. What are you going to do if someone rings your doorbell and tells you some bull crap story that your phone is out or you have an electrical problem, or your TV is out? What are you going to do?"

She smiled and said, "I'm to push this button."

"Very good. Now don't forget to do it, because if you don't, I won't know what's happening."

"Don't worry. I got it."

He smiled and relaxed for the first time. "Good. I don't mean to worry you, but it never hurts to be prepared."

Harlbager dropped Virginia at her aunt's house and waited until she was safely inside. He drove to the nearest hotel and rented a room near to the house. Since he didn't know how long he'd be renting the room, he gave the man his credit card as security. He had his laptop with him, loaded with movies or he could watch the Mets or Yankees through his sling box. Now it all came down to patience, and he had a lot of patience. He felt in his gut that something would happen. He didn't know what, but he had the feeling it would happen soon and he wanted to be close when it did.

Jenkins waited until all the passengers deplaned and were at the luggage carousel. Jenkins couldn't understand where she could have gone. He walked to the Delta ticket counter and asked them to check on the status of a Virginia Hayes who was on flight 442. The woman checked her computer. No, she wasn't on this flight. She arrived on an earlier flight, which arrived two hours ago.

"I see." he said, clearly disappointed. He had her aunt's address, so he decided he'd go there to see her. What could she do? Throw him out? Not likely. He rented a car with a GPS in it and punched in the address. Callicoon is on the banks of the historic Delaware River in Sullivan County, New York. Jenkins programmed the GPS in his rented Lincoln. It was a two-hour trip to Virginia's aunt's house, and the car told him how to get there.

Jenkins arrived at the correct address. It was easy these days driving with a GPS in your car. It certainly earned its keep with sales associates because instead of them driving in circles trying to find a customer's address, the GPS took you right to their front door and announced in understandable English, *"You have arrived at your destination."*

A frightened voice came over Harlbager's earpiece just as he was about to take a bite out of the donut he had in his hand. *"What are you doing here? What do you want? How dare you come here?"* It was Virginia's frightened voice he was listening to. He looked at the house and noticed for the first time a strange car parked in front of it. *How the hell did I allow that to happen?* He thought. Harlbager was already out of his car, even as the thought flicked through his mind. The donut fell to the street, forgotten, as he raced toward the house. Harlbager bounded up the front steps, two at a time, and stopped to listen for a moment before turning the door handle. It was unlocked, and it opened when he turned the knob. Jenkins didn't hear the door opening. He was busy trying to explain to the two frightened women he meant no harm. He just wanted to talk to Virginia to explain his feelings to her. That was all. He was using his entire charming con man persona to calm the ladies down, but to no avail.

"Let's go down to the corner and get a cup of coffee and talk about this. Come on, what do you say?"

Instead of Virginia answering him, Harlbager answered the question for her. "The lady says she doesn't want to go with you. She also says that she doesn't like you. She wants you to leave her alone. That's what she says."

Jenkins turned to see where the voice was coming from. It surprised him to see a very large man standing behind him with his jacket open, revealing a very large gun attached to a holster on his belt.

"Who are you?" Jenkins asked.

"I'm her friend. That's who I am. Now let's go."

"Where are we going?"

"Me? I'm going nowhere. I'm staying right here. You? You're getting in your car and driving away from here right now. Consider yourself lucky I'm letting you off easy. But if I ever see or hear of you bothering this lady again, I won't be so pleasant. I promise you that if I ever see you again, you'll rue the day you ever met her. And that's a promise you can take to the bank. Get out of here. *NOW!*" Harlbager watched Jenkins get in his car and drive away. Once he was out of sight, Harlbager went back into the house. "You did the right thing, ma'am. I don't think he wanted to hurt you. It looked to me as if he was smitten by you. Seems like he's got it real bad for you. Well, that's too bad for him. I wonder if he had any hand in framing your fiancé?"

CHAPTER FIFTEEN

After listening with interest to a satisfying brief dialogue, Sweeney hung up the phone. “The call was from Dan Harlbager, the agent I assigned to watch your daughter. My hunch was right. Jenkins followed Virginia to New York. When he discovered she took an earlier New York Delta flight, he made a beeline straight to your sister’s home. What alerted my agent was that he heard Virginia’s voice asking Jenkins what he was doing there.”

Hayes interrupted Sweeney. “I don’t understand. How he could hear her? How did he do that?”

“Dan gave her a transmitter to carry on her at all times and showed her how to use it. He told her she was never to go anywhere without it. If anyone came to the door, and he meant anyone, she was to press a small button that activated the transmitter, which allowed him to hear what she was saying. The button allowed her to carry on private conversations without him listening to what she was saying. But if anyone rang her bell or knocked on her door, she was to press the button before encountering that person. And she did just that. Dan heard her frightened voice quavering as she talked to Jenkins and he immediately rushed over and confronted him.”

“And?” Hayes asked.

“And Dan ordered him to leave and to never come back... or else. Jenkins had no choice but to do as he was told. He left the house sulking, then he got in his car and he took off.”

“Do you think he’ll come back?”

“No. I don’t think he will, but you never know about these kooks. That’s why I told Dan to remain on the job a little longer. Just in case Jenkins comes back, he’ll be there waiting for him.”

Sweeney remained with Hayes, just to make sure nothing further happened to him. Hayes worked his business just as he did when he first started. Hayes was so deep in debt; the man didn't know if he could reverse the downward slide. Hayes spent weeks streamlining each office. Downsizing when he needed to and hiring when the need arose. But it was like steering the Titanic. He just didn't know where the iceberg was. McCormack had done an almost perfect job of sabotaging his business, but not perfect enough. He saw a glimmer of daylight at the end of the endless tunnel, and if he could get his sales a little higher, he could hold out until the economy picked up again. Hayes knew he couldn't keep Sweeney on the payroll, but he could keep him on for a little while longer without it breaking him.

CHAPTER SIXTEEN

The slot opened and they passed a dish looking something like beef stew through. The old man took the tray to his bunk and took a spoonful, then spit it out. No way, this was beef stew. It might have been rabbit or it could have been rat. Guards at these off-the-radar and out-of-the-way prisons sometimes fed rat to a prisoner as punishment. He knew he had to eat something, so he took another spoonful. As he was about to put it in his mouth, he felt a sharp pain in his chest and the spoon dropped to the floor as his hand clutched his chest. After a few minutes, the pain abated. *Damn*, he thought as he picked up his spoon. *I've got to get some good food in me. This prison grub is giving me stomach problems. my old ulcer acting up again,* he thought. *I've got to have better food or my stomach will never get better.*

His symptoms today were very similar to the symptoms he had a few years back when he checked himself into a local hospital, thinking he was having a heart attack. When they completed his tests, and they stabilized him, the doctors found he had a large ulcer, which they attributed to nerves and a poor diet consisting of overindulgence in spicy Mexican foods, which he always topped off with plenty of red chili pepper. His problem this time, though, was far more serious than he realized. He knew he had a heart problem… something to do with a faulty valve. Doctors told him he didn't have to have it fixed right now, but he had to have it attended to soon. Well, ten years had passed since the doctors told him to have the valve in his heart fixed.

When the guard left for the night, the old man bent down to pull the rock out of the wall. As he tugged on it, a god-awful pain shot up into his chest and ran down his arm. He got on his knees and pressed his chest against the metal rim of his cot, trying to relieve some of the pressure of the terrible pain he was feeling in his chest. Then, as he tried to stand, so he could get to his cot to lie down until the pain went away, he passed out. He couldn't remember anything after that, unless he felt a pillow being placed under his head. He opened his eyes, and he was staring at the concerned face of John W.

John W said, "I waited for you, but when you didn't show up, I became worried, so I came to see if anything was wrong and I found you lying on the floor unconscious. What happened to you, old man?"

Dutch Henry gasped as he spoke. "I wanted to get out of this prison so bad, that my body couldn't keep the promise my mind made. I have these terrible pains in my chest that just won't let up." The old man gasped for breath, as he attempted to tell John W something important before his time ran out. "Come closer. I ... don't have… much time," he said through his pain. "I thought it was my old ulcer acting up. But I was wrong. It's my heart." He lifted his arm and, with a trembling hand, he pointed to his shoe. "Get my shoe - the left shoe–and... bring ... it here."

John leaned over, grabbed his left shoe, and tried to hand it to him, thinking Dutch Henry wanted to put it on. He wondered why he only wanted to put on his left shoe. "Do you want me to put it on for you, Dutch Henry?"

"No - No not… to put on. Turn the heel–there's a map - in - the heel. It's the lost Four Peaks - Gold Mine - take it. I want - you - to have - it." The old man's eyes grew wide as he grimaced from the pain. He grabbed John's shirt and pulled him toward him with a strength he didn't think the old man was capable of. He pulled John close, he whispered in his ear, and with his dying breath, he told him, "In the heel of my right shoe - a - twenty dollar gold piece. Use it - get to the - mine. You must - get out of here. You have to - do it - by yourself - now. The lever to the door - is in plain sight on the right wall - facing the desert. Pull it - down and the door - will open. Don't -(gasp) - worry - it will open. Go - now - and remember your promise - get those bastards." The old man's body shuddered - he gasped in a last struggle for breath. "You best be goi...," He never finished the sentence. Dutch Henry's head slumped against his chest and John heard the death rattle as his last breath left him.

In the short time John W knew the old man, he came to love him as much as the father he lost. His body was still warm, as if he were asleep, when John picked him up and placed him on his cot. John said a silent prayer over him, then he turned and crawled back through the tunnel to his cell.

Still on his hands and knees, he crawled across his cell and into the tunnel to the hidden room. John checked every part of the room to see if he missed anything. Without the old man, this room was sort of spooky, but it was nothing more than a cave or a mine, and nothing in it would ever spook Dutch Henry. Not even the grinning skeleton sitting in the chair, staring at them as they prepared to leave. John W kept putting off a last-minute chore he had to do, and it wasn't something he looked forward to doing. He had to pump up his nerve a notch in order to do it. John knew he had to see what the skeleton had in his pockets. He started with his shirt pocket. He felt something and took it out. It was a picture of a young woman, his girlfriend, or his wife, or maybe his sister, although a sister didn't seem likely. most likely his girlfriend, but who could tell what this woman was to him? John put the picture in his shirt pocket, fearing he might forget it, then he bent down behind the dead man. He looked through the back of the chair at his pants and noticed a bulge in the back pocket. He reached through the chairs slats and tried to open the button, but the skeleton slid off the chair and fell in a clatter to the floor. This spooked John and he sprang back, falling on his haunches. His heart was beating like a drum. Man, was he spooked, staring at the skeleton with his bones lying in pieces on the floor and his skull resting eschew on top staring back at him? John couldn't wait to get away from this place. *That solved that problem,* he thought. At least now he could open his back pocket. John removed his wallet and opened it. They must have just paid him, or maybe he had nowhere to spend his money because his wallet contained $285.00 in cash, which in those days was about four months' pay. If he could just get this balloon in the air, this money would help him better than the gold piece. John kept the guard's wallet with his badge secured to it. The badge may help if law enforcement stopped him, and the information in his wallet would allow John to inform the guard's kin about what happened to him. John was glad that he searched his clothes and he was about to walk away when he realized he didn't check the front pockets. He discovered a small Buck-folding penknife in his front trouser pocket, which he placed in *his* pocket. The knife was important, and he knew he would use this old knife before the night was over.

It was time to leave. It was dark and there were no guards in sight. He guessed they were upstairs playing cards like they usually did this time of the night. He lit up the forge and waited until it was burning. Then, as he got to work, laying out the hose that fed air into the balloon, he noticed another switch in the corner that the hose on the wall, diagonal to the wall that contained the handle, had hidden. He stopped what he was doing, walked over to it, and stared at it for a minute, trying to figure out what it was for. The handle was vertical, just like the handle that opened the hidden back door. Without thinking, he pulled the handle down. He heard a rumble, and he noticed the hose spring to life. He pushed the small handle to its original position and walked over to the hose. "I'll be damned," he said to himself. Smith was a genius. They had electricity back then and Smith figured a way to hook the fan up to electricity. Boy, that have surprised the old man, if he saw this? No time for that now. He had to get himself out of here. He pulled the cage toward the door and then he pulled the large lever down, praying that after all these years, it would still open the back door. But would it? He wondered. For a moment, nothing happened. He waited a few seconds - still nothing happened. He thought maybe the electricity to the door could have been disconnected. A wire could have come free. Maybe it didn't work with electricity. Maybe pressure would open it. He didn't know what to think. He had to do something. In desperation, he leaned against the wall near the lever and pushed with all of his might. To his surprise, after grating a bit, the wall moved a little. Then it appeared to free itself and move. The section that opened was about the size of an average door, and Smith designed it to slide into the upper portion of the wall. John took a moment to study the locking mechanism. He smiled, realizing that he stumbled upon the correct process of opening the door. By putting pressure on the wall, it moved the locking mechanism on the bottom about an inch. That abrupt movement released the tension on the door's locking mechanism, freeing it - thus allowing it to slide up along the channel. Once you left, this door could not slide back down; Smith didn't design it to work that way. It would have to be reset by hand. Outside the door, there was what appeared to be a shaft with a series of metal rungs bolted to the wall on the right that led to the surface. Old Willard Smith had lined the top of the shaft with cut stone that blended in with the rest of the structure. They secured the stone on a three foot by six-foot sheet of wood with hinges. The wood sheet covered the hidden door from the outside and it had a lock on the underside where someone who was escaping could slide the latch open and push up on the wood covering. If everything worked the way Smith planned, it would open on its hinges. John pulled the latch, but it was stuck shut and it wouldn't budge. He climbed back down the opening and looked for something heavy with which to tap the latch. Finding nothing, he used the butt of the guard's gun he carried on his belt. -This should work, he thought. He climbed back up, pulled out his gun, and tapped the latch with the butt. Nothing. Then he tapped a little harder a second time, and it rewarded him as the latch slid open. John put his shoulder against the wood and pushed hard. The wooden enclosure resisted for a moment, but then, as if it were spring loaded, it opened. John wasted no time. He hooked a rope to the cage and pulled it out of the room, up the shaft, and onto the desert sands. He did the same with the canvas. Once they were on solid ground, he placed the canvas in a neat row alongside the cage so that when he blew air into the balloon, it would inflate over the cage. This was a three-man job, and he didn't know how he would manage it alone, but he had to try.

He thought of Smith, and he knew he must have known something like this could happen, and he must have planned a way around it. But for the life of him, he couldn't figure out what Smith's plan might have been. He held his breath as he pulled down on the small lever, activating the fan. He expected a loud noise, which he feared would have alerted the guards. But the fan, being rather small, was quiet. Since from where he stood he heard nothing, he reasoned that the guards, being higher in an enclosed room, wouldn't hear anything either. John placed the can of propane in the cage, making sure he placed the flint striker to ignite the flame beside the propane.

As he was about to climb back down into the hidden room, John spotted two rungs similar to the ones on the shaft leading to the surface. They attached these two rungs to the bottom part of the outside wall in the prison's rear. Anyone looking at them would not understand what purpose they might have served. Since they had no function and served no purpose other than being decorative, they wouldn't give them a second thought. Standing alongside the cage, he thought about how he almost missed the two rungs that were secured to the base of the outer wall, eight feet apart. This answered the question of what Willard Smith's solution would be if only one man escaped. Smith placed the two rungs there in case one man had to secure the balloon. Smith had thought of everything, even the eventuality of someone escaping alone. John tied down the canvas balloon to the two discovered rungs so when the balloon inflated, it wouldn't become airborne without him. Smith's two rungs allowed him to tie down the balloon by himself and made escaping alone much easier. It was as if the fates were guiding him - showing him what had to be done and the proper sequence of how to do it.

When the balloon was about two-thirds full, he shut off the fan and placed the hose over the forge. He pushed and pulled the bellows, which filled the rest of the balloon with hot air. John looked around to make sure he forgot nothing. He took special notice of the fuses tied to the dynamite. They appeared to be set securely, so he bent down and lit the main fuse. Once it was lit, he paused a moment to make sure the flame didn't go out. Satisfied that it was burning, he rushed to the hidden door, climbed the rungs, and then hurried to the balloon. John lit the burner to push more hot air into the balloon to increase its lift. He jumped into the cage, but before cutting the lines tied to the two rungs, he looked at the fuse one last time. Then he let out a breath and relaxed as he watched the fuse burning toward the dynamite. He cut the ropes, freeing the balloon. The balloon lurched upward, causing the makeshift cage to jolt and sway for a moment, and then it stabilized. When the balloon drifted higher above the prison, the desert winds caused the cage to sway at first, but then it settled down as it reached the colder higher levels. John put his sweater and pants on and he felt better knowing he wouldn't freeze at the higher altitudes. He kept his eyes on the prison as it shrunk away in the distance as the balloon gained altitude and soared higher into the night sky.

The explosion lit the desert sky, turning night into day until turning black again. The blast had no effect on the balloon because it continued to soar steadily in a straight line away from the prison. John hoped that when it landed, it would be near a town.

John hunkered down in the cage, hungry and cold, but very grateful for Willard Smith's ingenuity. If he found Dutch Henry's gold mine, he would care for his granddaughter. He felt he owed Smith that much. He would also keep his promise to old Dutch Henry. John thought about the bandy-legged old man with the tuft of unruly white hair, who smiled, showing a mouth with a few missing teeth. The balloon drifted for what seemed like hours to John, but might have been a full day because he slept a good part of the time. As if he had an internal alarm clock, John awoke to ignite the flame that kept the balloon in the air. The balloon was holding up well, better than John expected. He realized Smith designed the balloon to last much longer than to just to fly him out of the desert.

John looked into the dark night and at the stars surrounding the curve of the Earth and noticed the beginnings of a pink glow. Sunrise! He scanned the horizon and spotted lights twinkling in the distance. The wind was taking him toward the lights, and it thrilled him he'd be a free man soon. When he estimated he was about a mile from the town, he allowed the balloon to cool and drift toward the desert floor. The hard landing didn't affect him because he rolled with it. He collected the canvas, rolled it into a ball, and then buried it in the sand. He left the cage, figuring it would be a long time before someone found it. And if anyone stumbled upon the cage, or the canvas balloon, they would assume because of its material and the way they constructed it, the balloon had been laying in the desert for over a hundred years. John felt good about that because the balloon would never become an issue in revealing how he escaped. His priority now was to get to town and figure out a way to find the gold, then remove it from the mine with no one knowing, and take it to a safe location. Once he secured the gold, he would find buyers to sell it to.

The town, from high above, looked to be about an hour's walk from where he landed, but he realized now that wasn't true because he had misjudged the distance to the town from the air. He walked all day, and he still hadn't reached the town. The scorching desert sun was relentless. His legs felt as if they were going to give out on him. Where the hell was that town? He saw it. He knew he saw it. It wasn't an illusion; at least he didn't think it was. He wasn't sure of anything, just that he saw a town about a mile from where the balloon landed. Could it have been a mirage? No, he reasoned, it couldn't be. Not in the air. A mirage would have occurred on the ground in the desert. He knew the desert heat sometimes made things appear closer than they were. He walked all day and into the night. It was dark, and he still hadn't reached the town. He was so tired that he couldn't walk another step. Exhaustion and exposure caused him to drop to the ground. He closed his eyes. As soon as he hit the ground, he drifted into a deep sleep. He woke with a start. It was daytime. He struggled to get to his feet and when his head cleared; he looked around to determine which direction was the town. It was no use. John was lost, and he was very thirsty. He did not know in which direction to go. The young man knew that walking somewhere was better than dying nowhere, so he forced himself to get on his feet and start walking. He walked for six hours before fatigue overcome him. He became delirious and collapsed; sure he was going to die. That thought lingered on his mind as he lost consciousness and passed out.

Something was nudging him. He tried reaching for his gun, thinking it might be a mountain lion. But when he opened his eyes, he was in the shade lying under an umbrella, staring into the face of an old man. He thought it must be a dream because it was Dutch Henry, but as his head cleared, he could see it was someone else. Someone who looked very much like Dutch Henry.

"Take it easy, son. Here, take a sip of this water. Not too much now, just a sip. You're dehydrated."

The water refreshed John W, and he felt his strength returning. "Who are you - and how did you find me?"

"My name is Sam Reed, but my friends call me 'Persistent.' I found you out here in the desert. I thought you were dead, but you weren't. Almost, though," he said, chuckling. "What in tarnation were you doing out here in the desert?"

John W's voice rasped from dryness, whispering rather than to speak actual words. "It's a long story, Persistent. I'll tell you all about it when I get my voice back." Persistent handed him his canteen and John W took another long pull. He swallowed the water, and then he handed the canteen back to the old man, handed him a slice of beef jerky.

"Here Eat this. It's loaded with salt and protein, which you need. You depleted most of the salt in your body, walking and sweating in the sun with no protection. This jerky will help replace the salt."

John took it and scarfed it. The protein in the meat and the salt renewed his strength, and he felt more like himself. He found he had his voice back. "Why are you called 'Persistent'? That's an odd name for someone to be called."

"I'm called Persistent because I'm the most persistent cuss you'll ever have the good fortune to meet. I'm persistent in everything I do. I've been especially persistent in searching for gold in the Mazatzal Mountains for over forty years now."

"And did you ever find any gold?"

"Some. But I never hit it big. I found enough for a few grubstakes and maybe just enough to get by on, but I never hit the big one. I'd give anything to find either the Lost Dutchman or the Four Peaks Mine - and I'm persistent enough to keep trying."

"Well, hang in there, partner, could be your luck is about to change. You know, you remind me of a friend of mine."

"Yeah, and who would that be?"

"You wouldn't know him. He was an old prospector like you. He searched for years looking for the Four Peaks Mine."

"Now you have gotten my interest, son. What would this friend of yours be called?"

"His name was Dutch Henry."

"Dutch Henry? You knew that ornery old coot?"

"Yeah, I did. He was my best friend."

Persistent slapped his thigh and laughed. "I knew that old bugger too. Knew him well. Him and me, we searched these mountains for years." Persistent pointed to the mountains behind us. "I searched these mountains over here and Dutch Henry, he searched those over there. Tell me. How's he doing?"

"Not good. His heart gave out, and he died a few days ago."

Persistent felt bad and hung his head. "It's too bad he died before he found that ole gold mine."

John tried smiling, but his cracked lips hurt when he smiled. "I have news for you," he said as he took his hanky and wiped blood from his cracked lip. "He found that mine."

Persistent's eyes lit up. "You mean he found the Four Peaks Gold Mine for a fact?"

"That's an absolute fact, Persistent. He found it. He gave me the map to the mine before he died."

"Oh, my God. Oh, my God. Please tell me you're not joshing me." "I'm not. It's a fact. He found the old lost Four Peaks Mine. If you calm down for a minute, you might want to hear a proposition I have for you. How would you like it if I cut you in for a 10% share of the lost Four Peaks gold? Would that interest you?"

Persistent was beside himself with excitement. "What king of fool question is that? Of course, I'd be interested! But, I got to be careful. I don't want all this excitement to cause this ole heart of mine to give out on me like it did ole Dutch Henry. But, for sure, I'll listen to any proposition you have on your mind. As long as it leads me to that ornery damned Four Peaks Gold Mine."

CHAPTER SEVENTEEN

Persistent checked the map, making sure they were heading in the right direction. John told him about how he became acquainted with Dutch Henry and the reason Governor Wilson put Dutch in this prison. Then he took his time telling Persistent *his* story, about how someone planted drugs in the old mine on his property, and how they sentenced him to fifty years in prison. He told Persistent how he was pretty sure the Governor had something to do with it. He said that he didn't have answers yet, but he'd have them soon. All he needed was money. If Dutch Henry was right, and he had found the lost Four Peaks Gold Mine, then he'd have all the money he needed to get back at whoever framed him. Then they'd feel the revenge of John W. John felt better knowing that with Dutch Henry's gold, the old man could rest easy. There was no way he was going to let the Governor and his accomplices get away with the terrible injustice they did to him and Dutch Henry.

Talking to Persistent was pleasant and relaxing, even in the heat, as they walked in cadence to the sound of equipment clanging against the sides of the sure-footed burros. Persistent rode an old nag. He explained to John that Daisy Mae had been with him for many years, and she was as sure-footed an animal as any he'd seen. But Daisy Mae was getting old now, like him, and he knew he'd have to put her out to pasture soon. That meant digging up enough dust to get himself another horse. Of course, if they found gold in Dutch Henry's mine, then that would take care of the horse problem.

Persistent told John that in the old days, the Indians would sometimes set traps to discourage treasure hunters who got close to their mines. Even though the Tonto Apache was no longer a threat to treasure hunters, you never could tell with the Apaches. They still kept a careful watch as they got closer to the mine. As they got closer, they had to find the slit in the mountain, which led to a ledge in a small valley. If it wasn't for the map, it would be like looking for a needle in a haystack. They searched for a day and a half before finding the cut that led through the mountain. A tree branch blocked the opening, making the cut in the mountain invisible to the naked eye. If they didn't know where to look, they would never have found it.

Thank God for the map, John thought. The opening was just large enough for a man on horseback to pass through. When the two men walked out of the narrow path that cut through the mountain, a variety of flowers greeted them, giving the lush green valley an "Oz" type of look. The green valley reminded him of the movie Shangri-La because, like the movie, the fertile valley was a surprising contrast to the stark desert they just left on the other side of the mountain. John pointed to a stream, which the map said to follow until they came to a cul-de-sac where the Mazatzal Mountains met and surrounded them on all sides. They scanned the mountains, looking for the ledge, which the map said was to their left.

Persistent pointed. "There it is; there's the ledge, John. Now it should be a simple matter to locate the cave." Dutch Henry had to have stumbled upon this lost mine by accident, because how he ever found it was beyond their imagination. John W looked at the map and noted where the cave was on the ledge. He spotted it right where the map showed it to be.

They tied the animals to a tree at the base of the cliff below the mouth of the cave. Persistent took a lantern and rope from his burro, and the two men followed a path to the base of the mountain. They climbed the short distance up the mountain to the ledge, but they didn't enter the cave. John took a moment and allowed his eyes to follow the ledge. He noticed it sloped downward on an incline and met with the valley floor in the distance. This was good for them, because if they found gold in this mine, it would make it easier and less time-consuming to have the burros walk the gold out of the valley, rather than try to lower the gold by rope to where they tethered their horses.

The two men looked at each other and wondered who would be the first to enter the cave. Finally, John W shrugged his shoulders and said, "We came all this way to find this cave, and so I guess I'll see what's in there." He walked into the cave. The old man held his lantern high and followed behind as they stepped into the darkness. The cave opening was small, but once you stepped inside, it was very large. A few steps into the chamber, John noticed a Spanish conquistador's helmet by the entrance. The helmet was a surprise because they did not know the Spaniards were ever involved with this mine. They noticed a lance leaning against the wall on the right and as they looked around the large room, they could see bits and pieces of Spanish armor on the floor. John motioned for Persistent to hand him the lantern. He took the lantern, pointed it in front of him, and walked to the rear of the cave. Where he thought the chamber ended, he found it veered to the left. They followed the path, which led to another chamber.

When they entered the chamber, John held the lantern high, and the room lit up. The reflection of gold dancing off the ceiling and walls bombarded them with gold dancing off the ceiling and walls. Old Dutch Henry had melted down the gold he found into gold bars. He had stacked them in neat rows against the wall. There were so many of them, it looked as if the walls on both sides of the were made of gold. It must have taken Dutch Henry years to accomplish this.

Persistent stood with his mouth open. "I would have never have believed this if I didn't see it with my own eyes. This is more gold than I ever dreamed of finding. My God, it's real. It's all real. The rumors about this old mine were all true."

John W just smiled. "Come on. Let's see what's back there," he said, pointing to the back of the chamber. When he reached the end of the chamber, there was an opening leading into a third chamber. John stepped into the chamber and lifted his lantern. The chamber exploded in a kaleidoscope of colors, as millions of twinkling stars reflected off of the ceiling and walls. He was so mesmerized by the dance of colored lights he was reluctant to look for its source. He lowered the lantern and found light caused the light show reflecting off of hundreds of colored stones that littered the ground. John noticed that the quantity of precious stones was more abundant near several large chests, as if someone had dug into the chest with their hands, looking for something, spilling the stones on the floor.

Some chests were open, and some were closed, but all had human skulls on top of them. Persistent said that the Tonto Apaches placed the skulls on top of the chests to scare off intruders.

The two men walked through the large chamber and couldn't believe their eyes. There was a lot of Spanish armor and weapons spread among the human bones in this room, most likely Spanish soldiers. John leaned his hand against the wall and took a deep breath. He thought of the second chamber, which contained a room full of gold, and this chamber contained so many jewels and precious stones that he didn't think they could count them all. They spread the jewels all over the place. The Indians did not know the value of the stones. They thought they were just pretty-colored stones and, when the novelty wore off, they cast them aside.

From the look of the chamber, John figured Dutch Henry must have picked up many of the precious stones and put them back in the chests, because he had swept this part of the chamber floor clean. There were still so many stones lying around. He picked up an emerald the size of a walnut and shined his light on it. Its effect was immediate, causing a cascade of shimmering green light to float along the ceiling and walls so that even Persistent stopped what he was doing to admire the dancing green light as it played along the walls and ceiling.

Apaches must have killed the Spaniards for attempting to take their gold. The Spaniards brought the chests of precious stones here. John assumed they must have looted every village they passed as they worked their way through Mexico and into North America. This could even have been Montezuma's treasure. John could just imagine what the Spaniards must have thought when they heard of the vast gold mines that the Indians found. The Spaniards must have had all of this jewelry ready to ship to Spain when they heard of the Tonto Apache gold mines. They must have salivated at the thought of bringing all that gold back to Spain. The logical assumption was that before they shipped the jewels back to Spain, they'd find the Indian gold mines. So, John surmised, they must have taken the jewels with them, thinking they would find the Indians' gold, take it from them, and then ship both the jewels and the gold to Spain. How else could they explain these chests of precious gems, and the Spanish armor among the bones of the conquistadors?

Persistent dropped a ruby he was admiring into a chest and walked over to John W. "Did you ever in your wildest dreams ever think you'd find this much wealth in one place?"

"No. Never in a million years would I ever have thought I'd see anything as wonderful as this."

"Yep. That's the right word, all right. Wonderful. And wonderful is what it is."

John W reached down and opened the chest in which Persistent had dropped the ruby and gasped. It was full to the brim with rubies of different sizes. They set some in gold rings, broaches, and even necklaces and earrings. He opened the next chest, and this one held emeralds and even some diamonds. They mixed some chests with other precious stones; all of them were worth a king's ransom. This find would make John one of the richest men in the world. He had to get the gold and jewels out of the cave and into a bank or repository where the treasure would be safe.

"Hey, Persistent," John yelled. "Come on over here for a minute."

Persistent ambled over to where John was squatting over a chest. "Oh, my God. Good Lord, but that's beautiful."

"Do you think you would have enough with this to keep you happy in your old age, Persistent?" John gave a mischievous smile, and said, "It's too bad this is all there is. I'd hate to run short of cash, you know." They both laughed at the ludicrousness of the remark. There was enough money here in this cave to fund nations. This could surpass the wealth of Solomon. "Here's what we're going to do. We're going to take an assortment of jewels from the chests. Enough for the animals to carry without tiring them. Once we convert some of it into cash, we'll buy a 4-wheel drive truck and maybe a large box truck to transport the animals in. We'll buy provisions and equipment, put them in the truck, and drive out here. It will take us a while for us to get all the gold and jewels into the trucks. Then, we'll drive the trucks to a safe place. Look, Persistent. I don't want anyone else involved in this. Let's just keep this between the two of us, if that's all right with you."

"Sure, it's all right with me. I agree with you, It's better to keep this just between us. You don't want something like this to get out, because sure as there's a God above, someone will try to take this from us.."

"I agree," John said. "Well, Persistent, you found the gold mine you've been looking for all of your life. And now you're a rich man. What do you say we finish the job?"

"Let's do it, partner."

CHAPTER EIGHTEEN

John W sold the twenty-dollar gold piece in Phoenix for its historical and not its intrinsic value, which amounted to fifty-five hundred dollars. He bought the most expensive suit he could find, then he went to the largest jewelry store in Phoenix and asked to see the owner. They escorted him into an impressive office that reeked of money.

Mr. David Greenwald, the owner of the business, greeted him. "Yes, sir. What can I do for you?" he asked.

"I have a few items I'd like to show you I think you might be interested in." John W opened his brand new attaché case, which exhibited a black velvet material covering something bulky. He removed the velvet, revealing several black velvet pouches, each containing different colored, glittering jewels. John W opened the first three velvet bags, one at a time, and spread the stones onto the small black velvet jeweler's apron he placed on the desk.

Greenwald recognized the immense value of what Mr. Christo had just placed before him. Mr. Greenwald took his loop from his pocket and asked John for his permission to examine them.

"Please, by all means. Take your time and scrutinize them."

Greenwald examined each item with a professional eye until finally he sat back and placed the loop on his desk. "I need a drink. Can I offer you one too?"

"Sure. Let's have a drink and celebrate our new relationship."

Greenwald looked at John and asked, "Would you know how old these jewels are?"

"I estimate the seventeenth century, but they could be older."

"That's what I think too, but I can't be sure. What do you want for them, or maybe a better question would be… What do you want *from* me?"

John smiled slyly. "Mr. Greenwald, these jewels are but a small sample of what I actually own. What if I told you I have seven large chests filled with jewels, just like these? And what if I told you I want you to find buyers for my gems and act as my agent? As quickly as possible, I would like to convert as many of these stones into cash. I know little about you, Mr. Greenwald. I imagine you are successful in your business and you've probably accumulated a lot of money over the years, but if you partner with me, I will make you wealthy beyond your wildest dreams. Think of me as Solomon, only my wealth exceeds his."

Greenwald poured them both another drink. "What kind of percentage did you say I would get?"

"I didn't say, but if we talk about a figure of one billion dollars, what would one-half percent of that be?"

"That would be, let's see now, that would be five million dollars."

"I'll give you that and I'll double it if you convert half or more of what I give you into cash. Now, does that interest you, Mr. Greenwald?"

"Well, if my commission were to be… let's say, one percent, then I believe I can help you Mr. . . . ?"

"Call me Mr. Christo, John Christo. And I will give you one percent commission, but with a condition."

Greenwald nodded. "Before you tell me your condition, I'd like you to know that my family owns a rather large jewelry exchange in New York City's financial district. I'll call them and tell them about the jewels, and if it's all right with you, I'll either have them fly in to see the jewels or we can go see them."

"Listen, Mr. Greenwald. Besides the percentage you're receiving, you will get my jewels far below their historical value. You will make money on every aspect of this transaction. I want to walk away with a billion dollars, minimum, in my bank from this first deal of ours. Here's my condition. Sell one billion dollars of my jewels and the one percent is yours. Sell any less and you only get one half of a percent. Remember, not only will you get the percentage I'm giving you, you'll also get a commission on every gem and all the gold you sell. Your end could amount to a hundred million dollars just on the first billion. Do you agree to my terms, Mr. Greenwald?"

The enormity of this transaction just walking into his store and dropping in his lap was difficult for Greenwald to believe, but it was real, and it was just handed to him on a golden platter. "I agree, and I'll do my best to get you your billion dollars, Mr. Christo."

John looked at him without smiling and told him. "Just so we understand ourselves. This billion dollars you will negotiate for me does not represent one percent of my holdings. If you handle this small transaction, I will give you another billion dollars in jewels. When we complete that transaction, we will deal in gold. More gold than you might imagine." John said this with such conviction, Greenwald hadn't realized that he had been holding his breath. "Think of this: any future deal is contingent on this lot being sold. Do you understand? And let me give you a little advice. Never fuck me. I'm the last man in the world you want to fuck. Do that and I will destroy you, but if you treat me right, as I told you before, I'll make you richer than you ever dreamed possible, and you'll thank god for the day you met me. Do we have a deal? And do we understand each other?"

"Before I leave, I have one other question for you."

"Yes? What is the question?"

"Do you have a secure vault where I can store some of my gold?"

"Yes, we have a vault downstairs and we have one in our New York facility. Can I ask how much gold you intend to store with us?"

"Yes. I have about three thousand fifty-pound bars of gold."

Greenwald took out his handkerchief and wiped his brow. "Did you say… three thousand fifty-pound bars of pure gold?"

"Yes, but it could be more. I haven't counted them. I just estimated the amount of bars I have. By the way, what's gold going for these days?"

"Wholesale, I estimate about fifteen hundred dollars an ounce."

"Why don't you include some of those gold bars of mine? They should fetch a good price right about now, right?"

"How many bars do you want to sell?"

"Sell as many as you can. I was figuring on ten of them, but if you could sell a hundred, well, that would be fine with me. I'll leave it up to you, but try not to flood the gold market and drive the price down. Maybe you should sell a little at a time, but that's your business and I will not tell you how to run it. I'll leave the details of what's right and what's wrong with you."

Greenwald agreed with John. "I'll need a sample. Could you get me one?"

"Sure, I have a sample in my car. I'll get it. John locked his attaché case, then he left. A few minutes later, he returned, carrying a heavy box. He placed it on Greenwald's desk and opened the box, then he lifted the gold bar out of the box and laid it on his desk. "Here it is. This should be a good enough sample."

"My god, it's just like you said it was." Greenwald picked up the gold bar and laid it on a scale. Fifty point two ounces.

"Look, Mr. Greenwald. Some of these bars will weigh over fifty pounds and some a little less. We melted the gold down ourselves and we used the crudest methods available to us, so just take each bar as a separate unit, unique unto itself. By the way, why don't you test the gold to make sure it's as pure as I say it is? Oh! One more thing, let's keep this strictly between us. I don't want any surprise visits from any government agency or the tax people, and I don't want to be surprised by anyone looking to take what's mine. Do you understand?"

Greenwald was sweating. If he told anyone about Mr. Christo, he'd lose a fortune for his stupidity. "Yes, I understand completely. Don't worry. I won't let you down. I believe this is the start of a beautiful business relationship, Mr. Christo, and one I do not want to see end before it starts."

Christo smiled. "Good. Keep your word to me and you will be one hundred times richer that you are right now."

CHAPTER NINETEEN

It took a full month to get the gold and jewels out of the cave, down the mountain, and into the truck. Persistent bought a fresh burro that he also named Daisy Mae. It made him feel as though his old burro was still with him. He used the same burro he'd been using for years. He was still young and strong. The burro was used to Persistent's ways, and Persistent with his. When they brought the gold down the mountain, they used the burro to transport it to the truck, which John then drove to Greenwald's bank in Phoenix.

Greenwald couldn't believe the amount of gold John Christo was storing in the bank. After each load, he would ask, "Is this it, John?"

"No, Dave, this is just the beginning."

God, everything this young man told him was true. He had to be the richest man in the world, thought Greenwald. Greenwald sold the first shipment of jewels and gold and delivered the first one billion dollars that John asked him to get as a condition for his earning the one percent commission.

The following day, John was on a plane for Switzerland to open a Swiss account. John informed the account manager, a Mr. Lenoire, when they spoke on the phone the previous Monday that he'd be coming to his bank to open an account on Tuesday of this week. John told him he was carrying a substantial amount of money to be deposited into his new account. He chose The Credit Suisse Group AG, a Swiss multinational financial services company headquartered in Zurich, because it operated in over 50 countries, making it easier for him to manage his money.

John sat back in a comfortable leather chair, opposite the large desk behind which Mr. Lenoire sat.

"It was pleasant speaking with you last week, Mr. Christo. What is the amount you wish to deposit?"

John reached into the inside pocket of his three thousand dollar custom-made suit and handed the envelope to Senior Vice-President Charles Lenoire. When he opened the envelope and saw the amount, he sat bolt upright. He was used to large deposits, but this was the first billion dollar deposit from a civilian depositor. Even though he tried to hide it, his hand shook, and he hoped Mr. Christo hadn't noticed. Christo hadn't noticed his momentary lapse in composure.

In reality, John had noticed the shaking of Lenoire's hand, and he smiled.

"This is a substantial deposit, Mr. Christo. I'll set the account up for you immediately."

"Thank you, Mr. Lenoire, but this is only a small fraction of what I intend to deposit in your bank if I'm satisfied with your service."

Lenoire, who had just gotten up from his seat, sat back down. "Are you saying that this deposit, the one I'm holding in my hand, is a small amount of what you intend to deposit in this bank? Is this what I heard you say?"

"Yes. Why?" John acted casually, knowing the amount of the check was staggering. He intended to have a minimum of at least ten billion dollars in this bank before long.

When they set the account up, John shook Lenoire's hand. As he was about to leave, he said, "I plan on depositing another billion dollars, possibly next week. Can you handle that amount?"

"Yes, sir. I assure you that any amount you deposit will be no problem for our bank. You know we have over 250 branch offices in Switzerland and we operate in fifty countries."

"Fine! But I expect preferential treatment as long as I'm dealing with your bank. I want you to keep me informed of any changes in interest rates and I want the luxury of being able to move my money in and out of any account, in any of your branches, if the need arises. Will this be a problem, Mr. Lenoire?"

"No, not at all. I will keep you informed of any interest rate fluctuations. And you certainly may deposit, transfer, or withdraw any amount of money you wish in any of our branch offices whenever you need to."

"Good. Then I see no problem in doing business with you." Mr. Christo left the bank. Mr. Lenoire couldn't believe that with this one deposit, he just added a billion dollars to his bank's net worth.

John remained in Europe. He stayed at the finest hotels and ate at the best restaurants. He bought his clothes in Italy, in a little store in Florence, where the proprietor gave him the address of his grandson's store in Manhattan. John took elocution lessons to learn how to comport himself when amongst society or royalty. His wealth opened doors that would have remained closed to others and his hunger to learn gave him the confidence he lacked growing up.

John had not seen Virginia or her father for over seven years. He was three months shy of his twenty-eighth birthday and the sides of his hair were turning grey. He had grown a fashionable mustache and beard, and he was unrecognizable to anyone who had known him in the past. It was time to return to America and find out what happened to them.

Persistent was content with having one hundred million dollars to spend. He loved the desert and would never think of leaving it, so he did what all the rich men who loved the desert did: he bought a little ranch near Death Valley. John had become good friends with him in the short time they knew one another and he promised him he'd spend some time with him when he returned from Europe.

Persistent had taken Dutch Henry's place in his life and he lessened the pain John felt at the loss of his friend. The first thing John did when he returned home was to spend quality time with the old man.

"My god, boy. You look wonderful. Whatever you were doing over in Europe, keep doing here, because it sure agrees with you."

John laughed. He felt good just being himself, and not having to pretend to be this other person. When he knew it was time to leave, he spent a month with Persistent. He had unfinished business to take care of.

"I'll see you soon, Persistent."

"You better, you young whipper-snapper. And if you need this old man for anything, you just call me and I'll come running, you hear? Now, don't you go forgettin' who your friends are."

John smiled. He loved the old man. "Don't worry, Persistent. You're the only friend I have now, and I'll never forget you. And don't you worry. I'll call you if I need you and if I call, you better come running, you hear?" John played with Persistent's words, but he meant what he said. "Good bye, old friend. I'll see you soon."

John hired a private jet and flew to Phoenix to visit Mr. Hayes to see how he was doing. When the limo pulled up in front of the Hayes Real Estate office, Mr. John Christo stepped out into the scorching Arizona sun. He looked at his old office and sighed. *So much water under the bridge*, he thought. He opened the door, and it surprised him to see there was no one working there. The back door opened, and Mr. Hayes stepped out. "Can I help you with something?"

"Yes, I was looking to purchase a piece of property and I heard you were the man to see."

Hayes smiled. "Once upon a time, maybe, but not anymore."

"Why, what happened? Didn't you have other offices?"

"Yes. I had three in Mohave County and I opened an office in Flagstaff, but then things went wrong. But why am I telling you this? I'm sorry to bore you with my troubles."

"You're not boring me at all, Mr. Hayes. I'm always interested in hearing anything you have to say."

"Why is that, Mr. Christo?"

"I heard good things about you from others. Didn't you used to have a young man who worked for you? I heard he just about ran this place."

"You heard right. You're talking about John W. Hardin. The nicest young man I ever met, and it's too bad because I loved him like a son."

"What happened to him?"

"Some land-grabbing monster took it all away from him and his mother. Then they used trumped-up charges to put him in jail so they could take his land away from him."

John's ears perked up. He didn't know any of this. "Well, wasn't his land worthless? Why would they want worthless land?"

"That's just it. The land wasn't worthless. The thieves wanted the old mine on the property. They took the land and reopened the mine and before long, they hit the mother lode. They took billions of dollars in gold out of that mine and poor John and his mother didn't see a dime."

"Speaking of his mother, whatever happened to her?"

"That's a whole other story. She died of a broken heart. She used to call me once a month, asking about her son. When I didn't hear from her, I drove out to see her. That's when I found her dead in her home.

"McCormack, that's the man who took their land away from them, and convinced Abigail Hardin, John's mother, to sell him her land for a fully furnished mobile home up near the Grand Canyon, along with one hundred twenty-five thousand dollars. He told her what she thought she knew. That her land was worthless, and he was just giving her the home and money to help her because he felt sorry for her. He made national headlines as her benefactor. They ever mentioned nothing about the old gold mine he reopened. I couldn't keep up fighting him, and trying my best to get John W out of prison. I went broke trying. You know, I never could find out where they were keeping poor John W. No one would tell me. All I know is that I was told that he died in a prison accident, which killed two prisoners, one of which was him, and severely injured three guards."

"I hired me an honest private detective who helped save my daughter Virginia from a fellow John warned me not to hire. John said he didn't trust the man, but I didn't listen to him. I hired him anyway, to my eternal regret. He ran the Flagstaff office into the ground. He turned down deals my sales agents worked hard to get. Then he paid them with McCormack's money so they wouldn't quit. Jason Sweeney, the detective I hired, found out about it and he told me. Then he came with me when I fired him. My troubles didn't stop there, but I don't want to bore you any longer by telling you my troubles."

"Mr. Hayes, I believe your luck is about to change. Do you have any debt, Mr. Hayes?"

"Yes, I do. A lot of debt, but I don't enjoy talking about it to a stranger."

John looked at his old benefactor for a long moment. Then he finally said, "I want you to take me to your bank. I assume it's a bank that you're having all the trouble with?"

"Yes, you're right. It is a bank."

"Please take me there. I'd like to talk to the bank manager." Hayes didn't know why, but he agreed to take Mr. Christo to see his bank manager.

Christo walked into the bank, looking like the billionaire he was, and he took a seat without being asked. He looked the bank manager in the eye and didn't mince words. "How much money does Mr. Hayes owe your bank?"

The manager a Mr. Stern, looked at Hayes, who nodded, then he looked at Christo and told him, "Mr. Hayes owes this bank two hundred twenty-five thousand dollars."

"I see," John said, and reached into the inner pocket of his suit, taking out his checkbook. John wrote something on the check, tore it out, and handed it to the bank manager.

The man looked at it, then at John. "What is this check for, Mr. Christo?"

"Please deposit that check into Mr. Hayes's account. Pay off his debt and leave the rest in his account. Is that understood, Mr. Stern?"

"Yes. Yes it is. I'll do it right now." He pressed the intercom button. "Marian, please come in to my office." He handed her the one million two hundred fifty thousand dollar check, together with a deposit slip. "Please deposit this check in Mr. Hayes's account."

John looked at Mr. Stern. "From now on, I'll be underwriting Mr. Hayes in anything he does. Here's my card. Check my references and then never bother Mr. Hayes again. You'll call me on my private number or my bank's number. Do you understand?"

When they were outside, Hayes asked John why he did that. "Why would you help a perfect stranger?"

"That's a fair question, Mr. Hayes, and one that deserves an answer. I knew John Hardin. Like him, I too they sent unfairly to prison, and I met him when he first arrived at the prison. I was an inmate too, and he told me all about you. He told me how much you meant to him. I promised him if I ever got out of prison, if you needed help, then I would help you. As you can see, I've done very well in life. I have wealth and stature. I can not spend all the money I have and I wanted to keep my word to John Hardin. Here's my card, Mr. Hayes. If you should ever need me, call me no matter how small a matter you feel about it is and I will help you without reservation. Any friend of John's is a friend of mine and I know he only had one friend and that was you, Mr. Hayes. Just so you know, John loved you like a father. He wanted you to know that. Now, before I leave, I want to ask you about your daughter, Virginia. I'd like to know what happened to her."

"She went up North to live with her Aunt Harriet, my sister. Virginia waited for John, hoping he would return. It has depressed ever her since she was told that they killed him in prison."

"If you talk to her, tell her she'll receive news soon. That will cheer her up. She was always such a happy girl. She doesn't deserve to be sad."

"How do you know she was always happy, Mr. Christo?"

"John told me all about her. I feel as though I have always known her. Well, thank you for your time. I'll be seeing you real soon. And remember, if you should ever need me, you have my card. Don't lose it. Goodbye, Mr. Hayes. We'll see each other again soon."

CHAPTER TWENTY

On a bright Sunday morning, a woman wearing a plain dress and an apron answered her door when the doorbell rang. It surprised her to see a very well dressed, elegant bearded young man standing in the doorway. “Yes, can I help you?”

“Yes, you can. I’m looking for a Lee Flowers. Does he live here?”

“Yes, he does. Can I ask what you want to see him about?”

“I’m afraid that’s personal, ma’am, but it’s nothing bad. In fact, I think he’ll be rather pleased to hear what I have to tell him.” Reassured by his pleasant personality and prosperous appearance, she opened the door a little wider and said, “Please come in. I’ll get him.” She escorted John W. into her small living room and asked him to have a seat while she went for her son.

A few minutes later, Lee Flowers walked in, wearing a shirt and tie and holding a jacket over his arm. He looked the stranger up and down, trying to get a read on him. “I’m Lee Flowers. What can I do for you?” Lee looked to be in his late twenties or early thirties with blonde hair, about six feet in height, with a slim, muscular body.

John W answered his question. “You helped a friend of mine once when he had no friends. You showed him a kindness that no one else offered him.”

“Wait, a minute. You don’t mean that kid they put out in that prison that they re-opened in the middle of the Gila Bend Desert, do you?”

“Yes, that’s the one. Word got back to me what you did for him. He asked that I come and see you to tell you how much that meant to him.”

“Yeah, well. That act of kindness got me fired. I mean, I tried to do the right thing, but you know… it just ain’t right for a man not to be allowed to talk to his mother.” Mrs. Flowers came into the room and heard the last part of what Lee said.

"What mother are you talking about, Lee?"

"Well, there was this boy who they locked up in the god-forsaken prison in the middle of the desert that they assigned me to. He asked me if I'd do him a favor and inquire about his mother. He was worried about her and he asked me to see how she was getting along. I tried. I went to my supervisor and asked about her, but he prevented me from looking into it. When I asked him why, he fired me, just like that."

"I see," John said. "What are you doing for work now?"

"Nothing. I was about to go out for a job interview, that's why the shirt and tie. I haven't worked since they fired me. You know what I think?"

"No. Tell me what you think."

"I think they black-balled me. They fired me and then put the word out throughout the security field that they were not to hire me. I can't think of any other reason I'm not being hired. I have the experience. Hell, it's all I've ever done since I got out of the army. I was an MP in the service and it carried over into my private life. Security work is the only work I know and the only thing I'm good at."

John W nodded his head in understanding. "I understand what you're saying. Now I have an offer for you. It's a job offer, if you want a job."

Lee's eyebrows lifted in anticipation, waiting to hear what the job offer entailed. "Well, it's no secret that I could use a job. What do you have in mind?"

"I want to hire you as my assistant. Sort of bodyguard, gofer-type job, but it pays well, and I think you'll like it."

Mrs. Flowers stood and said, "I insist you stay and have something. Would you care for a fresh cup of coffee and donuts?"

"That would really hit the spot, ma'am."

"Then if you'll excuse me for a minute, I'll go put a pot on. I'll pour you a cup as soon as it's ready and come right back in here. I don't want to miss what you have to say to Lee, so say nothing till I get back."

"All right then. We'll wait for your mother to return, then I'll have a cup of coffee and tell you what I have in mind for you." A few minutes later, Mrs. Flowers came back, carrying a tray with two cups of coffee and donuts on it. She set it down and handed John his coffee, and then she poured one for Lee.

"I didn't know how you take your coffee, Mr.… Mr.…? What did you say your name was?"

"It's Christo, ma'am. John Christo."

"Well then, Mr. Christo, enjoy your coffee. Now what were you about to say to Lee?"

"Thank you, Mrs. Flowers. I take it black." He took a sip and remarked. "Hmm this is excellent coffee. What kind is it?"

"I like Dunkin' Donuts coffee, so that's what I buy."

John agreed with her. "It's excellent. Now, as for the job, I have in mind for your son. Let me start by giving him something." John pulled an envelope out of his inner suit jacket and handed it to Lee.

Lee opened the envelope and his eyes lit up. "Holy shit, what the hell is this for?" He looked at his mother. "Sorry for cussin', Ma."

His mother acted as if she hadn't heard what he said. She reached over and took the envelope out of his hand. She opened it, looked at what was in it, and gasped. "Oh my lord," she said. "Is this all Lee's?"

"Yes, ma'am. It's all his."

"But this check is for one hundred thousand dollars."

"Yes, it is. And it's all Lee's."

"But what's it for? Why are you giving him this much money?"

"Because he did a kindness to someone who was without hope. A person who they framed for the crime they charged him with, a person who had no one to turn to. There was no one who offered to help this boy, except your son, Lee. That boy in prison didn't forget that kindness, and he was sad when he heard the one man who offered to help him they fired from his job for just asking one question. I knew the young man. He was a friend, and he told me to look you up. He asked me to help you if you needed help. I'm very wealthy, and I can afford this. I want you to have it. It's yours and there will be no further discussion about it. As for the job offer, if you decide to accept my offer and come to work for me, I will pay you well."

Lee wanted to ask him some questions, but he felt as if he were looking a gift horse in the mouth and would appear ungrateful. He finally got the courage to ask, "What will my duties be, and what will you pay me if I decide to work for you?"

"Before I answer that question, tell me what you were being paid as a guard."

"I made about fifty thousand dollars a year, plus overtime."

John nodded in understanding. "I'll double that. I'll pay you one hundred thousand dollars a year and I'll guarantee you a year's employment. If I like the way you work and if you like working for me, then I'll take good care of you. In fact, you can say that you would have a job for life."

"When would I start?" Lee asked.

"Well how soon *could* you start?"

"I could start tomorrow. I'm doing nothing right now, and I'm itching to get back to work."

"Okay, it's settled. We have a deal, then. My car will stop by to pick you up tomorrow morning at eight thirty. Oh! And make sure you deposit that check today because you won't have time to do it tomorrow."

CHAPTER TWENTY-ONE

The private jet landed at LaGuardia Airport in Queens, New York. Two passengers got off the plane and walked to the waiting limousine. The driver checked to be sure his passengers were comfortable, Then he put the car in gear and headed for Manhattan.

"Where are we going, Mr. Christo?" Lee asked.

"Our first stop is Valentino Maximus, a men's shop where I buy my clothing and that's where you'll buy your suits from now on. They're the finest men's store on this side of the Atlantic. I want the men working for me to look their best, so from now on you will look the part."

The driver pulled up to the curb in front of the store on Spring Street and remained in the car while his passengers stepped out of the car. Lee stood there for a moment, looking at the sign "Valentino Maximus" above the entrance to the store. *It's a strange name*, he thought, and wondered about its origin.

Valentino, a young Italian man in Florence, Italy taught by Flavio, his father, the secrets of fine tailoring, and because of his father's patience, he became not just a good tailor or an average tailor but the finest tailor in all of Florence. The young man had heard stories about America, such as how they paved the streets in gold. After he was an accomplished tailor with a growing reputation, he envisioned the store he would someday open in America, and he went there to seek his fortune. He asked his father to come with him, but Flavio refused to leave his beloved Florence. However, he encouraged his son to follow his dream. Valentino arrived in America and he opened a little men's store on Spring Street in downtown Manhattan in 1958 with the money his father had given him when he left Italy. He named his store "Valentino Maximus." "Valentino" after his first name and "Maximus," A Roman general's name, to add a little mystery as the last name of his business.

The quality of his work spread by word of mouth. Even though the store grew, it remained small compared to the larger men's stores. But the business grew despite that and when it was time, they handed it down from father to son, to its current owner, Carlo, the grandson of the Italian patriarch who taught his son the trade his father had taught him. The quality of the suits had never wavered as they passed the skills down from generation to generation and today, celebrities, actors, sports figures, and men of wealth sought after their suits.

A sales associate greeted them as they entered the store. "Welcome to Valentino Maximus, gentlemen. What can I do for you today?"

John W observed the man before speaking. "I'd like Carlo to take care of us, if he's available."

"I'm sorry, sir, but Carlo is out of the store at the moment. I'm the manager. Can I help you?"

It disappointed John, but he had his day planned, and he didn't want to come back later, so he agreed. "We need five suits as soon as possible, and this young man wants to wear one of them when we leave."

Five suits were a decent sale for any salesperson who worked on commission, but being the manager, he worked on salary and not commission. He recognized Mr. Christo from his prior visit and he knew he appreciated exemplary service. Since Valentino was famous for its service and the quality of its suits, he was determined to provide it.

"Follow me, please. If you have questions, just ask me. My name is Samuel, and I'll be happy to answer them for you." Then he turned and walked to the rear of the store to a rack of suits. They enclosed each suit in a custom zippered bag with the Valentino logo on it. "Giorgio!" he called. A man turned and saw his manager motioning to him. He dropped what he was doing and walked over to him. "Yes, Mr. Bramonte, did you want to see me?"

"Yes, Giorgio. This man needs five suits, and he wants to wear one of them when he leaves here. I want you to assist him."

Giorgio appreciated what his manager just gave him. He gave him a customer that would earn him a good commission and, in return, he expected Giorgio to give them the best service possible.

"Take good care of these gentlemen, Giorgio. I'll check back in a few minutes to see if they require anything else."

Giorgio explained to the men, "As you know, we specialize in creating men's custom suits, but we have excellent off the rack suits available for someone who needs a suit in a hurry. Now come over to this rack, pick the suit you like, and I'll see that you'll be wearing it when you leave the store. As for the other four suits, let me show you the ones that are currently in vogue, and you can point out any four you would like us to make for you."

John liked Giorgio's suggestion.

"I'll show you the ready-made suits first," Giorgio said. He asked John and Lee to follow him as he walked along a rack of suits and stopped when he came to the size suit he thought would fit the young man.

John W spotted it right away and pointed to a subdued black pinstriped suit. "This one. This is the one I want him to wear today."

Giorgio smiled. "Good choice, sir. Very elegant." He turned and snapped his fingers to get the attention of a young man putting a suit back on a rack. "Salvatore, come here, please. Take this gentleman to the fitting room and have him try on this suit. It must fit him. If it needs an alteration, call Willard and have him make the change." Giorgio turned to Lee and John. "Willard is our tailor and, between us, he's the best in the business, and he knows it." Then he whispered, "His reputation is going to his head, and he struts around the store like a peacock." He sighed. "But there's no denying it. He is the best of the best of all the tailors in New York City, except, of course, for Carlo. Now if you'll come with me, sir, this won't take long. I must take your friend's measurements, then we can make your suits. When they're finished, I'll have them delivered to you."

Mr. Christo added, "We'll need three sport jackets, four pairs of shoes, seven of your finest Italian silk shirts, and whatever accessories you feel he needs to finish the ensemble. When you complete the order, have someone bring them to my office." He handed Giorgio his card. "My office is on the top floor." Giorgio looked at the card and was confused. "Sir, this card doesn't say what room you are in."

"I own the building and my office is the entire top floor. I'll instruct my secretary to expect a delivery from you, and when it arrives, she'll have it taken to my office."

Lee tried the sports jackets on and found they fit him. When they were ready to leave, he carried the shirts, ties, sport jackets, shoes, and socks with him, but as they approached the exit, John stopped by the jewelry counter to look at Rolex's watches.

"Giorgio, can you come here a moment, please?" Giorgio was worried something may have displeased Mr. Christo and quickly came to see what the problem was. "Is something wrong, sir?"

"What? Oh, no, nothing's wrong. I want to see a few gold Rolex watches, that's all."

Lee placed his clothes on the chair next to the jewelry counter and observed John W. as he examined the watches that Giorgio had placed on the counter.

"Which one do you like, Lee?"

Lee pointed to the gold Yacht Master with a black face and said, "This one. It's a beauty."

"Good. Try it on."

The watch needed a link removed and Giorgio had his jeweler stop what he was doing to take it out.

"Do you have another one?"

Giorgio gulped, thinking of the commission he'd had with two Rolexes added to Christo's bill. "I have another Yacht Master, but that one has a gold face."

"That will do. If my man prefers a black face, I'll have him stop by and you can have your jeweler change the face."

"Very good, sir," Giorgio said, smiling. he was calculating the enormous commission he'd make on this sale. "Have a good day, sir, and come again soon." He watched the car as it drove away, then the usually very reserved Giorgio pumped his fist in the air in an up and down motion. *"YES!"*

The black pinstriped suit fit Lee like a glove and looked elegant on him. He felt like a celebrity when he walked out of the store. When they opened the doors to the car, both men looked as if they stepped off the cover of *GQ* magazine, getting admiring glances from passersby. The limousine didn't take long to get to John's building, but on the drive there, John studied the driver. The way he handled himself interested him. When John stepped out of the car, he asked the driver. "What's your name?"

"Angelo, Mr. Christo."

"Do you enjoy working for this company, Angelo?"

"It's a living, sir."

John W liked the guy. He didn't stretch the truth and only said enough to answer the question. John could tell by the scar tissue over his eyes that Angelo took a few punches in his time. "Angelo, I'm going to ask you a few questions if it's all right with you. I have my reasons, and it's not because I'm nosy."

"Go ahead, Mr. Christo. Ask your questions."

"Are you honest?"

Angelo blanched as if insulted. "You're goddamned right. I am. I'm a lot of things but I'm not a thief."

"How much do you make a year working for this outfit?"

Angelo shrugged his shoulders. "Forty-five thousand plus tips. I guess maybe fifty-five or sixty thousand, after tips, would be about right. Why do you want to know if I'm honest, and how much money I make, Mr. Christo?"

"Well, I'd like you to come to work for me. I need a driver and the pay is good, and if you accept my job offer, I'll double your salary. Before you say anything, were you ever arrested?"

"Twice," Angelo answered. "Both times for disorderly conduct. I had a couple of bar fights and the cops arrested me."

"Did you win the fights?"

The bored look left Angelo's face, and he smiled for the first time since being asked questions. He said, but with a hint of pride, "Yeah, I won both fights."

John nodded. "Good. Next question. Are you a drinker, and do you use drugs?"

"Yeah, I have a few drinks once in a while, but drugs, no way. Look, where I come from, it was survival of the fittest and if you took that shit, pardon the expression, but if you take that shit, you ain't gonna be the fittest. So no. I don't take drugs, never have, but I enjoy a drink once in a while."

John looked at the scar tissue above his eyes. "Did you ever box?"

"Yeah, how'd'ya know? I was a middleweight fighter. Had thirty-five professional fights. Won twenty-nine of them."

"You're hired. Here's a hundred dollars. Take the car back. Quit that job, take a cab back here, and come to my office. Here's my card. If security stops you on the way in, tell them to call me." John reached into his inside suit pocket and pulled out his checkbook. He scratched something on it and handed it to Angelo.

Angelo looked at the check, then he looked at John. "What is this for?"

"For your bills, get rid of them. Consider the rest of the money a starting bonus."

Angelo didn't seem impressed; his face showed no emotion. "Thanks, Mr. Christo. I'll hand in my notice effective immediately. I should be back here in a couple of hours."

"Good, that's settled then. I'll see you in my office later."

John and Lee had lunch in John's office. John ordered enough food for a third man, figuring Angelo might be hungry. An hour later, the elevator door opened and Angelo came sauntering in. "I'm a free man now, Mr. Christo, and ready for work."

"Good... sit down and have a bite to eat, then we'll talk about your duties." John turned to Lee. "Lee, after we finish lunch, I want you to find out everything you can about the men on this list. These are the men who put that poor bastard in jail for fifty years so they could steal his property. They framed the Hardin boy for a crime he didn't commit and that demands justice. And didn't they fire you when you asked about his mother?"

Lee nodded. "They sure did."

"I want revenge," John said. "If either of you don't agree with me, or if you don't want to take part with what I have in mind, which by the way will be perfectly legal, then you're free to go, and I will compensate you for your time." He looked at both men and waited. Angelo looked bored and Lee looked interested. "I take it you both are with me on this?" The two men looked at each other and they both nodded in agreement. "Good. Here's the list, Lee. Spend as much money as you need to, but find their weaknesses. Find out if they ever did time, summonses, traffic tickets, fights with their wives or girlfriends they're going out with. I need to know everything about them, including the flaws in their character, and the weaknesses they have."

Lee looked at the names on the list. "Geez, the Governor himself, eh?"

"That's right, the Governor. Read the names back, Lee. I want Angelo to hear them. Lee looked at the list, then he read off the names. "Well, we know about the Governor. Next is Jack McCormack, the President of McCormack Industries, then Rutgar Kleinst, and last, but not least, Tom Jenkins. These are the only four men you want me to check out?"

"That's right. Those four are dirty and they have to pay." John reached into his desk drawer and pulled out two bank cards with each man's name on it.

"Take these bank cards, gentlemen. They have a one hundred thousand dollar limit on them. Whatever you do from now on, you will use this card. It's a company write-off. I don't want you to use your own money for anything. Consider the card as another bonus, a perk of working for me. But there's one thing I insist on, and that is loyalty. I'll back you till my dying breath, and I expect you to do the same for me. Loyalty. Remember that word, because that, and trust, are the only words I believe in. Keep in mind that what we say here stays here. In the words of Barnum, 'Never smarten up a chump.' I don't want these four men to know I'm coming after them."

Lee spoke. "Mr. Christo, McCormack is a very wealthy man. It's going to be tough getting to him."

"That's right, but his wealth is mostly corporate. His company is worth billions, not him. It's true that he's personally worth millions, but understand this gentleman, you're working for the third richest man in the world and the way things are going, I may be Number One soon, and for your information, that's the best kept secret in the world."

Lee and Angelo gave each other a look of disbelief. They hadn't realized the extent of Mr. Christo's wealth.

"McCormack covets money, and that is how we'll get him. Lee, I want you to concentrate on finding out where he keeps his money. I need to know that. Governor Wilson, we'll get with his greed. He wanted a gold mine. Well, I'm going to give him a gold mine. One that he's going to love, and that will be his downfall. He owns a chain of hardware stores, which may be on the stock exchange. If it is on any of the exchanges, find out what the stock is selling for, then let's see if we can cause it to crash. I'd like to see that bastard ruined and disgraced."

"As for you, Angelo, I want you to buy a couple of cars today. I need a stretch limo and a Lincoln town car or maybe a Navigator. Yeah, I think we'll go with the Navigator, a loaded black Lincoln Navigator with dark tinted windows. Don't use your card to buy the cars. Have the dealership call me on my cell phone. It's on my business card." He handed both men his private card with his numbers on them. Then he remembered the business card Mr. Hayes gave him. He took it out of his pocket and read the name on it. *Jason Sweeney, Private Detective.* "Lee, I'm going to have you work with another man. He'll make your job easier. Do nothing until we meet with him later today.

John called Sweeney and told him Mr. William Hayes referred him, and John wanted to meet with Sweeney at his earliest convenience to discuss a job opportunity. "This afternoon, if possible." Sweeney agreed to meet with him at his office between two and three. Then, John Christo addressed Angelo and Lee. "Look guys. Give me your trust and be loyal to me and I'll be the best friend you ever had. If you ever need anything, all you have to do is ask and you'll have it. If you have problems, I'll make them go away. I'll always be there for you. But never fuck me. Because if you do, you'll wish you were never born, because I'll bury you alive. I hate a rat, any kind of rat, but especially a rat who works for me." He gave his two men a look that could fry eggs. "I needed to get that off of my chest, so remember what I just told you."

John W had a problem. The young man was a man who had been dirt poor and never had a dime, to his name, and now he was one of the richest men in the world. He couldn't spend all the money he had, and so he lavished it on anyone who needed his help. He didn't have to spend money on Lee or Angelo, but he did it because he could. The money he spent wouldn't put a dent in his bank account, but he knew he had to control his urges, especially his spending urges. He had an image to maintain and anyone associated with him had to be part of that image, so he justified his generosity with his need to maintain a proper image. He watched as Angelo stood to leave, but stopped him.

"Wait a minute, Angelo. Come over here. When you accepted my job offer, I had the card I gave you made while you were out. Now try this on."

Angelo stared at the Rolex in disbelief. He always wanted a Rolex, but could never afford one. "You want me to try this watch on?"

"Yes. Put it on. Let's see if you need any links taken off." He found that with his thick wrists that he needed a link added to it. "Do you like the watch, Angelo?"

"Are you kidding, Mr. Christo? What's not to like about it?"

"Good, that's settled, then. While you're out buying my cars, stop by Valentino Maximus and have their jeweler add a link to the watch. You might as well buy a few suits while you're there. I'll call Giorgio after you leave and tell him to duplicate Lee's order and to charge it to my account. I told Lee, and now I'm telling you. I'm building a core group of men who will work closely with me, and since you'll be representing me, I insist you wear the finest clothes money can buy. That's why I wanted you to have the Rolex. I want anyone who meets you to envy you, but in order to do that, dress the part. Just remember this, when we're in the car I don't want you looking like my chauffeur. I want you to look like my banker. Do you understand where I'm coming from? And don't think for a minute that I'm a Pollyanna throwing my money away foolishly, because I'm not. I'm investing it in my men and right now, everything I gave you is a business write off. But, I expect a return on my investment and I will get it, and never doubt it. Now get out of here and buy me a couple of cars."

While riding down the elevator, Angelo thought to himself as he admired his brand new solid gold Rolex. *Christ, what's not to like about this job? This guy spends money like it was water.*

CHAPTER TWENTY-TWO

McCormack put down the report. "It blew up?"

"Yep."

"Just like that?"

"Just like that," the Governor said, smiling. "These things happen sometimes. The consensus is that there must have been a lot of dynamite left over after they built the prison. They think they buried it with the dirt used to fill the spaces between the cells, rather than turning it back in and filling out a lot of forms."

"You're probably right. But what did they need the dynamite for?" McCormack asked.

"They sent crews to the mountains, and they used dynamite to blast for the rocks, and those rocks were used to build the prison."

McCormack was confused. "So, if they buried the dynamite. Why would it be a problem?"

"You don't understand. I think the dynamite was safe while it remained buried in the desert but when the workers dug out the prison and sunlight hit the prison, well when you leave dynamite in the heat it becomes unstable and sweats and it releases nitro glycerin, which could cause it to explode. The temperature at the prison site is over 120 degrees in the summer. It's a wonder that it didn't blow long before this." The Governor smiled. "The explosion did me a big favor because it got rid of my two biggest problems. I was afraid that someday someone would ask me why I put those men in that prison."

"But won't you still have to explain why they were there when the prison was supposed to be closed?"

"Nah. I officially opened that prison so that argument won't hold water. But I feel a lot better now that those two pains in the ass are dead. Now, if anyone asks why I opened the prison, I can tell them we started a pilot program with two prisoners to see if it paid for the state to keep the old prison open. Besides, as Governor I have the power to open or close any prison I want."

"Makes it easier for me too," McCormack chimed in. "With the kid gone, I don't have to worry about him hiring a lawyer or maybe some fancy ass high-priced detective coming around and asking me a lot of questions about why I bought his mother's property. If the kid were alive, he would've had to conclude that I knew there was still gold in that old mine or I wouldn't have gone to the trouble of getting rid of him and finagling the property from the old lady. Now I don't have to worry about anyone asking questions about how I gained that property. Besides, even if the kid didn't die in the explosion, I didn't see how he could hurt me. He was an uneducated kid that couldn't rub two nickels together, so tell me, how the hell could he ever hurt me? But knowing he's dead makes that question moot, and I feel a lot better about it. I'd like to drink to our good fortune. This is great news for both of us, don't you agree?"

"You bet I do. Now pour the drinks and let's toast to the dead."

Sweeney showed up at two thirty.

"Glad you could make it, Mr. Sweeney."

"Nice to meet you, Mr. Christo. Call me Jason, please. Now, what can I do for you?"

"I'd like you to bring me up to date on the work you did for Mr. Hayes. He said many good things about you and that makes me feel comfortable about telling you what I have in mind. He explained what you did for him, but I'd like to hear it from you, and please leave nothing out. I want to hear all of it."

For the next hour, Jason explained everything he did for Mr. Hayes, including how his agent protected Virginia from Tom Jenkins, when he barged into her aunt's home.

"Whew, that's some story. It seems Hayes chose the right man for the job, and that's why I want to hire you. Jason, I'd like to introduce you to Lee Flowers. Lee handles security for me. I gave him an assignment that may be better suited for you, so let me get right to the point. I'd like to hire you to work in a partnership with Lee to look into the backgrounds of four men. All four are enemies of mine."

Jason put his hands up. “I’ll research the four men for you, but I’m not a gunman and I don’t go after anyone’s enemies.”

“I’m not asking you to do that, Jason. I don’t break laws. I work within them. Lee, show Jason the list I gave you.”

Jason read the names and then his eyes opened wide in surprise.

“I thought these names would interest you. Do you recognize them?”

“Governor Wilson. He’s the one who put that nice kid who worked for Hayes in prison, then McCormack stole their property from his mother. Jenkins destroyed Hayes’s business, and Rutgar Kleinst is the strong-armed bastard who does all of McCormack’s dirty work for him. I hadn’t realized these men were your enemies, Mr. Christo. You can count on me. I never liked those bastards, but I was powerless to take them on by myself. Mr. Hayes just about ran out of money trying to pay me to find out what happened to that poor Hardin kid.”

“And did you find anything out about him, Jason?”

“No. They stopped me every step of the way. No one would tell me where they took him. I heard they moved him to a few different prisons before he completely disappeared. I’m an excellent investigator, Mr. Christo, but this was the first time I couldn’t get one bit of information from anyone, on someone I’m investigating.”

John turned to Lee. “Why don’t you tell Jason how you met John W. Hardin?”

“Well, at the time I was an Arizona State prison guard, so I guess the right place to start is when I was told I was being transferred to the Gila Bend Prison that the state was reopening. I never heard of a prison in the Gila Desert, and neither did any of the guys who went out there with me. I thought they were kidding me when they told me about it, but they weren’t; they were dead serious. There were eight of us assigned to that prison, and we were to work until twelve noon. We weren’t worried about anyone escaping because there was no place to escape to. There were the prison’s bars, and the walls, and then there was the desert. No man could have walked out of that prison because if they tried, they’d be dead men. It was the same with Yuma when they first opened it. You want to escape. Be my guest, go. The desert is waiting for you, with miles of nothing in front of you but sand."

"Anyway, we traveled deep into the desert, and I didn't believe it at first, but there was the prison staring back at me - and believe me, it was an ugly-looking place. Most of the prison was buried under the sand to keep it cool. There were two floors above ground. The first level under ground held regular prisoners, but the next level was for the incorrigible prisoners, the troublemakers. After we got there, we were told to get a cell ready for a new prisoner. I found out that we already had one prisoner and he'd been there for quite a while. We were the relief team. The others couldn't wait to get away from that place. Anyway, when the new prisoner arrived, I took him down to the second level. The boy looked scared. I put myself in his place, and I couldn't help feeling sorry for him. I wondered what this poor kid did to get himself put into this god-awful place. My Captain told me when I arrived there, not to become involved with the prisoners because they would just use you. Here was this kid asking me to find out about his mother. Now I ask you, how can that be using me, and it didn't seem to me like he was taking advantage of me? He was worried about his mother, was all. I remember telling him I wouldn't put myself in a position where they would fire me over something he wanted me to do. But I told him if I had the chance, I would find out about his mother for him, but only if I could, mind you. That morning, I asked the Captain about the boy's mother, and before the words left my lips, he fired me. I wanted to help that boy and they fired me for asking about her. Well, that's my story. That's how I met John W. Hardin. It's too bad they killed him. I would like to have met him under better circumstances."

Jason chimed in. "That goes double for me. The way Mr. Hayes spoke of him, he must have been quite a guy."

Lee looked at John. "How about you, Mr. Christo? Did you ever meet him?"

"Yes. Perhaps when I know you gentlemen better, I'll tell you my history with John W. Hardin, kin to the famous shootist, John Wesley Hardin. Until then, I have to remain silent with that young man."

CHAPTER TWENTY-THREE

"What do you think of Jason, Lee?"

"He's a damned good detective. He taught me a few things I never knew, but you have to understand that I wasn't in the investigative end of security. I learned a few things from Sweeney, which will come in handy while working for you."

"That's good to hear," John said. "Now have you discovered anything useful?"

"Well, we found out that Tom Jenkins is working with Rutgar Kleinst as his assistant and it's no secret that Kleinst reports to McCormack. We discovered that everyone but the governor works out of that location. Now that we know that, what do you suggest for our next move?"

John smiled a mirthless smile and said, "Did you ever hunt turkey, Lee?"

Lee shook his head and said, "No, I never have."

John smiled and said, "Well, when you hunt turkey and you come across a group of turkeys, they walk in a line. So, if you take your bead on the last one and pick him off, the first ones in front of him won't know it. Then you pick off the last one in the line. When only the lead bird remains, you take him down because he has no idea the ones behind him are down. I suggest we go on a turkey hunt. The last turkey in the line is Tom Jenkins so we'll take him first. Did you discover his weaknesses like I asked you to?

"Jenkins and Kleinst are small fry. I can destroy them quickly and be done with it. But I feel like the big tomcat that sees two mice, and he's has to decide which one he's going to play with before he eats him. No! We'll play with Jenkins for a little while and then we'll destroy him. Tell me about him, Lee."

Flowers turned a page on his pad. "Here we are. He's a nice-looking guy and he fancies himself as a ladies man. In fact, he's known as 'Fancy Tom Jenkins.' He's certain no woman can resist him. That's why he had it so bad for Hayes's daughter. She saw past his bullshit and she pegged him for what he was, a goddamned con man. Fancy Tom couldn't believe that a woman could resist his charms and refuse him when he asked her out on a harmless date. This guy thinks he's a modern day Casanova. His other glaring weakness is his love for the con.

"He loves putting together small scams, like fleecing a newly wedded couple or some old folks by taking their life savings from them. In his mind, he's not destroying someone's future or security. He sees it as another clever con he successfully pulled off. Usually he picks a city like Miami where there are a lot of rich widows and he'll stay there until he completes a con. Then he'll leave that state and go to a city in another state, like Phoenix, where there are a lot of retirees. He'll set up another scam, and once he's fleeced his mark, he'll get out of Dodge to repeat the scam in city after city. After a year or two, he'll return to a state he's been to in the past where the heat's simmered down. Then he'll start all over again. He's been a doctor, a lawyer, real estate agent, a priest, and he's even been a rabbi a few times. He'll be anybody and do anything to pull off a successful con."

John W motioned with his hand for Lee to stop. He wanted to ask a question. "Is this guy Jenkins good at the con?"

"Good? I'll tell you how good he is. He's so good, he can con a mark into believing that the winter air in the tires need to be changed to summer air or they'll fall off. Then he'll convince the guy to pay him to change the air and after . . . thank him for the great job he's done - that's how good he is."

John laughed and slapped his desk. "That good, eh."

"Yep, he's that good. He was making dough and doing all right, until he got a call out of the blue from his friend Rutgar, who he hadn't seen or heard from in years. Rutgar asked him what he was doing and after listening to him talk for a while, he asked Jenkins if he'd like to change careers. He had a well-paying job with no risk and lots of reward for him if he was interested. Well, at the time, things were heating for Fancy Tom and he jumped at the offer to work for Kleinst. McCormack hired him on Kleinst's recommendation. He's been working for them ever since. McCormack likes the guy and he feels comfortable with him. They're like two peas in a pod, except that one's a bigger con man than the other. McCormack was the one paying Jenkins when he ruined Hayes's real estate business. He was even subsidizing the other sales people in Hayes's office to make sure they didn't quit before Hayes's business was destroyed and he was deep in debt. Jenkins was supposed to take over Hayes's business; that was the deal McCormack made with him. Jack didn't care about the real estate business but once he realized that every once in a while a valuable property turned up, like the Hardin mine, where he could make a bushel full of money, that's when he decided it might pay to keep that business open."

John W digested what Lee just told him. "Hmm this is interesting. I think the best approach is to put out some bait and let Jenkins find it. We'll make the bait juicy enough so that he'll have to bring it to Kleinst. There's a chain of command and he wouldn't bypass Kleinst and go directly to McCormack. No, he'll bring the bait to Kleinst and Kleinst will take it to McCormack. I would prefer going to a turkey shoot with Jenkins as my first kill, but if we get one of the other guys first, I'll take it."

"I still like the turkey shoot idea," Lee said.

John W continued brainstorming. "But what if we combined the two ideas. We can set the bait and have Jenkins find it. Once he takes it to Kleinst, then we can take him down because he'll be of no further use to us. Then we can go after McCormack, who won't have the men he trusts around to protect him."

"What do you think, Lee?"

"I agree. It's simpler and once Jenkins does his job, then we'll take care of him and that will be one less man to worry about."

"Okay, that's what we'll do then. Now we have to figure a way to set the bait for Jenkins to take."

CHAPTER TWENTY-FOUR

"Persistent. It's John. How are you?"

"Doing great, young fella. The question is, how are you doing? The last time we were together, you said you had some unfinished business to take care of. Did you get to finish it?"

"No. That's why I'm calling. Do you have a few minutes to talk?"

"Son, I have all the time in the world. I can't wait for you to finish your business, so you can come out here for a proper visit. Then we can relax, have a few drinks, smoke a cigar or two, and enjoy the desert air. How's that sound?"

John laughed. "I'd like that, but first I have the little matter of that unfinished business to attend to. That's what I wanted to talk to you about. I need you to do something very important for me, and I can't trust anyone else but you to do it."

Persistent's face lit up like a street lamp. "You know I'd do anything for you, son. Just ask, and consider it done."

"Good. I was hoping you'd say that."

"Tarnation's, son. What gave you the idea I'd say anything different? Now tell me what you want me to do, because the suspense is driving me mad."

"I need you to make another trip into the desert. Are you up for that?"

Persistent smiled like he was the Joker in a *Batman* movie. He clapped his hands and he shuffled his feet. He put the phone back to his ear, still grinning, and said, "It's like you read my mind, son, 'cause I was just lookin' for a reason to go back into the desert again. I been itching to do it, but now that we struck it rich I had no reason to."

"I need you to go back to the Four Peaks Gold Mine again, Persistent. Do you think you could find it without me?" John said it jokingly, though Persistent thought he was serious.

"Sure. How could I forget after all the trips I made there

taking gold out of those mountains? But why do you want me to go back? We've left nothing but rock there."

"I need you to salt the Four Peaks Mine. It's got to look real or my plan won't work. There can't be a hint of a lie when I bring a certain party there to see the mine. He has to believe there's plenty of gold in that mine. If you can do it, then let me know how much gold dust or nuggets you need and I'll see that you get it. If you say you can't do it, then I'll scrap the plan and find another way of getting those rats. But you're the expert, you have to tell me If you can or can't do it, because I don't have a clue how to salt a mine. So the big question is - can you do it? Can you make that mine look as if it still has plenty of gold in it?"

Persistent chuckled. "Heh - heh. Son, I haven't spent the last forty years of my life digging for gold without learning a few tricks. 'Cause when I'm done with that mine, you'll think you were in King Solomon's mine, that's how rich it'll look. I'll get Daisy Mae out of her stable and get Conchita, my new burro, and I'll put them to work."

"Persistent, don't spend your money on the gold, I'll finance this little adventure of ours, and maybe I'll send one of my men out to help you."

"What, you're thinkin' of sending me a tenderfoot? Why, hell, he'd only slow me down. No, I'll handle this on my own. Just Conchita, Daisy Mae, and me. As for you financing me, why, tarnation, son, I have so much money now, I don't know how I'm ever going to spend it all. And believe me, I'm trying real hard to do just that." Then, as if he were imparting a great secret, Persistent said in a low voice, "You know, John. I think I liked it better when I was broke. All this money takes away a man's initiative, gives him no incentive to work."

John hadn't expected that and he burst out laughing. "That's why I love you, Persistent. You're not at all predictable. In fact, I should call you 'Predictable' instead of 'Persistent.' I have to get off the phone now. Call me when you've completed the job. Take care of yourself, Persistent, and thanks." He hung up the phone, shaking his head and laughing. "Takin' away a man's initiative." He laughed again, but this time harder. He laughed until his sides hurt, but it felt so good.

One month later, Persistent called him. "It's all done, John, and I have to tell ya, it was enjoyable being out alone in the desert again. As for the mine, I did such a mighty good job of salting it, even *you* would think there was gold in that mine. Tell whoever it is that you want to impress to bring along some high priced assayers, and a few mining engineers, cause they're gonna think they hit the mother lode."

"Good work, Persistent. I'll get to work on my end now. I'll let you know what happens."

"Good. Now don't be a stranger. You hear?"

"Don't worry. I won't. Take care, Persistent, I'll talk to you soon, because I'm going to need you again." John hung up the phone and said to Lee. "Now you're gonna do your part."

"What do you have in mind, Mr. Christo?" John reached into his jacket pocket, pulled out his wallet, and took out the map, which was on a small piece of bleached animal skin and handed it to Lee. "Lee, since you have the file on Fancy Tom Jenkins, you must know where his favorite watering hole is."

"Yeah, I do. It's a small bar in Phoenix called 'The Dew Drop Inn.' What do you want me to do?"

"Fly out to Phoenix and make The Dew Drop Inn your home. Stay there until you make friends with Fancy Tom and somehow get him to trust you. When the two of you are having drinks and telling each other sad stories, mention to him that you have a problem, and that you don't know how to handle it. He may not fall for the bait at first, but if you act sincere, he'll go for it. Especially if you mention this problem could make you rich. Don't you worry. He's a con man and when you mention the word 'rich,' he'll bite. There's no one easier to con, than a con man."

"When do you want me to leave?"

John handed Lee an envelope with his flight information. "You're leaving tomorrow morning on a Delta flight to Phoenix, so wear regular clothing, You know, dungarees, a western shirt, a cowboy hat, and some cowboy boots. Tell him the truth. You were a guard in the old Gila Bend prison and you were fired because you asked about a prisoner's mother. That should get Jenkins's attention, 'cause he'll know it's true. After he's hooked, tell him there was second prisoner with a failing heart and before he died, he gave you an envelope to give to his nephew. That happened shortly before you were fired. When you gave his nephew the envelope, he asked you if you knew your way around the desert and you told him you did. Then tell Jenkins how he opened the envelope and took out a map and handed it to you to look at. Then to impress him, show him your Rolex, and say that the old man's nephew gave it to you just for bringing him the envelope. Now you're in a position where you can have the treasure, but you have no idea how to get the gold out of the mountains. You could even mention that the guy told you the map was supposed to be the location of the lost Four Peaks Gold Mine. If that doesn't get their attention, then nothing will. My guess is Jenkins will check out your story. When he finds out you really were a guard at the prison, and were fired for the reason you told him, he'll take you to see Kleinst. Kleinst will ask you some questions and when he's satisfied your story is true, he'll take you to McCormack and that son of a bitch will sweet talk you, and try to seduce you, by promising that with him involved, you'll make a ton of money, which of course you'd never see. When they're completely hooked, give them my telephone number. Tell them you have a prospector who knows the desert and these mountains like the palm of his hand. And, Lee, that would be no lie. The man does know the desert and the mountains like no one you'll ever know. Tell McCormack that I grubstaked Dutch Henry, and became concerned when I hadn't heard from him. Remember, you don't know anything about mining and you have to find a company to help you take the gold out of the mine. Mention that your prospector knows the desert and he can lead you to the gold. Now all you need is the right mining company."

Lee flew to Phoenix and made the Dew Drop Inn his home. He spotted Fancy Tom saunter into the bar a number of times, but the timing wasn't right to approach him. This time, Fancy Tom took a seat at the end of the bar, and Lee knew this was his opportunity so he took advantage of it. He walked to the bar and seated himself beside Jenkins. He started a conversation with the barmaid, a lovely young lady with a beautiful smile who was not yet jaded by years of listening to bullshit artists, and scammers. As she walked away to get his drink, Lee casually leaned his head in Jenkins's direction as men sometimes do, while he watched her shapely derrière sway like a pendulum.

Lee said to Jenkins without looking at him, "She's some looker ain't she?"

Tom, who always admired a good looking woman, agreed, "She sure is, partner." The two men talked for a while until the waitress came with Lee's drink.

Lee pushed a twenty towards her along with a friendly smile and told her, "That's for you." He pushed another twenty in her direction. "Give me another round and give my friend here whatever he's drinking."

Tom looked at Lee. "You must be new. I haven't seen you before and I come in here almost every day."

"Well, you haven't been looking very hard because I've been sitting back there."

The waitress just returned with their drinks and heard what Lee said to him. "He's right," she said. "He's been coming here for about a week now. Isn't that right, stranger?"

Lee nodded. "I thought it was longer, but it could've been a week. My name is Lee and I come here to drown my sorrows and forget my troubles." He said it with a sad smile and Tom bit.

"Sorrows? Troubles? What kind of trouble?"

That was the opening Lee was hoping for. "I have a problem I'm trying to work it out, so I come here where it's quiet and I can think."

"A problem, you say?" Lee looked sadly at his drink.

"Yeah, and the best part is it could mean a fortune to me if I could just work it out."

That did it. That got the con man's attention. "Tell me about it Lee. Maybe I can help."

So Lee explained about being a guard at the Gila Bend prison and he told him about the two prisoners he guarded.

Tom heard about this from McCormack, but when Lee mentioned the map, Jenkins almost fell off his seat. "Do you have the map?" he asked.

"No. It was just an envelope and I didn't know the map was in it. It was addressed to a man in New York City. I called information and got his number, and then I telephoned him and said I had an envelope for him. I mentioned who gave it to me and said I'd mail it tomorrow. He told me not to mail it; he said to bring it to him in New York. I told him I couldn't do that because I didn't have money for a plane ticket and he told me not to worry about it. He asked me for my address. The next day, I received an overnight envelope with plane tickets and a thousand dollars expense money in it."

Tom was riveted to every word Lee said. "Man, that guy must have some money."

"Money?" Lee said. "Why he's one of the richest men in the world, and one of the nicest guys I've ever met. Look at the watch he gave me just for bringing him the envelope."

"Hey! That's a gold Rolex, wow."

"Yeah, I couldn't believe it myself. I thought it might be a knock-off, so I took it to a jeweler and was I surprised when he told me it was real. I never in a million years thought I'd ever own a real gold Rolex."

Tom's mind was racing now and he thought of McCormack. He was a rich man too, but he was far from nice. "So go ahead," he said. "What happened next?"

"He opened the letter right in front of me and shook his head. 'Look here,' he says. 'A map to a lost gold mine.' He handed it to me. It was a map all right. It showed the way to a lost gold mine called The Four Peaks Mine."

"Wow, you could have kept the envelope, and the mine would have been all yours."

"Nah, it wasn't mine to begin with and I don't take what isn't mine. That map belonged to someone else."

"Okay, so he had the map. What happened then?" Lee knew that greed was getting to Jenkins. "Well, go ahead. What happened?"

"I told you, nothing. I have an old prospector who told me he could take me to the mine if he had the map."

Tom asked him. "Do you have the map?"

"No, but I could get it. Look that's the problem, that's what I've been trying to work out. Don't you get it, even if I had the map, I don't know the first thing about taking gold out of a mountain, except maybe I could ask the old prospector to help me. But I don't know if I could trust him, and besides I don't want a partner. I just want to pay him for his time."

"Well, what about this rich guy who owns the map? Why doesn't he help you?"

"I told you. This guy doesn't give a damn about the gold. He thinks it's all bullshit, the gold, the map and the story of the Four Peaks Mine. He doesn't think the mine ever existed, and I think if it did exist, he'd rather have another company mine the gold and give him a generous percentage of it."

From what Lee just told him, Jenkins thought this could work out fine for him. He was aware of the Governor's obsession for the lost gold mine, and he had an idea. He wanted part of the treasure, and somehow he'd figure a way to get it. "Listen to me, Lee. I work for a very rich man myself, and I'm friends with a very powerful politician who's been searching many years for a lost gold mine. That map could lead him to the very mine he's been looking for. Let me help you with this and I'll give you the piece of the puzzle you're missing."

Lee put a look on his face as if he wasn't sure, as if he were thinking about what Jenkins just said to him, but inside he was jumping with joy. He tried not to show it. "Well, I don't know, Tom. The man told me not to tell anybody about the mine and while I was telling you about my problem, it kinda slipped out by accident. But now that you know about it, let's take it slow. I'll be in here tomorrow at the same time. If you come up with anything, let me know and maybe something will work out. Well, I have to go now. I'll see you tomorrow."

"So long, Lee. See you tomorrow right here at the same time, right? Right?" Tom said nervously, wanting to see Lee tomorrow, but afraid he wouldn't show up.

"Right," Lee said, as he headed for the door. Lee walked slowly down the street and once he turned the corner, he jumped up in the air, waved his cowboy hat, and clicked the heels of his new cowboy boots. He whooped at the same time, scaring the daylights out of an elderly woman who happened to be walking past him.

Lee called John W as soon as he got to his hotel. "Good news. Fancy Tom took the bait. I can't believe how he swallowed the story I gave him. I guess greed clouds common sense."

John said, "The bottom line is he bought the story hook, line, and sinker."

"You got that right. He couldn't wait to tell me that he has two powerful friends. One is his very rich employer and the other is a very powerful politician who's been searching for a lost gold mine himself. We don't have to guess who that is."

John agreed. "It's no secret who that politician is."

Lee continued telling the story. "Guess what he said. He wants to go in partnership with me. I played it down, like I was hard to get, like I wasn't interested in a deal. But I left the door open by telling him to talk to his people. Now I'm at a logger jam. You have to tell me how you want me to handle this."

John W smiled outwardly. "Here's what you'll do. Tomorrow, when you meet him, tell him that you spoke to the old man's rich nephew: me. And he said he might be interested in discussing it with Jenkins people. But they'd have to fly out to see him. He's much to busy to go to them. Tell them that. And before your friend leaves to give his people the good news, make sure you give him one of my business cards. I want them to check me out before they come east. Got that?"

"Yeah, boss, I got it."

CHAPTER TWENTY-FIVE

"Are you positive? You actually met the guard who worked at the prison we sent the kid and the old man to?" McCormack couldn't believe the run of luck he was having. First, the kids claim and now the legendary lost Four Peaks Gold Mine. "I want you to bring this guy in to see me. I want to hear it from him myself. Then you'll bring in the nephew, and we'll see if we can relieve him of his gold mine."

Fancy Tom just stood, shaking his head. "No good, boss. This guy Lee told me if you want to speak to the old man's nephew, you'll have to fly east to see him."

"What? I'll never do that. Who the hell does this guy think he is? He'll come to me if he wants to get the gold out of those mountains. I may even cut him in for a piece of the action if he doesn't piss me off."

Jenkins was getting antsy. He could see his end of the deal disappearing like a puff of smoke if McCormack's demands turned off the kid. "Mr. McCormack, this guy Lee told me that the old man's nephew is one of the richest men in the world. This guy Lee is legit, that much I know. Look, let me bring him in to see you and you can ask him all the questions you want about the mine and the man he gave the map to."

McCormack calmed down. He saw the logic in meeting the man and it made sense. "You're right, Jenkins. I got a little carried away for a minute. I was acting as if I already had the map and those people were intruders, when it's the other way around. See if you can get him in here tomorrow. I want to have a long talk with him, and when I do, I want to look into his eyes to see if he's telling the truth. I have a sixth sense when someone's trying to con me, and I'll know right away. If that's the case, then Rutgar will do some very unpleasant things to him. Now get out of here, go find him, and bring him to me."

Fancy Tom Jenkins headed right over to the Dew Drop Inn

and looked for Lee Flowers, but he wasn't there. He walked to the bar and signaled Pamela, the barmaid, to come over. "Did that fella Lee come back here after I left?"

Pamela thought for a minute. "No. He left just before you did and he hasn't come back yet."

"Do you have a piece of paper?"

"Sure, hold on a minute." She went to the register, ripped a page from a pad, and handed it to Jenkins.

He wrote his number on it and said, "If Lee comes back tonight, tell him I have good news and have him call me at this number. If he comes in tomorrow instead of tonight, tell him to stick around until I get here, then call me at this number and I'll shoot right over. I don't want to miss him; it's important that I see him. Thanks, Pamela, see you later."

Lee didn't show up that night and Jenkins was beside himself, worrying that Lee might have left town. But at eleven the next morning, Lee strolled in and Fancy Tom Jenkins was there waiting for him. "Lee, my god. I thought you skipped out on me."

"No, I'm still here. What's happening? Why are you concerned I might have left town?"

"I have great news for you," Tom blurted out. "My boss is interested in underwriting your lost gold mine. He wants to talk to you about it. Come on, I told him I'd take you to see him."

"Well, hold on a minute, Tom. I don't know if I'm ready to talk to anyone yet."

Tom was breathing hard now. "Wait a minute, Lee. Don't go on making me look bad. The other day, you were all down in the face because you didn't know how you were going to get the gold out of the mountains. I took care of that problem for you. Don't let me down after I went out on a limb for you. Look, just do me a favor and don't let me look bad. I explained everything that you told me to my boss, and he sees a fit with his company. Just talk to him, and if you don't want to do the deal after speaking to him, then just leave. At least this way I won't look bad, and you'd be doing me a big favor. If you and he agree to a deal, then I'll look good, and maybe he'll throw me a little something. Come on. Take a walk with me and have a talk with my boss. You'll like him. I know you will."

Lee made as if he didn't want to go, but then acted as if he didn't want to make Jenkins look bad, so he agreed to do it for him.

McCormack Industries was just around the corner in the heart of Phoenix's business district. They took the elevator to the ninth floor and walked through glass doors with McCormack Industries written in large gold leaf letters on them. A secretary escorted the men to a large office at the end of the hall.

A big man sitting behind a large desk stood when they walked in and said, "Now who do we have here, Tom? Is this the young man you told me about?" McCormack said, putting on the charm.

"Yes, sir. Let me introduce you to Lee Flowers."

McCormack gave Lee his most ingratiating smile. "It's a genuine pleasure to meet you, Mr. Flowers. Please have a seat. Tom, get Mr. Flowers a cup of coffee. Would you like that, Mr. Flowers?"

"Yes, a cup of coffee sounds good. I have had none yet this morning."

"Good. Tom will see to it. Now let's discuss this lost gold mine you told Tom about."

Lee put a pained expression on his face, but not too much. After all, he didn't want to overdo it. "I really wish Tom hadn't told you about that map just yet. I don't want too many people to know about it until I had time to figure things out."

"Were you really a guard in a prison in the desert?"

"Yes, sir. Gila Bend prison. It had been closed for years, but they reactivated it on a trial basis."

"Did you have any prisoners there?"

"There was one prisoner already incarcerated in the prison when I got there. But shortly after I arrived, they brought another prisoner in. I took him down to the lower level. That's where they took the problematic prisoners. I don't know why they took those two men down there. They must have done some terrible things to be put in there."

"I see," McCormack said as he looked for a sign of deception. But Lee knew too much about the prison to be faking it. *No matter*, McCormack thought. He'd have Governor

Wilson check out his story. If it proved to be true, then he'd go after the gold mine. "Go on, Lee. Your story is intriguing. What happened next?"

"Well, when they brought the kid in, they had handcuffed him and had him in chains. I took him down to the 'Tombs,' as it was called. When I opened that old cell, the door was so rusty from being closed all those years it would hardly open. Well, I have to tell you, I was breathing hard after getting the door opened. When he was in his cell, he asked me what my name was and I told him it was Lee. He asked if I would do him a favor. I told him I didn't do favors for prisoners; it could get me fired. He said that all he wanted was to know how his mother was doing. I felt bad about that. Every man should be able to know about his mother if he wants to, so I said I would see what I could do as long as it didn't cost me my job. But it cost me my job because as soon as I inquired about his mother, the warden fired me."

"But what about the map?"

"Well, that happened the day before. The old man was very ill. He had a heart problem, and he knew he was dying. He handed me an envelope and asked if I would mail it to his nephew, John Christo, in New York City."

"Well, what happened then?"

"They fired me before I could mail it. When I got home, I forgot about the envelope for about a week. Then, when I was putting my uniform away, I was going through the pockets when I found the envelope. Instead of mailing it, I called information for John Christo's number. I called right away, told him about the letter, and said I would mail it the next day, but he told me not to. He told me to fly to New York and deliver it to him. When I explained to him I couldn't afford it, he asked me for my address and said he'd send me a ticket. The next day I get an overnight FedEx envelope with an airline ticket to New York in it along with a thousand dollars' expense money."

"And you went to New York and delivered the envelope to him?"

"Yes, sir. That's exactly what I did. The strange thing was that when he opened the envelope, there was a letter, which he took out and read. It included a map in the envelope, and he studied it for a minute or two. Then he handed it to me. If I had a photographic memory, I could have stolen the gold from him and he would never have known. But I'm an honest man and would do nothing like that. He told me that since I delivered his uncle's letter, he'd include me in this deal somewhere, and then he opened his desk drawer and took out a box and told me to open it."

"'That's for you," he said. 'For bringing me the envelope, I appreciate it.'" Lee showed McCormack his gold Rolex. "He gave me this just to deliver an envelope."

McCormack couldn't believe anyone would give someone a gold Rolex just for delivering a letter. *How rich could this guy be*? He thought. That thought hooked McCormack. He knew the story Lee told him was true. Lee *did* work in the prison and he knew they had fired him. Wilson would confirm the story when he called back with the information. "Who is this man you delivered the letter to? Did he give you a card?"

"Yes, he did." McCormack smiled. "Here it is." He motioned to Kleinst, who sat in the corner listening to everything that they said, to come over. "Take this card, Rutgar, and check out this man and his company for me. I must know with whom I am dealing. I have to know everything about him because when I meet with him, I want to be armed with information." McCormack turned to Lee. "You're sure the map shows the location of the Four Peaks Mine?"

"Yes, sir. I saw it written on the map."

"You're sure it's real?"

"I don't know about that, sir, but the old man was dying and I don't think he'd be playing a joke on someone from his deathbed."

McCormack had no reason to believe that Lee wasn't telling him the truth. "It's a very interesting story. I'm inclined to believe you. What do you want out of this?"

Lee was prepared for the question. "Look, Mr. McCormack. I'm not a greedy man, but I deserve to get something out of this. After all, I lost my job for no reason I can think of. Since I'm the only one who can get the map, it should entitle me to a share of the gold. Not much, mind you, but enough to make me well off. I'm tired of worrying about my bills or where my next meal is coming from, and with the money I get from this mine, I can do that. I can live a simple, debt-free life. What percentage do you think I should get, Mr. McCormack?" Lee threw the ball right back in McCormack's lap.

"I should think a few points would make you a rich man, Lee, don't you?"

"By a few points, you mean five or ten percent, don't you?"

McCormack puffed up and was about to lose his temper, but he caught himself. "Don't you think five or ten percent is a little high? I was figuring more like two or three percent."

"All right, Mr. McCormack. Three percent it is, then." McCormack clapped his hands in delight. He could smell a fortune coming his way. "Good. That's settled, then. That's a wise choice, Lee, and one you won't regret. Now, I want you to call this Mr. Christo and tell him to come out here as soon as he can and we'll discuss the logistics of putting together a team to find the mine."

"I'll get him on the phone, but I can guarantee you he won't come here."

McCormack appeared annoyed that they wouldn't carry out his order. He couldn't tolerate people who didn't bow down to him, and he made it a rule never to go to anyone else's office to discuss business. His office was where he conducted business. He pushed the intercom button to Kleinst's office. "Rutgar, have you found any information on this John Christo yet?"

"Yes, Jack. I have it here. I was just going to bring it to your office."

"What have you found out about, Christo?"

"It's like Flowers said. The guy is mega rich. Rich beyond anything you could imagine. He owns his office building, and he's buying up businesses and investing in growth companies, but the funny thing is he seems to have come out of nowhere. Nobody ever heard of the guy until recently. He must be a Howard Hughes type of guy who likes to keep his business private. But one thing is for sure."

"And what's that?" McCormack asked.

"This man's got the Midas touch. Everything he touches turns to gold."

McCormack rubbed his hands in an unconscious display of

satisfaction. "Good Rutgar. At least now, we know the man is legitimate, just as Lee said. He's so rich that he could not care less about his bothersome gold mine. I can't figure that out though, because if it was me, I'd want it all. Hand me a gold mine on a gold platter and I'd jump at the chance to increase my wealth."

Lee agreed. "That gold mine is the last thing on his mind. I think he'd sell it if he could make a profit on it. He feels he has better things to do with his time than to go traipsing around the desert, chasing after a dream."

McCormack's eyes lit up. "Are you telling me he might sell it to someone if the price was right?"

"Yeah. I think he would, if the price was right."

McCormack was thinking fast now. "Lee, about that three percent we agreed to. What if I made it ten percent? Would that make you happy?"

"Boy, it sure would, Mr. McCormack."

"Well, Lee. You said you saw the map. Am I correct?"

"Yes, I saw it. Why do you ask?"

"Do you think you could remember where the mine is located?"

"I don't know, Mr. McCormack. I just saw it once. But when I took the old man to see Mr. Christo, he had a good, long look at the map and he said he knew where to find the mine."

McCormack jumped out of his chair; he was so excited. "The old man saw the map, and he knows where the mine is located? Is that what you're saying?"

"Yes, sir. That's exactly what I'm saying."

"Look, Lee. I'm not trying to cheat Mr. Christo out of anything. I just want to confirm that the mine exists before I invest my money in this venture. That makes sense, doesn't it?"

"Well, yes. It does. What do you want me to do?"

"Can you get a hold of this old man and ask him to take us to see the mine?"

"I don't know about that. I don't want to do anything that's not in Mr. Christo's plans. And I certainly don't want him to find out that I've done anything underhanded behind his back. That's for sure."

McCormack was sweating, trying his damnedest to

convince Lee to talk the old man into taking them to the mine. "Look, Lee. Mr. Christo put you in charge of this gold mine, didn't he?"

"Well, yes. He did."

"Okay, by default, he gave you the authority to decide on his behalf. All I'm saying is you'd be doing him a big favor by having me make sure this mine has gold in it. Nobody buys something expensive without first examining it, right? He has to inspect what he's buying, doesn't he?"

Lee nodded. "Well, when you put it that way, yes, a person should inspect what he's gonna buy. He doesn't want to buy a pig in a poke, now. Does he?"

McCormack wiped his brow, pleased that he finally got Lee thinking along his lines. He wanted the mine, but he had to see it first. He wouldn't dream of cheating a powerful man like Mr. Christo like he would cheat just about anyone else in this world, but he always liked to have an edge before he committed to a deal, something he knew the other guy didn't. By seeing the mine firsthand and having Rutgar Kleinst, who was his mining engineer, confirm that there was gold in the mine. Kleinst was valuable to him for several reasons, and this was one of them. Kleinst would keep the knowledge of the mine within the family, so to speak. If he hired an outside engineer, there was always the possibility that in no time at all, the entire world would know about the mine. He was fortunate to have Kleinst, but he would never admit that to him.

"So what do you say, Lee? Are you in or are you out? Decide now, because I need to know where you stand."

Lee thought a moment, then he said, "The old prospector spent his whole life looking to hit it big, and he never did. With the map, it would be his chance to find the Four Peaks Mine or… maybe he *could* find it from memory. I'll talk to him. He might agree if there weren't too many people involved. I think he'd go for it if, let's say, it was just you, me, and Mr. Kleinst going with him. But I'm getting ahead of myself. First, I have to find out if the old man remembers where the mine is located. He said he knew approximately where it was, and thought he could find the mine, but I have to tell you, those mountains are confusing, and without a map, it would be like looking for a needle in a haystack. You know, maybe I could talk Mr. Christo into loaning us the map, so we wouldn't have a problem finding it."

McCormack jumped out of his seat. "NO! Don't even think of doing that. I don't want Christo to know I'm interested in his mine, not yet. I have to see it first before I commit to buying it."

Lee backed up a bit and said, "Yeah, I see what you mean. Okay, I'll contact the old man and tell him I have a potential buyer for the mine, but the buyer wants to make sure there's gold in the mine before he buys it. How's that sound?"

"Good. Now when can you talk to the old man, and how soon after do you think we can we get started?"

"I don't know. If he agrees to take us - then pretty fast, I guess."

"When will you contact him?"

"As soon as I get back to my hotel. I left his phone number in my jacket. But I'll call him and then I'll call you back to tell you what he said."

"Good. I'll wait for your call. I'm an impatient man when I want something, so don't keep me waiting too long."

"Don't worry, Mr. McCormack. I'll call you as soon as I finish talking to him."

When Lee left, McCormack asked Rutgar what he thought of the man.

"I don't think he was lying. I talked to the Governor, and he worked at the prison. They fired him because he asked about the kid's mother, so we know he was telling us the truth about that. There were two prisoners that he mentioned. One was the old man, and the other was the kid, so he wasn't lying about that either. The question is, was he lying about the map? He said the old man gave the map to him to give to his nephew? Why would he accept a letter from a dying man when he could get fired for getting close to the prisoners?"

McCormack thought about that. "Well, no one would know the old man gave him an envelope and besides, if he was telling us the truth about everything else, why would he lie about the map? It makes little sense to think he'd lie about that and nothing else. And wouldn't we find out if he was telling us the truth after meeting with Mr. Christo and actually seeing the map? If we find gold, then by definition, he must have been telling us the truth about everything else. Don't you agree?"

"Yeah, I guess. But something doesn't feel right about this. I can't put my finger on it. It's just a feeling, but I've learned to listen to my feelings when I get them."

"The trouble with you, Rutgar, is you worry too much? This is all self-explanatory. If we find the mine, then it's true. It's true if we find the gold. If we talk to Christo and he agrees to sell the mine to us without knowing we already checked it out, then that's also true."

CHAPTER TWENTY-SIX

Lee called John W from his hotel room and told him what they had said at the meeting.

Christo listened with interest to every word Lee told him. "From what you just told me, it was a very productive meeting, Lee. When you call McCormack, tell him that Persistent said he'd take them, but only if he blindfolded them when they got close to the mine. Say that the old man feels he'd be betraying my trust if they knew how to get to the mine. But if he blindfolded them and they didn't know where the mine was, then he has no problem taking them there."

The two men discussed various approaches they could take until they agreed on a simple plan. John asked Lee to hold while he conference-called Persistent so they could have a three-way conversation. After talking to Christo, Lee knew what to say to McCormack. Now they had to nail down Persistent's part. Christo instructed Persistent on what to say and do, but he advised him to relax and be himself. The conversation was productive, and the men agreed to a plan, which was like a well-choreographed play where each man knew his part and committed it to memory. Satisfied with the plan, John told Persistent to get a room in Payson and, in a few days, McCormack, Kleinst, and Lee would meet him there.

Lee called McCormack and said he had spoken to the old man. "He told me he knew the general location of the mine and he agreed to take you to it, but he had a condition."

McCormack asked what the condition was.

Lee told him. "The old man insists that he blindfold you fellas when we get close to the mine so you won't know where the mine is." Lee explained to McCormack that this was Mr. Christo's mine and if they want to see it for themselves he'd take them, but they would have to be blindfolded part of the way. McCormack didn't like the idea of being blindfolded and neither did Kleinst, but if they wanted to see the mine, they had no choice but to agree to the old man's condition.

The three men drove to Payson, a little town that is nestled among the majestic mountains of the Mogollan rim, a 7,000 foot, 200-mile long escarpment that sits at an elevation of 5,000 feet. Persistent told them to meet him at the Rodeo. He said he'd be wearing a sombrero and a red cowboy shirt, with a red bandana around his neck. Lee knew what he looked like, having met him once, but the others had no clue what he looked like.

"Persistent!" Lee spotted him and yelled out to him, and the old man turned with a smile. "Hi, there, Lee. I wondered if you'd find me among all these people. He looked at the two men. "These must be your friends, the ones you told me about."

"They sure are. Persistent, I want you to meet Mr. McCormack and his associate, Mr. Kleinst. These are the men who are interested in buying that lost mine."

The men shook hands, and then McCormack asked Persistent a question. "Can you remember how to find the mine?"

"I only saw the map once, but I studied it real hard, hoping to remember it. But I recognized certain landmarks that most persons wouldn't know from a hole in the ground, but to answer your question, yes. I believe I can find it."

The Mazatzals Mountains are treacherous if you don't know what you're doing. There was a time when Tonto Indians would kill a man if he stumbled on their gold mine, but that was in the past. Many prospectors have searched the Mazatzals for the lost Four Peaks Gold Mine. Most of them ended up dead. At least two accounts tell of a rich, gold-bearing quartz deposit somewhere along the western flanks of the Four Peaks. In one case, a pair of prospectors discovered the lode, but the Tonto Apaches later killed them. In the second case, a cowboy stumbled on the gold deposit while searching for cattle. But he could never find the mine again.

"Let me give you a rough idea of where we're going. From Payson, we're gonna head south about 15 miles to the Arizona Highway 188 junction. We'll turn left there and follow Highway 188 south for about 14 miles. This will take us to the south end of the Punkin Center Business Road. This road takes off to the left and goes east. It's a paved road, so it makes traveling to that point a lot easier. Then we're gonna take Forest Road 409, which is a dirt road and we'll follow it west for 1 ½ to 2 miles to where it forks. The left fork drops off the mesa and goes a short distance to the Park Creek Trailhead while the right fork heads to Camp Reno. We're taking the left fork and that's all I'm gonna tell you for now. I'm a little strapped for cash, but I reserved a rig to carry four horses and Conchita."

"Who the hell is Conchita?" McCormack asked.

"Sorry about that. She's my burro. I keep forgetting she's a burro. She's like family to me."

"When could we get started?" McCormack asked.

"Tomorrow morning, we'll get an early start. Today, we're gonna take it easy and enjoy ourselves by watching the longest continuous rodeo."

Persistent explained the history of this rodeo. He told them a man called Arizona Charlie Meadows started it and he lived to be one hundred and two years of age. "There were no chutes in those early days. The cowboys dragged or lead the broncs to the middle of the street and a couple of cowboys eared them down. Then, someone would cinch a rig onto the horse's back and a bronc rider stepped onboard. This wasn't a timed event; that came years later."

Even though McCormack and Kleinst were in a hurry to get started, they were caught up in Persistent's story, and to their surprise, they were enjoying it. "The cowboys brought their own horse to those first rodeos, and they rode them until his head came up or the horse threw the rider. The cowboys also rode the broncs of their competitors, as well as their own, so that it was a fair contest where everyone got a fair shake. Now if you don't mind, I'd prefer we don't talk business right now. I suggest we all just sit back and enjoy the rodeo."

CHAPTER TWENTY-SEVEN

At eight a.m., the journey to the Four Peaks Mine began. Kleinst rode with Persistent, who drove the truck that carried the animals, tools, and equipment. Lee followed in the Range Rover while McCormack sat in the passenger seat. They left the paved road and were now driving on dirt roads. The dirt roads were rough, but they did not know what rough was until they made a turn at the base of the Mazatzals mountains. They drove for another two hours on a road in which a gopher wouldn't dig a hole until the lead truck pulled off the road and onto a dirt clearing at the base of the mountain and stopped.

"Everyone out!" Persistent yelled. "Help me get the animals out of the truck and let's saddle them up. If you've never saddled a horse before, then leave it and I'll do it. It wouldn't do to put the cinch on wrong and fell off your horse and hitting your head on a rock."

Lee nodded and told him, "I know how to saddle a horse."

"So do I," Kleinst added.

"Good," Persistent said. "Then let's get to puttin' saddles on these dumb critters."

McCormack was the only one who had not only never put a saddle on a horse, but he had never ridden one. He felt helpless, and he didn't like it. The feeling passed when he heard Persistent say that if he remembered the location correctly, they should locate the mine later this afternoon.

"Are you sure you can find this mine, Persistent?" McCormack asked again. McCormack asked that question every ten minutes.

"I'll know for sure, Mr. McCormack, when I find the landmarks I'm looking for. When they present themselves to me, then I'll know we're near the mine."

Persistent ordered the men to dismount, and then he led them along a narrow path that extended up the mountain. The air was cooler, and the going was tough on everyone except for Conchita and Persistent. They were like Billy goats as they climbed the mountain path. Kleinst was in excellent condition, so the climb didn't bother him and the same applied to Lee. The only one having trouble was Jack McCormack. He wasn't used to this much physical activity, and to make matters worse, he was out of condition.

"Hold on a minute, guys," he said. "Let's take a breather for a few minutes. I need to catch my breath."

Persistent apologized for pushing them. He said that he'd like to get to the mine while there was still daylight. But it was embarrassing to McCormack to hear him say that because Persistent was a good 20 years older and the climb didn't seem to bother him at all. They took a ten-minute break to give McCormack a chance to regain his strength, while the animals ate grass that grew on both sides of the narrow path.

Persistent knew where the mine was, but since the terrain looked the same for miles around, he led the men in circles until he felt it was time to head toward the mine. When they were close to the cleft, which they had walked past twice but from different angles, Persistent put his up hand to signal *stop* and they halted at the base of the mountain.

"Okay, boys, we're close to the mine. Let's mount up," Persistent ordered, and then said, "Take out the sacks I gave you. It's time to put them on. I want to see them covering your faces. I'm gonna check each one to make sure they're on right… so do it right the first time. Then I'm going to tie your horses in a way so that each horse must follow the one in front of it. Okay then, just relax, and let your horse do the work." He entered the cleft, leading the small troupe of men through the mountain. When they exited, he continued to lead them along a narrow ledge for about one hundred and fifty yards, until they approached a clearing that led to a fork. The right fork led to a lush green valley, brimming with varieties of multi-colored flowers and abundant wildlife. It was a virtual paradise, but they didn't take the right fork; they took the left fork, which led them to a narrow ledge with a path below it that ran parallel to the ledge. The path followed the base of the mountain for almost a quarter of a mile until it ended at a gap in the mountain, facing a cave that was almost completely covered with vegetation. The men still had the sacks on their heads while the horses, led by Persistent, walked ahead for another ten minutes. Persistent halted the horses and turned to the men.

"Okay, boys, you can take the sacks off now. We've arrived."

McCormack ripped his hood off and looked around but didn't see the mine. "Where's the mine? I don't see any mine," McCormack asked.

Persistent clapped his hands. "You didn't think I could find it, did you? But, I found it. I found the Lost Four Peaks Tonto Apache Gold Mine."

The men looked around.

McCormack looked too, but they saw nothing. "Are you pulling my leg? Because I sure as hell don't see any mine."

Persistent looked at McCormack and shook his head. "You hear, but you don't listen. You look, but you don't see. We're standing in front of the mine, Mr. McCormack, and you're so close to it you can touch it… and you still don't see it."

McCormack looked around again and he still couldn't see the mine. "Where the hell is it? I don't see a damn thing."

"Like I said, you look, but you don't see." Persistent said laughing as he performed a little dance like Walter Huston did in the movie, 'The Treasure of the Sierra Madre', then shaking his head while still laughing, he turned and walked over to a growth of vegetation that hung off the mountain, covering the opening like a curtain. He moved it aside, revealing the small opening to the cave. McCormack gaped at the opening, slack-jawed. "I'll be damned," he said.

"Take your lanterns with you and pray to whatever god you believe in that there's gold in this mine." Persistent led them through the entrance to the cave with a warning to be careful of the loose rocks littering the entrance. Once inside the cave, it opened up into a cavern. Flickering light from the lanterns reflected off of the Spanish helmets and breastplates. The men noticed the Spanish weaponry, lances, and swords that lined the walls. The light from the lanterns illuminated the skeletons, especially the skulls, that smiled up at them.

Persistent pointed to the skulls. "The Tonto Apaches put

them there to scare off intruders."

It pleased McCormack with what he saw, and he put his arm around Persistent's shoulders in an uncharacteristic show of affection. "I'm impressed, Persistent. Lee was right. You know the desert and you didn't even need the map. You found the mine from memory. Well, we have proof that the Spaniards were mining gold here, so this has to be the Lost Four Peaks Gold Mine."

Kleinst shined his light against the rear wall and didn't get a reflection. He realized there was another chamber in the back and he motioned for them to follow him into the dark extension of the chamber they were in. "Let's see what's in there."

They followed him into the room. As the lanterns lit up the room, the gold glittered off of the walls and the ceiling. Kleinst's keen eyes spotted loose nuggets on the floor. He bent down, picked up a few, took them outside, and tested the gold with a kit he removed from his jacket pocket. Rutgar shook his head after completing the test.

McCormack, who had followed him out, thought it signaled something bad and he asked, "What did you find, Rutgar?"

Rutgar paused a moment, then he looked at McCormack. "This is pure gold. It's some of the finest I've ever seen. If this is a sample of what's in this mine, then there's a fortune in gold here."

"You're sure about this, Rutgar?"

Kleinst looked at his boss and said, "Technology doesn't lie, Jack. I can only tell you what the tests tell me, and they're screaming that we're looking at pure gold. Maybe the richest I've ever tested."

"That's all I need to know," McCormack said. "Come on. Let's head home. I want to meet this Christo character and buy his mine from him." What the pair didn't know was John W had Persistent scour every area of the mine to make sure it was played out. Dutch Henry had taken every ounce of gold out of that old mine. It was dry. There was nothing left to mine. McCormack and Kleinst had taken the bait and had bitten down hard on it.

Persistent checked the sacks to make sure they covered their faces, and they tethered the horses the same as before. Persistent looked at the men seated on their horses to make sure they were ready to leave. Then he picked up the reins of the horse behind his and led the men back down the mountain through the hidden narrow cleft. When they were past the hidden break, Persistent kept the horses walking until the opening in the mountain was a suitable distance behind him. He looked back and smiled because the pass was invisible to the naked eye. “Okay, boys, you can remove the sacks now.” Then, with Persistent leading the way, the little troupe began the long slow trek back to their vehicles.

CHAPTER TWENTY-EIGHT

Persistent drove the big rental truck he used in which to transport the animals and equipment. He'd return it to the rental company when they returned to Phoenix. On the ride back, you could feel the excitement radiating from within the car. It was like sitting in the middle of a lightning storm. McCormack was as giddy as a new bride. He was sure he hit the mother lode with this mine and it wasn't even his yet, although he acted like it was.

"Well, what do you think now, Rutgar? Do you still have any doubts?"

Rutgers' initial doubts about this deal had all but subsided. However, somewhere deep inside him, a little voice was telling him to be wary. "No. I don't have any doubts, especially after seeing the high yield of the gold I tested."

"And what about the Spanish armor and weapons we found? That showed that the Spaniards must have taken a ton of gold out of the mine too."

Rutgar nodded. "Yeah, that too. What are you thinking of doing next, Jack?"

"Good question." He turned to Lee. "I want you to call your John Christo right now and set up a meeting for tomorrow."

Lee nodded. "I was going to make the call tomorrow, but I could do it now if that's what you want."

"That's what I want. Call him now and let's get the show on the road. I want to take control of the mine as soon as possible. Wait till I announce I found the Lost Four Peaks Gold Mine. That should drive our stock way the hell up. Man, I can't wait to see the expressions on my competitors' faces when they read about how Jack McCormack did it again."

Before he made the phone call, Lee asked McCormack a question. "Mr. McCormack, what do you think the mine will be worth?"

McCormack thought about it for a minute, then said, “Lee, that mine could be worth more than all of my other mines combined if we could take out all the gold I think is in there. Why do you ask?”

“Well, I was wondering what my ten percent would be worth after you make the announcement.”

McCormack didn’t know where this was going and he didn’t want to give Lee the impression he would make many millions with his ten percent. But now that he opened his big mouth and smartened up the kid, how could he deny it? Well, he’d just have to bluff the kid and see where he was going with this. “Why do you ask, Lee?”

“I was just wondering if you would consider buying my ten percent for, say, ten million dollars.”

McCormack let out a sigh of relief. All the kid wanted was ten million dollars. Normally, he would have given him nothing. He would have just taken it from him, since he didn’t have the money to fight him in court. But he still had to meet with John Christo and negotiate a price for the mine. He couldn’t afford to be seen cheating Lee because Christo not only would back out of the deal, but he had the wealth to fight him to a standstill. He didn’t want to leave money lying on the table, so instead of cheating Lee, he negotiated a better deal for himself. “That’s a lot of money, Lee. Especially when we don’t know how much gold we’ll be taking out of that mine. Besides, I couldn’t give you any money until I take control of the mine.”

Lee pretended to understand McCormack’s line of reasoning. “That’s all right, Mr. McCormack. I’ll just wait until the mine produces and I’ll probably make twenty times the ten million. I guess it’s better if I wait until the mine produces.”

McCormack didn’t like the sound of that either. He certainly didn’t want to pay Lee twenty times the ten million he asked for. Greed was getting the better of him now, just as John W had figured it would.

“You know, Mr. McCormack. When you make the deal with Mr. Christo, I’d like an agreement drawn up containing the terms you said I would receive. The agreement will eliminate any misunderstandings that may occur between us in the future. Don’t you agree?”

McCormack didn't want to do that. The last thing he wanted was an agreement with this kid. "Tell you what, Lee. I'm going to cut a check for five million dollars. The moment Mr. Christo gives me the map and relinquishes any rights to the mine, I will hand you the check. How does that sound? Is it a deal?"

"It sounds okay, Mr. McCormack, but I asked for ten million, not five. So I think it's better if I wait until the mine produces."

McCormack was between a rock and a hard place. He didn't want to give Lee ten million dollars, but more than that, he hated to see his ten percent giving him hundreds of millions more. McCormack was in a tough position, but he knew he had to choose between the best of two evils. He smiled at Lee and said, "Ten million dollars it is, Lee. I'll give you the check for ten million dollars the moment the Christo signs the deal, and he delivers the mine to me. You understand that you'll have to sign a release for your percentage of the mine when I give you the check."

"Sure, that's only fair, Mr. McCormack."

On the drive to Phoenix, Lee called John Christo with his cell phone and put it on speaker. When Christo picked up the phone, Lee told him he was on speaker and asked him if he would be available for a meeting tomorrow morning with Jack McCormack. Christo said his calendar wouldn't allow it, but he would be available the following morning. It disappointed McCormack, just as Christo figured he'd be. He was playing mind games with McCormack, setting the hook deeper. They confirmed the appointment for 10 a.m., the day after tomorrow.

Angelo picked up the men at LaGuardia Airport in the new black shiny stretch limo the company had just gained. The plan was for Angelo and Lee not to recognize one another; As far as anyone was concerned, they were strangers. Angelo held up a sign, chest high, with "McCormack" written on it. Lee walked over to him, looked at the sign, and said, "McCormack, that's our party."

Lee, McCormack, Kleinst, and Governor Wilson, who insisted on attending this meeting, stepped into the sleek black limo. Wilson reminded them he had a vested interest in this mine. If he hadn't locked up Dutch Henry, they wouldn't be riding to Manhattan in a limo. The trip should have taken 20 minutes, but because of the heavy cross-town traffic, it took almost an hour. Eventually, Angelo pulled to the curb in front of a building on Sixth Avenue that had, to the right of the door, a large elegant plaque with "CHRISTO" in large bold brass letters. They took the elevator to the top floor and when the elevator doors opened, a young pretty secretary got up from behind her desk and welcomed them to Christo Enterprises. Then she escorted them down the long hallway to Mr. Christo's office. All the new people and activity surprised Lee.

The young lady knocked once, then she opened the door and escorted the three men into a waiting room. She then approached another secretary seated behind a modern smoked glass and chrome horseshoe-shaped desk. "Monica, these gentlemen have a ten o'clock appointment with Mr. Christo."

"Thank you, Claudia. I'll take them into Mr. Christo's office as soon as he's off the phone." Claudia left the room. Monica, a pleasant smile on her face, asked the men to have a seat. "Mr. Christo will be with you in a moment. He's on the phone, but he should be off momentarily. Would you gentlemen care for a cup of coffee or tea?" The men declined her offer, except for Lee, who asked for a cup of black coffee. He said he needed the caffeine jolt to wake him up. Monica smiled and glided away to fetch his coffee. Just as she handed the cup to Lee, her intercom buzzed. After answering it, she motioned for the men to follow her.

Christo dressed in an elegant dark blue pinstriped suit. He wore his beard short, but long enough to disguise who he was. No one standing before him knew he was the poor frightened soul who they left in a prison to rot for the rest of his life. The man cultured man and everything about him reeked of wealth. He didn't flaunt it, but class just oozed from him. Governor Wilson, who was never at a loss for words, couldn't find anything to say. McCormack, always so sure of himself, felt intimidated by this man's presence. Only Christo thought his wealth didn't affect Kleinst, and that uncertain feeling was still with him, and he noticed it intensified now that he was in John Christo's presence.

"What can I do for you, gentlemen?" Christo asked,

smiling.

McCormack spoke for the group. "Lee, here, informed me he delivered a map to you. A bequest, as I understand it from an old miner who was in prison."

"Yes, Lee was a guard in that prison and was kind enough to do the dying man a favor, whom I might add, was my uncle. He honored my uncle's last request and brought me this envelope." He opened the desk drawer and took out the envelope. "This envelope contains a map to a lost gold mine. Lee tells me you have experience in mining gold."

That was the opening for which McCormack was waiting. "Mr. Christo, I am president of McCormack Industries and we specialize in mining precious metals such as gold, silver, copper, or any other valuable mineral that's in demand. We are a profitable company worth many millions. You can check us out for yourself."

"I'll do that." He pressed the intercom and told Monica to bring him a report on McCormack Industries as soon as possible. "It concerns my guests. Their time is valuable and I don't want to keep them any longer than I have to."

While Monica was preparing the report, McCormack asked, "Is this your building, Mr. Christo?"

"Yes, with the state of the economy in the shape it is, I was fortunate to have bought it at the right price."

"I see," McCormack said. "If I'm not being too personal, can I ask you who holds your mortgage?"

"I don't have a mortgage. The price was right, so I paid cash for it."

McCormack did a quick mental calculation and determined that this building must have cost Christo close to a billion dollars.

Monica came in with the report. Christo took his time to read the report page by page. "Yes, I see you have extensive mining properties, Mr. McCormack, and I can see where this mine would be a perfect fit for your company, if there's any gold in it. Are you looking for a partner, Mr. McCormack?"

McCormack's eyes widened. "Are you saying you'd be interested in partnering with me, Mr. Christo?"

"No, not at all. I thought there might be a possibility of Lee representing me, that was all." Christo had no intention of Lee acting in his stead. He just wanted to see McCormack's reaction. He wanted to break McCormack, not partner with him.

"No," McCormack said. "I'm afraid I'm not looking for a partner, but I am interested in buying the map from you."

John W had checked on McCormack's net worth, both business and personal. He wanted to take it all and annihilate him, the way McCormack had destroyed all the others from whom he had bilked and stolen. "Well, I have no interest in the mine. Whatever profit I'd make from the mine, I'd double here in six months without raising a sweat. But if you're interested in the mine, then I'm sure we could work out some sort of arrangement. What's your offer? I know you're interested in it or you wouldn't have flown here to see me. So how much is the lost Four Peaks Tonto Apache Gold Mine worth to you, gentlemen?"

"I'm the only one interested in buying the mine, Christo."

"It's Mr. Christo, if you please."

"Sorry. Mr. Christo."

"That's better. So you're the only one in this group interested in buying my mine, eh?"

"I'm interested in it too," Governor Wilson added.

Christo looked amused. "The two of you want it? Do each of you want it, or do you intend to be partners? Which is it?"

McCormack looked at Wilson and knew he'd have to have him as his partner or he'd prevent him from getting the mine. "Hell, Wilson, why didn't you tell me you wanted in?"

"I always wanted in and you know that."

"Let's not air our dirty laundry right now, Governor. We'll discuss this later when we're alone, but for now let's just say that if I get this mine, we'll be partners."

"Good. That's what I wanted to hear."

McCormack turned back to Christo. "We were talking about the mine."

"No, we were talking about how much you will pay for the mine. Now, give me your figure."

"Well, I'd have to have a look at the mine in order to place a value on it, then I could give you a better idea of how much I'd offer you for it."

"That will not happen. Gentlemen, I believe there's nothing more to say. Thank you for coming. I have someone else interested in the mine and he's willing to pay me cash for it, so let's not waste each other's time. Monica, will you show these gentlemen out?"

McCormack couldn't believe the man. He didn't care about money. He'd just as soon walk away from it than show him the damn mine. "Okay. Hold on a minute; let's not be hasty. What did the other guy offer you for the mine?"

"500 million dollars. Of course, that's after I have someone, maybe Lee, visit the mine and take out a few gold samples for his man to analyze. He gave me a good faith deposit of 50 million to bind the deal in case you weren't interested or couldn't come up with the money. I'm no fool, gentlemen. I knew the reason you came to see me was to buy the mine. Why else would the Governor of Arizona, and the president of an international mining company, visit me? To play chess? No. It's for the mine. So make up your minds. Do you want it or not? I have another buyer waiting and I have business to attend to."

"You said the man offered you 500 million for the mine?"

"That's right. I could show you the deposit he gave me if you'd like."

McCormack was sweating now. He didn't want to lose the mine to a competitor, and he didn't want to risk his company's money and his own fortune in a crap shoot. "Would you mind showing me the deposit the man gave you? I'd like to see it."

"No, not at all." John opened his desk drawer and removed an envelope. He opened it and took out a check. "Here it is. Look for yourself." He handed the check to McCormack. McCormack studied it for a moment, then handed it to Kleinst, and both he and the Governor examined the check, looking for any sign of deception, but they didn't see any. A Mr. Samuel Reed, President of the Last Chance Mining Company, made out the check. That should be easy enough to check out. He made a mental note to do it the moment they returned to the office. But John had already prepared for this figuring, they would do just that. The previous month he told Persistent to find a vacant office and have a sign painter paint a sign with the name of the company on the window, then get the phone company to put a line in and hire a temp to sit there and answer the phone in case it ever rang.

Kleinst handed the check back to Christo. "Would we offend you if we were to call him?"

"Not at all," Christo said. "In fact, you can call his office now if you would like." Christo seemed relaxed and assured. He had the look of a man who had everything and didn't care one way or the other if they made the call or they didn't, and the manner in which he comported himself spoke volumes. His visitors knew he had another buyer, and it looked to them as if he couldn't care less if McCormack bought the mine or if he didn't. It was all so very confusing to them. They were looking for a sign that something other than the truth was taking place, but there was no sign of anything amiss. It was almost as if he were playing with them, like a cat would a mouse. "If you want to call Mr. Reed's office, you can do it now. I'll leave the room and leave you gentlemen to your privacy. While you're using the phone, it will give me a chance to get some coffee." Christo left the room and walked through the first office door he came to and sat at the desk. He pressed a button attached to the phone and heard both ends of the conversation, unbeknownst to the men on the phone.

McCormack called the Last Chance Mining Company and a young lady answered the phone. "Last Chance Mining Company. How can I help you?"

McCormack asked to speak to Mr. Reed, and she informed him that Mr. Reed was out of the office, looking at a property.

"He'll be in later this afternoon. Leave a number and Mr. Reed will call you back."

"No, that's unnecessary. I'll call him later. Thank you."

John waited for a little while, then he poured himself a cup of coffee and walked back to his office.

"Well, gentlemen, I assume that you've called the number. Have you decided?"

McCormack answered, "Yes, I called that number, but Mr. Reed wasn't in. Maybe I'll call him later."

John shook his head. "Why would you call him later? By the time later comes, he'll already be the owner of the mine, because once you leave this office, I'm taking your offer off the table. I'll have no reason to meet with or speak to you again. You have your business to run, and I have mine and they are miles apart, so we'll part as friends."

CHAPTER TWENTY-NINE

"Could you excuse us for a moment, Mr. Christo? I'd like to discuss this with my associates."

John got up from behind the desk. "Not at all. I'll leave you gentlemen to discuss this among yourselves." He left the room and walked to the same office he visited before and sat behind the desk. This time he pushed a different button on the phone's console and the conversation they were having came flooding into the room as clear as if he were with them. He listened to them discussing amounts they thought he might accept for the mine. He heard offers of 100 million and 300 million, but Governor Wilson said, "Give him the 500 million and match the offer the other guy offered him."

McCormack whistled. "Man, that's a ton of money to give someone for one mine."

Wilson was tiring of this bantering back and forth. "For Christ's sake, man, decide. Either give him the goddamned 500 million and buy the mine or let's go home."

McCormack hung his head, knowing he had to do something. Did he want to invest all of his corporate money in this venture?

Wilson asked him, "Just how much money is your company worth? And how much of it can you invest?"

McCormack let out his breath and said, "I have 250 million in cash reserves I can use. I'll have to borrow another 150 million to match the offer he received from the Last Chance people, but if that's what I have to do, then I'll do it."

Christo heard enough. He walked out to the area where they kept the coffee and just as he finished pouring another cup for himself, McCormack found him.

"Finished with your talk, Jack?"

"Yeah, I've decided. Let's step back in your office."

The men settled themselves in their seats, waiting for the

discussion to begin. This time they had direction, and they were eager to have it conclude.

"Mr. Christo."

"Call me 'John.'"

"John, I've matched the offer Mr. Reed gave you."

"That's not good enough, Mr. McCormack - Jack. I already have a bid for 500 million, so if you want the mine, you'll have to outbid the other bidder."

McCormack looked crushed. He didn't want to admit that 500 million was stretching it, but he was stuck. They'd have to come up with a little more in his bid. He looked at his friend, the Governor. "You said you wanted to be my partner. How much cash can you come up with?"

"Me,? I can't come up with anything - but the state can. It will be a historical investment project that the state will finance. It will match the short fall you need to complete this deal."

Lee added. "And don't forget about my check, Mr. McCormack."

McCormack reached into his coat pocket to reassure himself that the check was still there. "To be honest, I forgot about that, Lee. But I have it with me and you'll have it when we agree to a deal."

"Okay, I'll make the offer 501 million."

Christo smiled. "Make it 510 million and we have a deal."

McCormack knew Wilson would have to come up with the rest of the money or he'd have no deal. "Holland, can the state underwrite 120 million dollars?"

"Why 120 million? I thought you needed 100 million."

"I promised Lee 10 percent of the mine, but he agreed instead to take a 10 million dollar buyout. I can only come up with 400 million. I need another 120 million, which includes Lee's ten million and the extra ten I had to add to the bid to complete the deal. That totals 520 million dollars needed to pay Christo. That's why I'm short 120 million."

Governor Wilson thought for a moment and said he would come up with the money. "My lawyers will make sure I do it legally," he said. "But, yes, the state can and will underwrite a 120 million dollar grant for the lost Four Peaks Gold Mine."

John W's plan was working to perfection. But he didn't

want to blow it so instead he suggested. "Look, Jack. How about we do this? I can see the Governor has to have some time to work out the financing for this project. So why don't you pay Lee the money you promised him and then give me a good faith deposit like the other fellow did? If you give me a firm date to pay me the rest of the money, we'll close the deal right now. Meanwhile, the mine is yours and I won't entertain any other offers, but I'll hold the map until I'm paid in full. Does that sound fair to you?"

"Yes, and I appreciate it." John's offer was something McCormack would never give to any of the people he screwed in the past, and he accepted it.

"How much are you giving me now?"

"I'll give you a check for 50 million dollars."

John interrupted him as he was about to write a check. "Not good enough, Jack. I heard you say you had 250 million available to you, and you can get the money right away and that's what I want."

"But - But I still have to give Lee the 10 million dollar check I'm holding for him and I'm still short another 100 million."

"Alright. That's a point well taken. Give him the check for 10 million and give me a good faith check for 240 million. Then, when you get your bank loan for the 150 million and the state funding, you'll pay me the balance owed me. That's the deal I want to see happen before you leave."

Jack looked at his friend, the Governor. "You're sure that you can get the 120 million to close this deal?"

Wilson smiled at him like the cat who was about to eat the mouse. "That depends, now, on what percentage you're gonna give me."

"Come on, Holland. Don't pull this shit with me now. Tell you what. I'll give you Lee's 10 percent. How's that sound?"

"It doesn't sound good at all. Make it 25 percent and we'll have a deal." The Governor just kept smiling. He knew he had Jack boxed into a corner.

"All right, you money-grubbing bastard, I don't like it, but you have a deal. When you give me the check, I'll give 25 percent share in the mine."

There wasn't a word said after Jack and the Governor spoke.

John W stood and put out his hand. "I'm waiting, Jack. I'd like you to give Lee the check you promised him and then write me a check for $240 million dollars. When I get the check, I'll sign this letter of intent for the mine. It will protect the good will deposit you're giving me." There was nothing further for Jack to say. The slick bastard John Christo had thought of everything. McCormack reached into his jacket, pulled out the envelope with Lee's check, and handed it to him. He was sweating as he wrote Christo a check for 240 million.

John told him, "Before I accept this check, I'd like you to tell me when I can expect the rest of my money. I didn't become a rich man by letting people take advantage of my good nature. When will I get my money, Jack?"

McCormack looked at him and knew he was not a man to trifle with. "I'll have it for you within ten days."

"In ten days, I'll expect all the money owed to me, even the Governor's grant, for which I hold you responsible." John turned to Governor Wilson. "When will you give Jack the grant money?" The two men weren't used to being spoken to or questioned like this by anyone, the way this man was doing.

Governor Holland Wilson wanted to kill John Christo. "Don't worry, Mr. Christo," he said. "You'll have your money within ten days."

"Good! Then there's nothing more to say. It was a pleasure doing business with you gentlemen. I wish you all the luck in the world in your new endeavor, Jack. Would you like my driver to take you to your hotel?"

McCormack nodded. "Yes. And if your driver could wait a few minutes while we get our luggage, we'd appreciate a lift to the airport.

John W pushed a button and Angelo came in. "Take these men to their hotel. Wait for them while they get their luggage, and then take them to LaGuardia. They have a plane to catch."

Lee remained seated as the men left the room. Lee didn't like being in their company any more than John W. did. When they left, Lee handed John W the envelope with the 10 million check in it. "It worked exactly as you said it would. You told me greed would get them and it did. I would have taken the 5 million when he offered it to me if you hadn't told me not to.

You told me he'd give a counteroffer, and he did. I memorized what I would say to it shocked him and me when he agreed to the 10 million dollars. You should have seen his face when I said I'd keep the 10 percent because it might be worth a lot more than the money I'll be getting from him."

Christo put the 10 million dollar check into his inside jacket pocket and settled back in his chair. "Now it's time we took care of Fancy Tom Jenkins." John W picked up the report Lee gave him earlier. "After reading this report, I'm shocked at the number of people he's scammed. This guy has to pay for the crimes he's committed over the years and because of that, he's about to get the shock of his life. He's gonna find himself in jail."

The following morning, John W and Lee were involved in a strategy meeting. John reached into his desk and pulled out a large bundle wrapped in brown paper and placed it on his desk. He was silent for a moment, and then he looked at Lee and pointed to the door. "Lee, ask Angelo to come in here. I'd like him to be a part of this discussion." Angelo came into the office and took a seat. "You wanted to speak to me, boss?"

John W nodded and said, "Have a seat. I'm going to tell you something that no one in the world knows but me. And I'm telling you this for a reason." He looked over at Lee, who was sitting on the sofa on the other side of the room. "Lee, come over here and take a seat. You might as well hear this, too."

"I need men I can trust. So, can I trust you guys? That's the big question, isn't it? Can I trust you two, especially when I don't trust anyone else except Persistent and Bill Hayes? You two, I'm just starting to trust you two. Do you know how I learn to trust someone?" They both shook their heads. "A friend is someone who's been tested and who's passed the test. Trust is based on the same test. Lee, you passed your test. Angelo here has yet to pass his, but his test is coming, but that's just part of what I want to tell you. This is a little hard for me to say, so bear with me for a moment." John sipped some water from a cup on his desk and looked at Lee. "If either of you tells anyone what I'm about to confide in you, I will destroy you so thoroughly, your mother will think she never gave birth to you." That warning caused looks between the two men. John looked at Lee and then at Angelo. Angelo rarely took this kind of shit from anyone, but he was curious about where Christo was going with this. "Do you understand what will happen to you if you betray my confidence and leak what I'm about to tell you to anyone?" They both said "yes" at the same time. "Okay, here goes. Lee, do you remember the prisoner who asked you to find out about his mother?"

"Yes, I remember him well. I didn't think it was right what they did to him, even if he was a prisoner."

"Good, Lee. Remember what you just said, because I'm going to get back to that in a moment. That boy was innocent of the crime they charged him with. His father passed away, leaving the mother and son with an 80-acre ranch to take care of without a dime in their pockets. Mr. Hayes sold them the property at a fair price. But when the Hardins couldn't keep up with the mortgage payments, it forced him to take it from them. Hayes was a good man, and he felt terrible having to evict the mother and son from their land. He met the Hardins one day, saying he had something to tell them. To make a long story short, he traded their equity for 40 acres of worthless desert property, which included a played out mine that wasn't worth anything. The miner's shack they lived in came with the property. The shack had no electricity and no plumbing, but it had an outhouse in good condition, and the mother and son were grateful they had a roof over their heads. It wasn't much of a home, but the Hardins loved it and they were grateful to Mr. Hayes.

"McCormack found out from the mining engineer who was working a mine on the other side of the mountain that there was a high-quality vein of gold hidden in the played out mine on the Hardins' property. McCormack ordered Kleinst and Jenkins to get rid of the boy who was working for Hayes. The boy helped open three branch offices, and he was about to open an office in Flagstaff when Jenkins came into the picture. Jenkins conned the old man by telling him he didn't want a salary; instead, he said he'd work on commission. The boy warned Hayes to be careful that he had a bad feeling about Jenkins, but the old man hired him despite the boy's warning. McCormack, Kleinst, and Jenkins had to get rid of the Hardin boy, so they planted drugs in his mine, his car, and his home. They then tipped off the police that he was dealing drugs to kids and they arrested him. They convicted him on planted evidence and sent him to prison. He wound up at the Gila Bend prison, which they reopened just for him and an old prospector by the name of Dutch Henry. Do you remember that old man, Lee?"

"Yeah, I sure do. He seemed like a harmless old man to me. I don't know what he did to get put in that piss hole of a prison."

"Well, I'll tell you what he did. He found a gold mine. The Lost Tonto Apache Four Peaks Gold Mine, the same one I'm selling to McCormack. He found the mine, and that's what Holland Wilson wanted from him. Wilson owned the hardware store that Dutch Henry bought his supplies from, and old Dutch always paid for his supplies in gold nuggets. Wilson wanted to know where Dutch Henry found the gold. He became obsessed with finding the source of the old man's gold. Wilson became the popular owner of a large chain of hardware stores and because of his popularity and McCormack's money, it wasn't long before he became governor of the great state of Arizona. That's when he learned he could control people's lives. He imprisoned that old man because he wanted his gold mine. But the old man was smart. He knew he was going to be put in that awful prison, so he researched it thoroughly. He tracked down the granddaughter of a prisoner, an ex-engineer who left a diary of his day-to-day building of the prison. The old man discovered in the diary that the builder, a convict by the name of Willard Smith, built a back door exit into the design."

It riveted both Angelo and Lee to every word he spoke. Angelo asked, "So what happened next, Mr. Christo? Did they get out of that prison?"

John nodded, and explained how the old man spent three years digging his way into John W's cell, and then he explained how they dug their way into the hidden room. John told them about the skeleton, the balloon, and how poor old Dutch Henry, as he lay dying, handed the boy his map.

"Dutch Henry died in my arms."

Lee looked up. "You? You were the boy who asked me to find out about his mother?"

John smiled. "Yes, that was me. And because of the

kindness you showed me while I was in that rotten cell, when I got out, I tracked you down. I wanted to repay you for what you did for me."

Lee blushed. "Shucks, Mr. Christo, I did nothing for you. I didn't find out about your mother for you."

"I know, Lee, but you made an attempt, and they fired you because you tried to help me. Now understand this. You and yours will never want for anything ever again in this life. That I promise you."

Angelo then spoke up. "So, how did you find the mine?"

"Sam Reed helped me find it. He knew the mountains like the back of his hand, and I was lucky to have found another honest man. When we have more time, I'll fill in the blanks for you. It's an interesting tale, but it has to wait. I'll tell it another time. Now you both can understand why I'm doing the things I am. I'm telling you my story because I can't do what I have to do by myself. I need help… your help. I dislike breaking the law, and I'm going to try hard not to break it, but I may have to bend it a little. Some things I may do are not legal. That's why I wanted you to know my motives. Angelo, go with Lee. You're gonna plant this package in Fancy Tom Jenkins's apartment. If you have a problem doing that, then don't worry about it, Lee, and I will do it. Now, Lee, are you with me?"

"Mr. Christo, that bastard should pay for all the bad he's done to so many people for so many years."

"Good. Now, what about you, Angelo? Are you in or out?"

Angelo was silent for a moment. Then he said, "Well, this is not what I signed on for, but never let it be said that Angelo Muscano walked away from a friend."

"I like that, Angelo. I like the part about not walking away from a friend, because you will always have a friend in me, and I don't have many friends except you two, Mr. Hayes, and old Persistent. You were told what happened to me. I was lost and buried in a dark hole away from everyone I cared for… my mother, Mr. Hayes. They destroyed my life, and all because of the greed of two men and two other men who helped them. I promised Dutch Henry I would get the man who imprisoned him, Governor Wilson. I intend to keep that promise. Besides putting Dutch Henry in that prison, Governor Wilson had me imprisoned on phony drug charges, and because of them, I went to prison.

"While I was in jail, my mother died. Jack McCormack and Rutgar Kleinst stole our land." He looked at Angelo. "Angelo, I'm telling you all of this because I intend to destroy those men, starting with Jenkins. He'll be the first to go. But I don't intend to rush the process. I want them to know what's happening and I want them to squirm. Kleinst will go the same way as Jenkins. I will disgrace governor Wilson while in office. They'll convict him of abusing his power and he'll go before a judge and they'll find him guilty of those crimes. I'll see that he spends time in one of his prisons. That's the promise I'll keep to old Dutch Henry. They will convict McCormack of misuse of corporate funds. All of them will wind up broke and they'll face long prison terms.

"Lee, you have Jenkins's file. When he leaves for work tomorrow, I want you to enter his home and plant this package in his attic, or under his bed, or in a closet. Put it somewhere where someone who they tipped off that there were drugs on the premises would find it, but with difficulty. Questions?"

"Just one," Angelo said.

"What's the question?"

"How are we supposed to get into his house without breaking down the door? And what if he has an alarm?"

"Glad you asked, Angelo." John reached into his desk drawer and pulled out a very expensive envelope for which he paid a rather unsavory but talented character. "Here, take this with you. It contains the alarm code and a key to his apartment. Make sure you put the alarm back on and lock the door when you leave. Questions? No? Alright, get going and call me as soon as it's done."

CHAPTER THIRTY

When Lee informed John W that they had successfully planted the package containing the drugs in Jenkins's home, he made an anonymous phone call to the police. He gave them the name and address of a drug dealer who was selling drugs and targeting children. He said he called them because he wanted to help stop the proliferation of drugs, spreading like a plague through this once quiet neighborhood.

Later that day, breaking news of the arrest of Fancy Tom Jenkins, they showed a major drug dealer in Phoenix repeatedly on all the major news outlets. The police told reporters they received the drug kingpin's address from a tip by a concerned citizen who preferred to remain anonymous, fearing for his life. After obtaining a search warrant, the police broke into Jenkins's home. After a thorough search, they discovered a large stash of drugs concealed under a tarp in a corner of his attic. Jenkins placed boxes over the drugs and covered the boxes with the tarp to make them more difficult to find. The police told reporters if it weren't for a drug enforcement canine who located the stash, they likely wouldn't have found the drugs. The police held Mr. Jenkins in jail with no bail. Witnesses who bought drugs from the suspect came forth, ready to testify against him.

John W. had worked hard for months on his plan to frame Jenkins. He wore a disguise when he met with mercenaries in a rented warehouse. He thought of telling them about Jenkins and the crimes he committed, but then decided against it because he knew that all these men were concerned about was the money he would pay them for this job. One man raised his hand and asked what the job entailed and how much will he pay them to do it.

"A reasonable question," John replied. "I'll pay each of you $50,000.00 up front and another $50,000.00 upon completion of the job." The men raised their eyebrows and looked at each other, wondering who this man was that would pay so much money for so simple a job, and it didn't even include murdering someone. "One thing, though." He placed his attaché case on the table and opened it so each of them could see that he filled it with stacks of hundred-dollar bills wrapped in $10,000.00 bundles. "I expect loyalty from each of you - at least until you complete this job. If I'm satisfied with your work, I'll keep your name on file in case I have need of your services in the future. This simple job that I'm hiring you to do is important to me, so don't disappoint me because that would make me angry. I will pay you fifty grand now and in a few days when you complete this job, I'll pay you the rest of your money. I think you'll agree that's a lot of money for so simple a job, but like I just said, the results are important to me. So don't disappoint me; just do the job and come back for the rest of your money." The men in the room were not men easily intimidated, but they made their living by working for men like John W. It wouldn't do if their reputations or integrity became damaged by rumors that they were trying to fuck him. Theirs was a small fraternity, and if word got out that they took money for a job they didn't complete, it would blackball them. He looked each of them in the eye as he handed each his $50,000.00.

One man, Terry Crawford, who John thought must be the spokesman for the group, looked him in the eye as he received his money and told him, "Don't worry about a thing, Mister-whatever-your-name is. Put your mind at ease; we'll do this job for you and none of us will fuck you. But, just so you know it, you pissed us off by insinuating we would. I'll call you when the job is done and we'll meet you here for the rest of our money. But here's a little advice for *you.* When we come back for the rest of our money, have it, and don't *you* fuck us."

John got it and replied, "Sounds fair to me."

Terry was the last man to leave. When the door closed behind him, John smiled, knowing he hired the right men for this job.

The mercs used drugs as bait. They started by convincing drug users to testify against Jenkins with the promise they would receive a large quantity of drugs of their choice in return, and it didn't stop there. The men tracked down many of

Jenkins's victims from the list Christo gave them and most were eager to testify against him.

"But, Mr. Christo, do you really think a jury will convict him?" Lee asked.

John W gave him a ghost of a smile. "Joe Stalin once said, '*People who cast the votes don't decide the election. People who count the votes do.'* Don't doubt me on this, Lee. I've counted the votes, and he's going away for a long, long time." Lee and Angelo looked at each other. They both realized that they've already decided Jenkins's fate long before they planted the drugs in his attic.

When the trial began, the prosecution called twenty-seven witnesses to testify against Jenkins. When it ended, they found him guilty on all charges and they sentenced him to 50 years in prison.

McCormack put down the paper in disgust after reading of the drug kingpin Fancy Tom Jenkins's sentencing. He knew Jenkins was a lot of things, but he wasn't a drug dealer. Somebody had set him up… but why? Sure, Fancy Tom had a lot of enemies, but he had been out of the con game for several years now. He thought, *Tom's been working for me for how long now? Three years? That's it. He's been working for me for three years and I know for a fact that he couldn't have been dealing drugs while he was on my payroll.* He dialed the private line. The Governor picked up. "Holland, it's Jack. Have you been following the Jenkins trial?"

"Yes, I have. Go figure. I never would have thought that the guy was into drugs."

McCormack's temper flared, and he yelled into the phone, "He wasn't into drugs, you fool. Get your head out of your ass and look at what happened. He was framed, plain, by someone who wanted him out of the way."

Governor Wilson was silent for a moment. "Framed, you say? But who would want to frame him?"

"I don't know, but it worries me when things happen without a reason. I asked myself the same question: who would want to frame Jenkins? I can't put my finger on what's going on here, but remember this: what happened to Jenkins could happen to you or me. Look, we need to get Jenkins out of jail;

he knows too much. Can you pardon him?"

"Are you crazy? If I pardoned him now, the voters would hang me. This isn't the right time for a pardon, Jack. I would love to pardon him, but things have to cool down a little before I can even think about it. Look, when things cool off, I'll quietly pardon him. That's the best I can do for now."

"I understand. I'll tell Tom what you just said. He'll understand. He won't like it, but he'll understand. Now, how's the funding for our project coming along?"

"It's just about completed. I should have a bank draft for you the day after tomorrow. It was a hard sell, but when the legislature realized the funding was for a partnership in the recently discovered Four Peaks Gold Mine, they approved the funding."

"Good. Once we pay off that bastard Christo, we'll control the mine. Then, when the mine shows a profit, we'll repay the state and then we'll both make millions."

"Yeah. Heh, heh heh. That old stubborn sombitch, Dutch Henry, wouldn't share his gold with me, and now he's dead and I have it, anyway."

"Be careful what you say on the phone, Holland. Someone could listen to us."

"Don't worry about that. This is a secure line."

"Good. I'm glad to see you're using your head. I gotta go now. Don't forget. Send me the check as soon as you get it."

"Don't worry. You'll have it the day after tomorrow. I want to send it to you as much as you want to get it. Talk to you then." McCormack hung up the phone and sat, contemplating what had happened to Fancy Tom Jenkins.

"Did you get it all?"

"Yes, sir. When you're tapping an encrypted phone line, it's tricky, but I think I got it all. When you're dealing with electronics, sometimes you get nothing."

"I don't want to hear that 'sometimes you get nothing' stuff. You're the best, and that's why I hired you. I want to hear that you got it all. You *got* it all, didn't you?"

"Yes, sir, I believe I did. I'll know for sure when we replay the tape."

"How soon will you be able to play it back for me?"

"It won't take long. Give me a few minutes and you'll hear everything that was recorded."

John W listened to the conversation between the two powerful men, Governor Wilson and Jack McCormack. He took the headphones off and put them down. "You did a good job, Jerry. The quality of the sound is perfect. I could hear every word clearly. Make a copy and give both tapes to me later."

Jerry Sutphin was an ex-C.I.A. expert and one of the best men in the business concerning surveillance and counter-surveillance. He had a backlog of clients to prove it *and* he hired out to anyone who could afford his exorbitant fees. John W read Sutphin's advertisement in *Soldier of Fortune Magazine,* where Sutphin kept a yearly ad running. When John contacted him, Sutphin said he wouldn't be available for six months. A moment of silence passed, and then John said, "Look, Mr. Sutphin, I have a job in Arizona that can't wait six months. Whatever your fee is, I'll double it, but you have to come now."

"Look, Mr. Christo, I'd have to give up a lot of work to drop what I'm doing to do yours."

"What if I tripled it? Would that make a difference?"

"Expenses?"

"I'll include expenses."

Money talks and bullshit walks because Jerry 'Soldier of Fortune' Sutphin put what jobs he could on hold, and the jobs he couldn't he gave to an associate. He showed up the very next day at John's office in Arizona with all of his gear ready for work.

"Lee, I want you dig into Rutgar Kleinst's past and find out all you can about him. Find out if he was ever in trouble with the law, especially when he was a kid growing up in Germany. He might have a record and if he does, I want to know what they arrested him for. If this is out of your area of expertise, I'll get Jason Sweeney to do the job."

Lee thought about Sweeney, and partnering with him seemed like a good idea. "I think you should call Sweeney, boss. We could get a lot more done if we worked together on this. Call him and see if he's available. I'd feel better having a partner with me in Germany. Jason may have more experience in this area, but my experience in other areas will complement his and it's better if we checked Kleinst out as a team rather than one of us going it alone."

John W thought a moment. "You're right, Lee. The two of you working together on this makes sense. I just hope he's available and not working on a case." Christo reached over and pressed a button on his console. "Monica, get Jason Sweeney on the phone for me. Please. Thank you, Monica." A few minutes later, his intercom buzzed.

"Mr. Sweeney is on Life One for you, Mr. Christo."

He picked up the phone. "Jason, how are you?"

"Good, Mr. Christo. What can I do for you?"

"Are you working on anything right now?"

"Actually, I am, but if it's important, I can have another agent complete this assignment. It's a husband - wife thing… not very exciting. What is it you need me to do?"

"I'd like you to accompany Lee to Germany to check out someone's background. You'd have to spend some time over there sorting through German police files. Is that a problem?"

"That's not a problem, Mr. Christo. In fact, I speak a little German. I was with the military police while in the army and I learned German while stationed in Berlin."

"Well, it looks like I called the right man then. How soon can you be here?"

Sweeney thought a moment and then he looked at his calendar. "My calendar looks good, but I'm putting you on hold a minute while I confirm it with my secretary." A minute later, he clicked back on. "I can be in Arizona the day after tomorrow." My secretary will fax you my flight itinerary."

"That's great, Jason. I'll have Angelo meet you at the airport. I'll have everything ready so that when you get to my office, you and Lee can get started right away." Knowing that Jason was on board took some of the pressure off. John leaned his head back on the plush cushion of his chair and turned to Lee, who had heard none of the conversation and was eager to know what Jason had said. "Jason will be here the day after tomorrow."

Lee was relieved, knowing that he'd be going to Germany with Jason and he got up from his chair. "Since Jason won't arrive for a couple of days, no sense in me hanging around when there's work to be done. I'm going to my office and logging on to the Internet. I'll see what I can find out about Rutgar, and while I'm at it, I'll perform a police background check on him."

"Good, that'll give you something to work on until Jason gets here."

One down, three to go, John W thought to himself. The stress of planning every move was weighing heavily on him and to relax a little, he emptied his mind and allowed his body to melt into his comfortable leather chair. He didn't relax for long, though, because Rutgar Kleinst suddenly appeared in his mind, which pleased him. He thought, with a grim smile, *You are next*. Even if Rutgar were clean, John would make sure that he wound up in jail just like Jenkins. The thought of Rutgar in prison increased his smile. It would happen slowly, he mused. Revenge *should* happen slowly so I can savor it. The revenge of John W *mus*t happen slowly and when his revenge was complete, he would pick up the shattered fragments of his past and try to return to a normal life, maybe even with Virginia. *She doesn't recognize me right now*, he thought, *but maybe after I explain what happened to the boy she once loved and who loved her, maybe we'll start over.*

CHAPTER THIRTY-ONE

John W stared at the manila folder lying on the desk in front of him as if it were too heavy to pick up. He looked at his men, then at the folder again, and then he reached down and picked it up. John hoped it contained the information he needed. He opened the folder, took out the report, and read. "Yes!" he said, pumping his fist up and down. "This is What I was hoping for. Did you have any problems with the police in Berlin?"

"No, Mr. Christo," Lee said. "We visited their headquarters at 23 Linden Street and spoke to Chief Otto Froedrick, who was very co-operative. He showed us the letter he received from the reclusive billionaire, John Christo, asking for his co-operation in a small background matter. The chief was most cooperative, and he assigned an attractive police officer to assist us, a Ms. Helga Borman. I have to tell you, boss, she was a knockout. I didn't want her to find anything on Kleinst, at least not for a few days, but unfortunately for us and great for you, she found a load of information almost as soon as she started tapping the keys on her computer. She didn't find any record of a Kleinst in her files, so I showed her a picture of him. She plugged it into her computer's facial recognition program and bingo - up he popped. Only his name isn't Kleinst, it's Rutgar Keisel, and he worked as a strong-arm man and a contract killer for the German mob. He protected drug dealers and made sure a rival mob did not impede their deliveries."

Sweeney interjected, "Ms. Borman told us he's wanted for a string of murders, including that of a cop. The police were about to pick him up, but he disappeared from their radar. She told me that if we find him and bring him back to Germany, they'll try him for murder."

Christo's eyebrow rose. "This is interesting stuff, guys. Your girl just gave us the answer I was looking for. When we grab him, we'll take him to her and she can handle it from there.

Okay, go on."

"After we had the information we needed, we visited his old address, but Helga told us they tore down the old section where he once lived, and they replaced it with high-rise apartments. She explained that the area used to be seedy, but after they built the high-rise apartments, it became a very nice neighborhood. It was too bad though - I would have liked to see where he grew up. Since we couldn't visit his childhood home, we decided that since there were two women mentioned in his file, the next best thing was to track them down and have a talk with them.

"One girl by the name of Brigitte Keinreck was a prostitute. Helga told us that the name 'Brigitte' means 'Exalted One' in German. I guess with a name like that, she picked the right profession. Anyway, she pressed charges against Kleinst for physical battery. He's a nasty drunk, because he got drunk one night and kicked the shit out of her. And it wasn't the first time he did it, but she was determined that it would be the last. She pressed charges against him, and had him arrested, then took him to court. As soon as she finished testifying, she left the witness stand, rushed out of the courthouse, and left town in a hurry. She didn't leave a forwarding address, so we had no way of finding her. Helga fired up her computer and tried to find her parents, but she discovered they were both dead."

"What about the other girl?"

Jason opened his notepad and turned a few pages. "Here it is. Freida Ernst. Our pretty police officer, Helga, brought up Freida's home address on her computer screen and printed it out for us. She pointed to the address and asked us if we knew how to get to there. We shook our heads, and to our delight, shapely Ms. Helga put on her uniform jacket and her hat and said she'd take us there."

John W. smiled. "That must have been disappointing for you guys, not driving there yourselves. Instead, you had to put up with a beautiful police woman to drive you there."

Lee smiled. "Of course, we would much rather have driven there ourselves, but, well, you know, we didn't want to offend the chief now, did we?"

"No I guess not," John said, smiling. "But go on." His smile grew wider.

"Jeez, John, you look like the Cheshire Cat with all those teeth showing."

"All right, I'll wipe the smile from my face," he said "Tell me what happened when you got there."

Jason skimmed through his notes. "She wasn't there, but her landlady told us where she worked. So Helga drove us there, to a large Blockbuster-type store that sold and rented movies and computer games. Freida was the day manager and when we inquired, a young clerk pointed to her office. She was a little surprised to see two strange men and a police officer enter her office and she wondered what we wanted. Helga handed her a file photo of Rutgar Kleinst, which she studied for a moment. She said, 'This is an old picture of Rutgar. Where did you get it?' Helga told her it was from his police file. 'What has he done now? No, don't tell me. I don't want to know. He's been out of my life for a long time now and I don't want to be reminded of him.' Helga insisted, 'I'm afraid we must ask you some questions and you must answer them. Give us five minutes of your time and we will leave.' Freida shook her head. 'I don't want to get involved with that man ever again. And I won't answer any of your questions. Do you think I'm mad? I don't want to worry about that man coming back to Germany to find me. I'm afraid I must ask you to leave.' Helga was polite but firm. 'Please. It would be better to answer our questions here in the privacy of your office, where we wouldn't take up much of your time. But, if you do not cooperate and you give us a hard time, then we will finish asking our questions at police headquarters, where it will take much longer and be a lot more unpleasant for you. Which is it to be?' Poor Freida didn't want any part of this, but she knew she had little choice in the matter. And she preferred to answer their questions here in her nice air-conditioned office than down at the dreary, unpleasant police headquarters. She'd been there once to bail Rutgar out, and she swore that she never wanted to visit that place again.

"'All right,' she said, 'Ask your questions.' She talked for twenty minutes, telling us about his friends and what he did for a living. Quite by accident I discovered what he did for these men. I overheard him talking to someone on the telephone and while he spoke low and tried not to say much on the phone, I understood what they said and I became frightened. I stopped seeing him. He did not know that I discovered what kind of man he was and he called me frequently, but I wouldn't talk to him.'"

Sweeney asked her when she saw Rutgar last. "'About four years ago, when the police questioned him about the murder of two men, but he had a contrived alibi, but Rutgar got away with it. But it became difficult for him to remain in Berlin. They knew he murdered two men, and they were looking for a reason to arrest him. The police had been following a drug dealer, because an informer told them they would deliver a large amount of drugs, but they didn't know when or where. They continued to follow Rutgar, figuring he'd lead them to the drugs, and that's when he made a mistake. They took him so completely by surprise that they almost captured him. He shot his way out, killing a police officer. He had to leave town fast, so he fled to America and sold his services to the highest bidder."

"'How do you know that?' Helga asked.

"'Because I knew that is what he did here. Killing was all he knew, so why would it be different in another country? He is a charming man when he wants to be, but he is very dangerous all the time. Be careful. Because if you intend to arrest him, and if you are not careful, he will kill you like a dog. Well, that is all I can tell you. Do you have any more questions?'"

John W scanned through his file. There were many murders that pointed to Kleinst, but they attributed them to Keisel and they couldn't prove them. They arrested him once on suspicion of murder, but they couldn't convict him because witnesses somehow never testified against him; they just seemed to disappear. *Hmm, so how can we use what's in this file against him?* He thought. John dropped the file on his desk and pondered his next move. It was important that he be right the first time. If Kleinst ever got a whiff that he was being set up, he'd bolt in a heartbeat - and once he was gone, he would be difficult, if not impossible, to find. Rutgar was an expert in disappearing. He was so good at disappearing, he could have given a college course on the subject. John W knew Rutgar was the one with whom he'd have to be extra careful. He knew with the other two he could use their weaknesses against them, but

Rutgar was different. He was a hunter, and he knew the signs of another of hunter, especially if that hunter considered him prey and was hunting him. Rutgar was a smooth operator who was always suspicious of everyone he met. He trusted his instincts, and he always looked over his shoulder. He was an expert at spotting a tail and he could spot one a mile away, but he did it surreptitiously so no one could tell he was checking to see if he was being followed. John W nodded in acknowledgement of this man's superb abilities as a clandestine operative. It didn't matter, though. They'd get him, no matter how good he was. He was still a man, albeit a powerful man, but still a man - and every man had a weakness. He picked up his file again and glanced through the pages. Kleinst was playing it close to the vest. He had a good thing going in Jack McCormack. He was making a good buck, and he wasn't straying far from McCormack, except for his brief forays, visiting his favorite prostitutes, which were his one weakness, and the only constant in his behavior. That was his recreational constant in Berlin and it was the same here, because as smart as he was, he never thought of his bordello visits as a risk.

John W pressed his intercom. "Have Angelo report to my office." Then he thought of something else and pressed the intercom again. "Monica, call Jason Sweeney and tell him I'd like to see him as soon as possible."

Angelo knocked once, opened the door, and walked in and took a seat. "What's up, boss?"

"Can you get away for a little while?"

"Sure, I have no family to speak of. A sister in New Jersey, but that's it. Why?"

"I'd like you to come to Arizona with me. I'm going to buy a building in Phoenix and I'll need a car, so while we're there, I want you to buy one for me and we'll keep it there. This way, we'll have something to drive around in whenever we visit Phoenix. I'll talk to Bill Hayes and I'll have him check on office buildings for me. Maybe if I ask him, he'll come in with us. We'll see. For now, pack a bag and be ready to leave at a moment's notice. Go down to Valentino Maximus on Spring Street and buy yourself three new suits, some shirts, shoes, and ties. I'll call down there and tell them you're coming. They'll know what to give you. Keep your cell phone on in case I need to talk to you."

"Got it. Anything else?"

"No, that's all for now."

An hour later, Sweeney walked in. "You wanted to see me, Mr. Christo?"

"Yes, Jason. I need you to fly out to Arizona and do something for me, and it's important that you start right away. The meter will run when you leave this office today. Now, here's what I want you to do. I want you to buy yourself a western outfit; boots, cowboy hat, western shirt, jacket, and anything else you need that will make you look like a local. Bring me the bill and I'll pick up your expenses, including whatever clothes you have to buy. Don't overdress. Look as if you belong there. I don't want anyone to think you're a dude, and I don't want you to stand out as a New Yorker. Either way, he'd spot you immediately. Dress like a local, and then follow Rutgar Kleinst wherever he goes. I'm only interested in the houses of prostitution he visits. Follow him and take notice if he visits a particular house more frequently than the others. Once you know his favorite house, then find out who his favorite girl is in that house. Get her name and find out where she lives. Once you have that information, call me and I'll fly to Phoenix on the first plane out. Questions?"

"Mr. Christo, this could take a month or more. Are you sure you want me to stay that long?"

"Do the job, Sweeney. That's what I'm paying you for. Get me a name and an address. Then I'll fly there, and we'll conclude this business."

CHAPTER THIRTY-TWO

Three weeks later, Sweeney called. "I have a name for you, Mr. Christo." Sweeney was always formal when he spoke to John W because business was business. He was being generously paid by Mr. John Christo and he would treat him with the respect he deserved. So it was always "Mr. Christo" whenever he addressed him.

"He sees a lot of women, but he favors one more than the others. Her name is Jane Spotta, and she works as a prostitute for a Madam Sophia who runs a fancy sporting house on the outskirts of Phoenix, heading toward the desert. Rutgar Kleinst is a busy man. Or I should say he's a 'horny' man with a very large libido. Anyway, she's the one you want to talk to and don't tell me why you have to talk to her, because what I don't know won't hurt me."

John laughed. "Relax, Jason. Nothing bad is going to happen. I'm just going to take him down a peg. You know, teach him a little humility. God knows he needs it. Good job. Send me your bill and I'll cut you a check."

Jason was silent a moment. "Look, I'm going to stick around until this is over. Don't worry about paying me for my time. It's on me. You may need me and besides, I'm kind of interested in how this plays out."

"I'll talk to you when I get there, but when I tell you what my plans are, you may not want to stay and help me. Besides, you may not have any say in the matter. I may surprise you and insist that you go home."

Jason laughed. "Let's talk about that when you get here. When can I expect you?"

"I'll have my secretary book us a flight for tomorrow morning, and I'll call you back with the details."

"Good. I'll wait to hear from you."

The Arizona Biltmore is a Waldorf-Astoria hotel and is at

2400 East Missouri Avenue in Phoenix. John W had his secretary, Monica, book four rooms for an undetermined stay. Everyone had heard of John Christo, the mysterious, reclusive young billionaire, and the staff was excited to have a man of his stature stay at their hotel. Of course, celebrities were not uncommon at their hotel, but even they were curious and wanted to know if he was handsome or homely, and what sort of man he was. Everyone wanted to get a peek at him, so it was with nervous trepidation that the hotel manager, Mr. Arthur Crumb, waited at the entrance with four bell hops to take Mr. Christo's luggage to his room, as soon as he stepped out of his limousine. A few minutes later, a black stretch limousine pulled up to the front entrance of the hotel. The driver got out of the car and opened the car door. By this time, a crowd had gathered wondering, who would step out of the car. Most knew the billionaire was expected, but many of the onlookers thought that maybe they'd have the good fortune to see Brad Pitt and Angelina Jolie. It disappointed them to see three regular looking men in beautiful suits step out of the limo one at a time. The fourth man stepped out, wearing a Brioni $6000.00 black pinstriped suit with an Italian white silk shirt, lavender Italian silk tie, and a lavender silk pocket hanky. The lights of the hotel reflected off his thick, slicked-black hair that he combed back like a movie star of the twenties. So this was the mysterious billionaire that everyone was talking about. Some in the crowd murmured. Every magazine and newspaper tried to have an interview with him, but he politely refused all interviews. Mr. Crumb rushed over and greeted him effusively, telling him that when he realized who he was, he switched the room he booked to the penthouse suite, of course at no extra cost to him. John W played the part of the billionaire to perfection. He was a humble man in an arrogant sort of way, but it was becoming on him. He acknowledged and smiled at everyone as a king or prince would at his subjects. The girls behind the reception desk strained to get a better look at the young man and when he noticed them, he smiled and waved to them.

Lee leaned over and whispered to him. "You're quite the celebrity. Everyone wants to get a look at you."

John nodded. "They're curious, that's all. I've been getting a lot of publicity and since I don't give interviews, people want to know more about me. I told you my background. I'm a simple guy who is living a complicated life, and I don't like it. Lee, you've hooked your star to me. Whatever I do when this is over, you'll be a part of it. Can you live with that?"

"Are you kidding? I was going nowhere when you first came to my house. Now I have a future and I'm living like I'm a millionaire. I've become somewhat of a mystery myself because of my closeness to you. Are you kidding, sure I can live with that."

"Good, because we've got more work to do before we can relax and have some fun." They spoke in whispers until they were in the penthouse.

"Angelo, I want you to buy us a car tomorrow. Make it a large car like a Lincoln Town car or a Navigator, like the one you bought up north. Yeah, let's buy another Navigator. I like that car, and it's large enough for all of us to fit in."

Angelo excused himself and walked to the phone on the other side of the room. He scanned through the phone book and found a Ford dealer. He spoke to a sales associate for a few minutes, and then he rejoined the conversation.

John W looked around the living room to make sure the four of them were within shouting range. "Get close, guys. I want to bring you up to date on what I'm planning to do." Lee, Angelo, and Jason sat on the leather couch and John W sat in his leather chair facing them. "Earlier, Jason gave me this file on Rutgar Kleinst," John said, holding the folder up for all to see. "Every Tuesday and Thursday, he visits a brothel just outside Phoenix's city limits. Sometimes he'll visit on a weekend, but not regularly. We know for a fact, thanks to Jason, he goes to the whorehouse to visit a certain young lady." John stopped what he was saying and put down the folder and his face took on a somber look. "I'm getting a little ahead of myself because I trust you guys. I'm talking to you from my heart or I wouldn't be discussing any of this with you. We're entering areas where I expect loyalty, so if any of you betray my trust, you'll wish you were never born." When he said that, it struck fear in each of them. He looked at each of them for a reaction. There was none. His demeanor lightened, and he was himself again.

"Okay, here's what I plan on doing." John spent the next hour going over his plan. When he finished, he looked at Jason. "Are you in?"

Jason didn't hesitate. "Sure, I'm in. I'm an honest guy, but if it means putting this guy away, then I'm with you all the way."

"Good. I was hoping you'd say that. How about the rest of you?" It was unanimous. The operation was on. John nodded to Angelo. "I saw you on the phone; did you buy us a car, Angelo?" John asked.

"Sure did. I ordered a black Navigator. They had one in stock and it's got all the bells and whistles. It's loaded; I made sure it has every available option. The sales associate told me it's a real beauty. When I told them who it was for and we'd pay for it in full when we got there, they told me to give them an hour to detail the car and we can pick it up later." Angelo loved working for John W. He enjoyed buying and maintaining cars. He liked the close camaraderie of working with Lee and John W, and even Jason, who was becoming a part of the group even though he wasn't aware of it yet. This was just another job to Jason, but what he didn't know was John W had been making discrete inquiries about buying his firm, which he thought would be a good fit with his. He liked the way Jason worked, and he wanted him on board with him, even if it meant buying his company from him.

Jason parked across the street, a few cars away from Madam Sophia's bordello. He was waiting for Kleinst to leave. It wasn't a long wait, but this is what he did. It wasn't unusual to spend days waiting for a target to leave a building, and then to follow him somewhere, only to wait longer at another location. This one was easy. Kleinst never spent the night in the bordello. He was in and out in an hour and, sure enough, one hour later, the door opened and Kleinst walked out, got in his car parked nearby, and drove away. Sweeney left his car and walked the short distance to the bordello. He rang the bell and Madam Sophia answered.

A customer made an appointment in advance to see one of her girls, so it was unusual for the doorbell to ring, as there was no one reserved on any of the girls' schedules. However, sometimes a new customer who heard about her establishment she would allow in. If she felt comfortable with him, she might accept him as a new customer. She looked at the big man standing in the doorway, sizing him up. He didn't look like trouble, but he also looked like he could handle trouble if it came his way.

"Yes, what can I do for you?"

Jason gave her a big smile, showing her a perfect set of expensive, capped white teeth. "I want to see one of your girls, Jane Spotta. Is she available?"

It impressed madam Sophia. Jane was getting a lot of attention these days. She was earning more than a few of the other girls combined. "Jane is available, but she is expensive."

"I figured as much," Jason said with a wide grin. "How much is 'expensive'?"

"$500.00 for one hour."

Jason pulled out his billfold, took out five crisp one hundred-dollar bills, and handed them to Madam Sophia, who couldn't help noticing the large amount of crisp one hundred-dollar bills still in his wallet.

Hmm, she thought, *why isn't this man a member of my establishment*? "When you're finished visiting Jane, please come and see me before you leave. I want to give you a gold card, which would make you an official member of my establishment. The card will not contain any information other than a member number and our telephone number. We have no need for any other information. The less we know about you, the better it is for all concerned. Go on up now. Jane's waiting for you. She's in Room 204."

When Jason entered the room, Jane was wearing a stunning, revealing negligee. He shook his head because she might as well be wearing nothing. As he stood with his mouth open, studying the outline of her breasts and her pert protruding nipples, he wondered if she did anything to make them as firm as they were. His eyes followed the curves of her hips to the place where her thighs beckoned invitingly at him. They bathed the room in red and the bed was a beautiful four-poster with the bedspread and decorative enclosure of the upper part of the bed in red and cream colors. The room was breathtaking. Jason's gaze drifted from the bed to Jane, and he took one long look at her. His eyes traveled up and down her body, undressing her mentally, and he knew why Kleinst chose her as the person he visited twice a week. He closed his eyes and said a fast prayer to St. Christopher, asking him to give him strength, make him strong, and keep him from becoming aroused, which was a very hard thing to do. Jason was a married man who had always been faithful to his wife, and he always resisted the temptations of the flesh, but he realized as he stared at Jane's flesh, it was really tough not to sample the forbidden fruit. *Come on, St. Christopher, you're supposed to be the patron saint of travelers and I'm a traveler - and I'm in a situation here and I could use a little help.*

He introduced himself to Jane, trying not to look flustered. Without saying a word, he pulled ten $100.00 bills from his billfold out and laid them on the table.

Jane looked at the money and said, "What's this money for? Didn't you pay Madam Sophia downstairs?"

"Look, Jane. You are the most beautiful girl I've ever almost had sex with. But I didn't come here for sex. I paid my money so I could talk to you in private for a few minutes." He looked at the money, and then he pointed to it. "This is yours, with no strings attached. Here's where I'm staying. If you are interested in making $100,000.00 for a few minutes of your time, call me at this number."

Jane was instantly interested and suspicious at the same time. "I won't do anything illegal. If you need me for a special party with your men friends, then that figure will work. I'll take on as many men as you can fit in the room, and you can include a few women too, but I will do nothing illegal other than having illegal sex. Do I make myself clear?"

Sweeney smiled. "There's no gang sex involved and there is nothing illegal involved." He stood and walked to the door. "If you're interested, call me at that number."

"Wait," she called out, just as he opened the door. "Come on. Tell me a little more. What the hell could it be that I could do for you to earn that kind of money? I'm not saying I will, but if I agree to anything, I want a large part of the money in advance. Now, come on, tell me what you want from me. As far as sex goes, I can do it all. I'll fulfill your every fantasy and give you everything you ever dreamed of and I'm good at it. So tell me, what it is you want from me?"

Sweeney said, "I can't tell you anything now, but if you tell me when you can be at my apartment, I'll have someone there who will explain everything to you. And don't be frightened, we're good men who can do you a lot of good, but for you to earn the $100,000.00, you must perform a very simple service that will require a few minutes of your time. Something only you are in the unique position to do."

Now that confused Jane. She was very confused. What the hell was it she could do for them, that none of the other girls couldn't? She had to hear for herself what this man wanted her to do. Sweeney knew he had her. She'd come, and he knew it. Just the way she looked when he mentioned the amount of money she'd get by performing a brief service for them. And it wasn't sex, which threw her because that's all she knew. That was what her expertise was in; sex, and they didn't want any of her sex. That deflated her a bit, but it also piqued her interest.

"All right. How about tonight? I get off early tonight because I don't have a sleepover."

"What's early?" Sweeney asked.

"I get off at 12, so how about if I get there at 12:30?"

"That's all right with me, but tomorrow morning also works for us."

"No. Now I'm so curious, I won't be able to sleep tonight if I don't find out what it is you want me to do. No, I'll see you tonight at 12:30. Make sure your friend is there and please don't waste my time, because my sleep is important to me. Do we understand one another?"

"You have my address and telephone number on the back of the Arizona Biltmore's card.

Jane hadn't looked at the face of the card, only the room number. "You're staying at the Arizona Biltmore?"

"Yep, take the elevator to the penthouse. We'll be waiting for you there and please, do not tell anyone about what I've just told you. If you mention this to anyone, we'll find someone else to give the $100,000.00 to. Remember, it's essential that you tell no one. Not your mother, your friends, your madam, or your boyfriend. Believe me, this will be the easiest money you ever earned." He had been half out the door while talking to her.

He left, closing the door behind him. Jane remained standing there, staring blankly at the door, unable to understand what had just taken place. She looked at the money on the table and wondered what man comes to a whorehouse, pays the madam $500.00, leaves another $1000.00 on a table, and then leaves without having sex. It was all very confusing, but she was determined to find out what was going on. She picked up the phone and was about to call Rutgar and ask for his advice, but after the warning, she thought better of it and she placed the phone back on its receiver. The money was more important to her than taking a chance on telling anyone, especially after he warned her not to.

CHAPTER THIRTY-THREE

Jane got off at the Penthouse level and rang the doorbell. Sweeney opened the door and invited her in. "Are you hungry?"

"No," she replied."

"A drink, perhaps?"

"No. Let's just get down to business. I'm here now, so tell me what I have to do to get the money?"

"It's simple," a voice said from the other side of the room. A light switched on and a man walked toward her, dressed elegantly. He was young, and he was very handsome, and above all, he reeked of money. "And you are?"

"Call me 'John.'"

"Are you the one who will pay me $100,000.00 to perform some sort of act for you?"

"Please, call it a service and not an act. Listen to what I have to say. If after hearing what I want you to do, you prefer not to help me, then I will give you another thousand dollars with your promise that you will not repeat what I asked of you to anyone. If you decide to help me, I will give you one hundred thousand dollars in cash. Twenty-five thousand now and the rest tomorrow when you complete your assignment."

"What do you want me to do?"

"Simple. I want you to invite Kleinst here to this very room. Tell him a rich client had to leave town, and he left the penthouse for you for the night."

Jane was suspicious now. She liked Kleinst. He was a regular and although he was a little rough with her, and he could be kinky, he paid her very well. She was reluctant to lose that income.

John sensed what she was thinking. "Where can you make this much money at one time? No matter how much Kleinst gives you, it will never amount to what I'll give you for five minutes' work."

Five minutes' work. *What could he want me to do for him that will take five minutes of my time?* She wondered. "Tell me what you want me to do."

"Like I said. Invite Rutgar here and pour him a drink, but put this in it first. Don't worry; it's a harmless sleeping potion. Once he's asleep, you can get dressed and leave."

She felt uncomfortable and looked at the two men. "You will not kill him, are you?"

John smiled patiently at her. "Jane, we're not murderers. We don't kill people, but Mr. Kleinst does."

"What? I don't believe you. How dare you accuse him of being a murderer?"

John pointed to the file on the table. "Jason, please bring me the file on the table?" Jason handed the file to John, who opened it. "Please sit by me, Jane. I want to show you the man you have been sleeping with." She sat beside him and snuggled closer than she intended, but she liked the feeling, so she remained close to him. John told her to read each page of his dossier. It was painful to watch her face as realization set in. When she finished, she said, "I did not know this man was capable of these crimes."

John smiled a shadow of a smile and told her, "I'm going to take a chance on you. I'm going to tell you something that no one but a few people know. Kleinst had me put in a prison that they did not mean me to leave. He robbed me of my property, but as you can see, I've done well for myself. It's a simple matter of revenge. He has to pay for his crimes, and I'm the tool that will make it happen. Your job is to put the liquid from this vial in his drink. It's odorless and tasteless. Once he's asleep, you will call me at this number. It's the room below this one. When I walk in the door and I find him asleep, I'll hand you a bag filled with the rest of your money… in cash. Then your job is done and you can leave. What's easier than that? Well, are you in or are you out?"

Jane thought for a minute, but she had decided after reading his file. The information frightened her and even if she walked away from this, she would never sleep with that man again. Never! "Okay, I'll do it."

John relaxed a bit. He hadn't realized that he had tensed up, waiting for her decision. "You see him on Tuesdays and Thursdays. Do you have his personal number?" "Yes. We're not supposed to keep any of our clients' phone numbers or addresses, but he insisted I have it, just in case I wasn't available. He wanted to know first. His is the only phone number of all my clients that I kept. I don't know why I did, but yes, I have his number."

"Call him and give him the good news. Do you have a drink during his visits?"

"Yes, many times he'll bring champagne and if he doesn't, I have liquor in my room and we'll have a gin and tonic or a rum and coke and once in a while he'll take a scotch and water. So, yes. We have a drink or two before sex."

"Since you're with us, make the call."

Jane called Rutgar on Wednesday morning, hoping Rutgar wasn't asleep. He was a night person, and he was wide-awake as he picked up the phone. "It's Jane." She said. Then she told him the good news. When he heard she was in the Arizona Biltmore penthouse, he was eager to see her, and the penthouse, so he said that he'd be over that night instead of Thursday. On the way there, Rutgar kept thinking of how different it was going to be having sex with her in the penthouse. It should have a bath large enough for two people and that was worth the trip there. He saw her today because people are sometimes fickle. The old man who rented the penthouse might decide to come back, and he wouldn't try something different with Jane. He reached over and checked the champagne to make sure it was still cold. Kleinst needn't have bothered because it was in a thermal bucket with dry ice to keep it cold, but he checked every few minutes, anyway. He was like a kid. Of all the women he had, he enjoyed sex with Jane better than any of the others. She was game for anything with sex, and he was the same. Tonight, though, would be the diamond in his crown.

When the door to the penthouse opened, Jane appeared in a slinky black nightgown that left little to the imagination. He kissed her on her lips, then stepped into the large living room. As was his way, he studied everything about the room. Then he began a thorough search of the other rooms. Old habits die hard. Checking out a building, house, or apartment came first before anything else. As much as he wanted to grab Jane and tear her clothes off, he needed to feel safe first. He knew he was safe here in America. This wasn't Germany, and he didn't have enemies looking to kill him here. But it was better to be safe than dead. When he finished, he returned to the living room and took the drink Jane handed him. He would switch drinks, but he was getting paranoid even thinking that. He reminded himself that he just had that mental discussion with himself a few minutes ago. But the clincher was that he had been with Jane hundreds of times and if she was a danger to him, she would have killed him long ago. That feeling returned. The feeling he always got when something wasn't right. This time, he didn't listen to it. Kleinst did a thorough check of the penthouse. He could see the girl wasn't armed, at least not in the usual sense. Kleinst smiled at his little joke.

He took the glass and raised a toast to Jane. "Here's to you, Janie girl. With you, I can relax and not worry about anything." He took his glass and downed the drink in one quick gulp.

She sipped her drink, waiting for the drug to take effect. She hoped it was fast working because he might hurt her once he realized she had drugged him.

"Come on," she said, as she took him by the hand and led him to the door on the other side of the living room, to a large round white bed in the bedroom. She jumped in bed and bounced on it. "Come on, slowpoke, get on the bed with me. I'm horny and you're keeping me waiting."

He took his shoes off, but was having trouble. "Damn I'm tired. These late hours must catch up to me." He took off his shoes, but fell over as he was about to step out of his pants.

Jane looked over the bed, reached down, and shook him. "Wake up sleepy head," she said. Rutgar was out cold. She quietly slid off the bed, thinking she'd wake him if she rushed and walked to the phone in the living room. She called the number John had given her.

CHAPTER THIRTY-FOUR

John entered the penthouse with Lee and Angelo and walked directly to the bedroom, past Jane and straight to Rutgar, who was unconscious on the floor. A cruel smile appeared on his face. "You did your job, Jane. Thank you. Jason has your money. He's in the living room."

Jane's $75,000.00 was in an attaché case on the table. John had asked Jason to deliver the money to her because he was the only one of the three men she knew.

She opened the attaché case and yelped. "My God," she said. "I've never seen so much money in all of my life."

Jason was concerned for her. "This is an awful lot of money to be carrying alone. Would you feel better if I took you home? It would be safer, you know."

She looked at him, as if deciding if she needed to do that. "No. I don't think that's necessary," she said. "I parked my car in the garage downstairs."

"Then I'll walk you to your car. I know nothing will happen, but it will make me feel better knowing you drove away without a problem."

"That's very kind of you, Jason. Thanks." While they were walking to her car, she said, "I never thought he'd give me this money. I helped him because I read the file and I didn't want Rutgar to hurt another woman. But this money… I didn't think he'd keep his word to me. I can't believe he gave it to me."

"John? Nah! I knew he'd give it to you. He's a funny guy that way. A real straight shooter and he doesn't lie. If he tells you he's gonna do something, you can make book on it. I'm glad you got the money, though. Put it someplace safe where you can't get at it because if you can, you'll spend it. Buy a business, or a house or condo, or just give it to a money manager, do anything with it, but remember to keep it where you can't get at it."

She smiled. "Thanks, Jason. It's too bad you're married. I would have liked to do you when you came to my room. The offer is still open, you know."

"Don't do this to me, Janie. You don't know how my resolve is weakening. I thought about you standing there in that sexy negligee, looking like you walked out of a dream, and the offer you made me, but I have a beautiful wife who trusts me and is waiting for me at home. But thanks for the offer, Jane. You're a very desirable woman and if I weren't a married man, right now you would be on your back, naked."

She laughed. "I kind of like the idea of being on my back naked with you on top of me." Jason didn't expect her comeback and his face turned crimson. She noticed his reaction and smiled. "Here's my card. Who knows, maybe someday you'll change your mind - or maybe you'll divorce your wife. Doesn't matter. The offer will remain open." When they got to her car, she stood on her toes and kissed him on his lips. "Goodbye, Jason. I'll look forward to you calling me someday."

Jason waved to her as he watched her speed down the long aisle to the exit, where she stopped for a moment and waved back. Then she left the garage and turned left. He watched her zoom out of sight in her Mercedes convertible.

"Help me up with him. Grab hold of his arms and let's stand him up." Angelo motioned to Lee. They had allowed the drug to partially wear off in the hotel so they could use his mobility to help get him down the stairs instead of carrying dead weight to the car. "Lee, take that arm and I'll take this one. Let's ease him out of here and get him down to the car and over to the airport. Mr. Christo is downstairs waiting for us." As he manhandled the semi-conscious, staggering Rutgar, Angelo whispered to Lee, "If anyone in the hotel sees us, we're just taking our drunken friend home from a party."

They had given Rutgar just enough drugs to keep him docile. Angelo was a street guy who was a graduate of the school of hard knocks, so the thought of Rutgar waking up with a headache brought a smile to his face. It didn't go unnoticed by Lee.

"What's the smile for?"

Angelo kept the smile and answered him. "I don't like this

guy. He might have gotten away with the shit he pulled where he came from, but if he ever pulled that crap in my old neighborhood, they'd find him gutted in an alley with his face gone. And I was just thinking that when he wakes up, he's gonna have one monstrous headache. That pleasant thought brought the smile to my face."

Christo had left the room soon after Jason had left to escort Jane to her car. He was waiting by the hotel's back entrance. As soon as he saw his men come through the exit, holding a semi-conscious Rutgar, he opened the door to the Navigator, and then rushed to help them. When they were in the car, Lee gave Rutgar another shot to put him to sleep.

Rutgar's head was throbbing as the sedative wore off and the altitude didn't help him any. He looked around and knew that Toto wasn't with him, and he wasn't in Kansas any longer. This aircraft wasn't the penthouse. The operative in him knew he was in deep trouble and he struggled to get free of his restraints. But that would not happen.

A voice from behind him said, "Don't even try it. Those cuffs are carbon steel and unless you have a welding torch in your pocket and you're wearing a parachute, you're not going anywhere. Besides, we're at thirty-five thousand feet, so relax and enjoy the flight."

Rutgar rubbed his eyes, trying to clear the cobwebs. "Where are you taking me?"

Angelo had the same smile on his face as before. "It's a big secret, a surprise, so put your head back and relax. You'll find out where we're headed soon enough."

John W knew Sweeney was married, so he told Lee, who wasn't, to call Officer Helga Borman of the Berlin Police Department using the phone on the plane. When she got on the line, Lee told her to meet him at the airport. When she asked why, he said he was going to get her a promotion. She laughed. *These Americans*, she thought, *always joking*. "Silly man, how can you get me a promotion?"

"When we land, I'll walk off the plane with Rutgar Kleinst, alias Rutgar Keisel, handcuffed to me, and I'll hand him over to you. That should make you happy, right? He's still wanted for the murder of a police officer, isn't he?"

Helga's heart beat faster with the realization that bringing in Keisel *could* mean a promotion for her. Maybe this time she'd make sergeant. Lee cut her thoughts of a promotion short by speaking to her again.

"Make sure you bring a large police officer with you. I don't want this guy to pull any stunts and escape from you."

She thought about it for a moment. "You're right, of course. I'll take Rudolph with me." She was referring to Sgt. Rudolph Schmidt. He was six foot three inches and ex-military. "Don't worry, Keisel won't get away from us. If he even so much as tries to escape, I'll shoot him like the dog he is."

Lee laughed. Here was this beautiful 5'4" woman saying she would shoot Keisel if he tried to escape. "Okay. You convinced me. Now get going and meet me at the airport. Oh! One more thing."

"Yes?" she asked.

"When you get off duty today, you and I are going to have dinner together and we're going to enjoy the rest of the evening with you showing me the sights."

Her face flushed as she laughed. "I'd like that, very much," she said.

CHAPTER THIRTY-FIVE

Officer Helga Borman of the Berlin Police Department, accompanied by Sargent. Rudolph Schmidt took official control of Rutgar Keisel, aka Rutgar Kleinst, as soon as he stepped onto the tarmac in Germany. Helga became Chief Froedrick's star when she brought in the killer that was sought all over the world and whom now everyone in Germany knew was behind bars. The country had Helga Borman to thank for it. She owed Lee big time for allowing her to take the credit for Kleinst's capture. Whenever the two met, Lee and Helga discovered they enjoyed one another's company - and after Lee gave her Keisel as a gift-wrapped present, it made her a star. How could she refuse when he asked her to visit him in Arizona? She told Lee that as soon as things quieted down, she would take some vacation time, and that she looked forward to visiting him. Lee would leave Germany and he thought it was far too soon for him to be separated from her. He thought of telling John that he'd like to stay in Germany for another week, but then thought better of it. He'd have to wait until she came to America to see her.

Lee hated to admit it, but when he and Jason left Germany after their first visit, he found he missed her more than he cared to admit, but the one consolation was that ever since John Christo walked into his life, he could afford many things - even a high-class woman like Helga. He thought of everything that had endeared her to him. She was an outstanding police officer, had a bubbly personality and a positive attitude. Besides that, she was a beautiful woman and since money was no longer a problem, Lee fantasized about the various ways he would spend it on her. He'd take her out to the best night spots, see the best shows, eat in the finest restaurants, and maybe, if she were willing, some high-quality intimacy, if she felt about him as he did her. But it had to wait until she arrived in the States. He pushed these thoughts from his mind and smiled because he was still here in Germany and he had a dinner date tonight with this beautiful woman.

Two down, two and two to go, John told himself. His plan in capturing Rutgar Keisel had worked, and no one got hurt even when they turned him over to the German police. Chief Froedrick assured John that no one kills a police officer in Germany and won't pay for it.

"Don't worry, Mr. Christo; Keisel will spend the rest of his life in prison," he assured John. Now John set his sights on Number Three, Governor Wilson. He decided Jack McCormack would be last. He wanted to savor McCormack's descent into hell, and that was what John W. was planning for him.

John picked up Wilson's file and studied it, deciding on the best way to take him down. According to Jason's report on Governor Wilson, there was no mention of him having Dutch Henry and John W. Hardin imprisoned in the Gila Bend desert prison. After the explosion, the Governor thought he was safe from an investigation. After all, the explosion destroyed the prison, and there was nothing left to investigate. And besides, Wilson had controlled the investigation from behind the scenes. It was nothing more than a sham show he had to put on in order to close the case. How could anything go wrong when there was no way of producing any evidence, and no one knew what went on in that old prison or who the prisoners were? Wilson figured that time would soon forget.

John W. Harden and Lee Flowers were in a meeting deciding the Governor's fate. At the meeting was Timothy Suttor, his new corporate attorney and full-time legal council. John asked him to attend the meeting because the attorney had drawn up some legal papers that needed to be discussed and signed at the meeting. Sutter drew up Lee Flowers's statement, detailing everything Lee witnessed while at the prison, up to and including his being fired.

"Read the statement, Lee, and if you agree with it, sign it," Tim advised.

Lee knew what was in the document because they discussed it at length earlier. But he scanned each page and read one part over a second time because they worded it in legalize, and he had trouble understanding it. When he finished reading it, he signed it and handed it to the attorney. Sutter handed Lee another document to sign, this time as a witness. This document explained everything that happened to John W Hardin from the time he arrived at the prison until the explosion. It was important that Lee corroborate his story. This document was John's statement, and he signed it as John Wesley Hardin. Governor Holland Wilson was in for a surprise when he took the stand at the trial because he was going to be sandbagged. He did not know that John W. Hardin was still alive and the explosion hadn't killed him. It was time to take down Governor Wilson, but first there was one other thing to attend to.

John told Sutter that he didn't want to appear at the trial. Instead, he offered the court a video statement, and the written statements that Sutter drew up. He even instructed Lee to take his fingerprints on a dated and notarized police fingerprint card. The state of Arizona had John's prints on file. These new prints would prove beyond a doubt that the person in the video was John W. Hardin, and he was alive.

John converted a large room at the opposite end of the top floor into a video studio, complete with three JVC high definition state-of-the-art professional broadcast video cameras and a high definition-editing suite. He also bought himself clothes similar to what he wore when he worked for Mr. Hayes. They comprised a blue western shirt, dungarees, western belt and buckle, and a pair of inexpensive western boots. He shaved his face. He allowed his hair to fall in a wild tangle, which was how he wore it back then. When he sat down for the interview, he looked nothing like the suave millionaire he had since become. He needed to keep his two identities separate. No one could know that he was like Dr. Jekyll and Mr. Hyde; two different distinct personalities wearing the same body. If they did this right, no one would ever suspect that the two men were the same person.

He sat down in a plain chair in front of a black curtain. Three professional klieg lights glowed at different angles, illuminating him on all sides the result of a famous director who John hired for this one job. The director positioned the lights himself and then re-adjusted the lights when the test sample he viewed didn't satisfy him. A second test satisfied him, and he was ready to proceed with the interview. The director listened as Mr. Christo told him the effect he wanted. He nodded in agreement and told John he didn't want a canned response. What he was looking for were spontaneous answers from the questions that scrolled down the teleprompter. The director instructed John not to look into the camera, but to the person sitting in a chair to the left of the camera so it would appear to the audience that John was looking straight at them, answering their questions, and not reading from a teleprompter.

After the first few questions, John shook his head and motioned for the cameras to stop. He told the director, "Let's not use the teleprompter. Just ask your questions and I'll answer them. I just don't feel comfortable looking at words scrolling down a screen. It feels phony to me."

The director shook his head, and John thought he was disagreeing with him, but he smiled and said, "I like it. Without the teleprompter, you'll come off a lot more naturally. Take your seat, Mr. Christo, and let's get this show on the road. I have a good feeling about this video." The shoot was a success.

After John changed back into his business suit, he called Sutter into his office. "Tim, I want you to call a few top marketing companies and set up meetings with them. You'll represent me at the meeting." John started rattling off instructions. Sutter held up his hands, stopping him the way a referee does at a football game, signaling time-out. Then, Sutter reached over to the chair next to him and picked up his legal pad. With a nod, John resumed rattling off instructions and Sutter began jotting down notes. "You'll tell them you represent a very wealthy client who has taken an interest in a young man's plight and if this meeting is successful, I'm allowing you to hire them." He continued giving Sutter instructions for the next ten minutes. "Did you get all of that, Tim?"

Sutter read back the salient points. He got them all, which satisfied John. John was eager to get started, so he instructed Sutter that if he hired a marketing firm, then he could proceed with the publicity campaign. Meanwhile, the firm of Jacob and Nash was just as eager to close the deal. A wealthy client meant a healthy fee, so they scheduled a meeting for the next morning at 10 am.

CHAPTER THIRTY-SIX

John scrutinized and critiqued, then approved the first commercials and newspaper ads to be released to all the major national newspapers and media outlets. He picked up the phone. "Tim, everything looks good. Go ahead with the campaign. Tell the firm you hired they should get this out as soon as possible. Let them know that I'm paying them a lot of money to get an indictment on the Governor. Tell them to keep the ads running until he's arrested and put in prison."

The television commercials and the newspaper articles broke at the same time and they kept appearing with no respite. Then, Tim called a news conference and since it concerned a sitting Governor who was being accused of multiple crimes, he knew there would be a lot of questions. Everyone was aware of the relentless TV commercials and newspaper editorials that were blitzing the state. It not only aroused public interest in the Governor's response, it also alerted the major media outlets, who smelled a major story. They swarmed to Phoenix like locusts.

The Governor was served with a warrant to appear before a grand jury to see if the charges against him were warranted, and his arrest was imminent. At the hearing, the attorney for the plaintiff presented the court with evidence against Governor Holland Wilson to answer charges brought by a person known as John W. Hardin and another person known as Dutch Henry. The case was remanded to a federal judge, who could not overlook the compelling evidence presented at the hearing. He ordered Governor Wilson to stand trial before a jury for the stated offenses. Wilson was released on one million dollars bail. The trial was scheduled to start in three weeks. Tim was empowered by John W to hire any lawyers he felt necessary, in order to obtain a conviction.

"Hire the best and put together a dream team." That was

what Mr. Christo told Tim, and that's what he did. He hired a dream team. That dream team ultimately destroyed Governor Wilson's credibility. The facts were irrefutable and John W. Hardin's video testimony was especially effective when it was shown to the judge and the jury and everyone in the crowded courtroom, and ultimately everyone in the nation. To the media, the trial was *mana* from heaven. The judge allowed cameras in his courtroom, which captured the drama taking place in the courtroom. The dream team, through the power of the subpoena, had somehow obtained the Arizona transfer papers for one John W. Hardin to the Gila Bend prison, which by order of Governor Wilson had been re-opened to house besides John W. Hardin, one other prisoner: one Dutch Henry, an old prospector.

When Wilson was questioned as to why Hardin was sent to that prison, a prison that had been closed for over 50 years, the Governor had no answer to the question. Oh, he had an answer: a lame one, "The man was a convicted criminal, and deserved to spend time there." When asked what he was convicted of, the Governor had a litany of charges that spewed from his mouth. But when he was cross examined and was asked if he knew a certain Rutgar Keisel, also known as Rutgar Kleinst, who had agreed to testify against the Governor for consideration of waiver of the death sentence to life in prison, Wilson denied knowing Kleinst. John's attorneys presented pictures of Governor Wilson and Rutgar Kleinst taken by Jason Sweeney, a licensed private detective, based in New York City, which were placed into evidence. The pictures proved the Governor lied under oath. They showed the defendant and Mr. Kleinst together at many locations: seated at a table having dinner in a restaurant, attending a fundraising event, cheering on horses at a race track, and rooting for their team at a baseball game. Evidence was presented in the form of an affidavit, showing that Governor Wilson knowingly sent an innocent man to prison under the promise of a share in John Hardin's mine. Wilson's lawyer tried to have the affidavit thrown out of court, but the judge overruled him and let the affidavit stand as evidence. When that didn't work, the lawyer tried to shift the blame to McCormack, which was exactly what Hardin hoped he would do. Now McCormack was named by two sources and linked directly to the crime. The first source was Rutgar Keisel from his prison cell and the second was Holland Wilson from his testimony while on the witness stand. The Governor was sweating profusely in the air-conditioned courtroom. He hadn't expected the trial to go in this direction. When he thought it couldn't get any worse, Hardin's attorney then asked the sergeant-at-arms to play the recording. Wilson sat back in the chair, waiting for the trapdoor to open, and then wondered if this was instead the sound of the guillotine about to strike. The attorney ordered Wilson to listen to the recording.

"I want you to listen carefully and tell me if this is your voice on the phone." Wilson, the judge, jury, and everyone in the audience listened to the recording of the telephone conversation. It was riveting to hear what was said between the two men.

When the recording ended, Tim asked him, "Wasn't that you talking to Mr. Jack McCormack? And wasn't he asking you to give a Mr. Jenkins, a convicted drug dealer, a pardon? And wasn't that *you* saying it was too soon, that you'd have to wait until things cooled down before you could pardon him? And wasn't it you bragging to McCormack that you stole Mr. Dutch Henry's mine to keep for yourself?"

Wilson jumped up from his seat. "Lies! They're all lies! Someone is trying to frame me! Someone made this up! It's not me talking on the phone."

Jerry Sutphin was brought in to testify that he recorded the phone conversation that took place between the two men. Other experts were brought in to corroborate that the voice on the recording was in fact Holland Wilson's. When testimony for the day ended, Holland was held without bail and remanded to the court's prison. Before leaving the courtroom, he asked to speak to Andy Connelly, the Attorney General, and because he was still the governor, the court agreed. When informed of the Governor's request, the Attorney General agreed to speak to him.

Wilson appointed Connelly to the job. When they met in the holding cell, Wilson was desperate and didn't mince words. He got right to the point. "I'm in a world of trouble, Andy. You have to help me."

"I'd love to help you, Holland, but my hands are tied. You dug yourself a deep hole this time but I might be able to convince the court to give you a lighter sentence if you were to help me get Jack McCormack."

Wilson sat with his face resting in the palm of both his hands, not saying a word for a long moment. He might have been crying and he lifted his head and looked at the DA with red rimmed eyes. "Why not? I don't see Jack McCormack running here to help me. What do you need from me?" Wilson's eyes were watery and glistened as if he would begin to cry at any moment. "I can't spend time in jail, Andy. It would kill me. I'm not a young man. Please, you must help me. I have no one else to turn to." His eyes looked pleadingly at the man whom he had appointed to the Attorney General's job, waiting for a sign - any sign - that his friend would help him. Only, Holland Wilson had no friends - not any longer. Whatever friends he had were leaving him like rats leaving a sinking ship. But his friend Andy wouldn't tell Wilson that. He wanted Wilson to believe that he'd do his best to help him if he turned on Jack McCormack.

In reality, Andy couldn't do anything to help the Governor. However, Wilson, without realizing it, could help him become the next governor. "Don't worry, Holland. I'll do what I can do to help you, but you have to help me. I need to bring Jack McCormack to his knees. It's out now and everyone knows what kind of man he is. Now I need proof of his crimes so I can put him in prison where he belongs."

CHAPTER THIRTY-SEVEN

McCormack made a beeline to his hideaway, high in the mountains of Arizona, as soon as he heard news that they convicted Governor Holland Wilson of misuse of power and of swindling the state of Arizona of millions of dollars. Jack spent a few sleepless nights worrying about his imminent arrest until he thought of a solution to his problem. He did not know how young Hardin had survived the explosion, but if he, along with that guard Lee Flowers, were to vanish, there wouldn't be a witness left to testify against him. The problem was, he didn't know where Hardin was hiding. McCormack tried putting himself in Hardin's place. He concluded Hardin was being very careful, and since he was familiar with the desert, he must know of a good place to hide. That much was obvious, because no one knew where to find him.

McCormack decided he would hire the best detectives money could buy and have them locate Hardin. He read that Lee Flowers had accepted a job as chief of security for the young billionaire John Christo. Well, at least he would be easy to find and eliminate, but first he'd have to find John Hardin, and he did not know where he could be.

McCormack dug for gold in many countries and he always kept track of men he might have use for in the future. Men who would murder anyone he pointed his finger at, if the price was right. Since Kleinst was no longer here to do the tough jobs for him, it was necessary to oversee this job himself. At least if he had a hands-on role, he knew the job would get done. The men he had contacted were meeting him at a nondescript hotel in Tucson. It was fortunate for him that the Governor had handed him the 210 million dollar check before they arrested him, because the moment he had the check in his hands, he had rushed to the bank, cashed it, and then deposited it. Now that the money was in his account, his attorney advised him that no one could get at it and they wouldn't freeze his bank accounts until his trial. Jack contacted his friend, the Attorney General. McCormack knew Andy Donnelly had plans on becoming the next governor and Andy would do whatever he could to help Jack McCormack because he could use his money and his support.

It surprised John Christo when his secretary told him that Jack McCormack was holding for him on Line One. "Jack, how are you?"

"You know how I am. I have these god damned trumped-up charges leveled against me and I won't be able to do anything until I straighten this mess out. But that's not what I called you about. I have the rest of your money and I'd like to complete our deal as soon as possible, so I can take gold out of that mine. Right now, gold is about the only thing that would make me look good to my shareholders. That's why I'm kinda in a hurry. You can understand why I'm in a hurry, can't you?"

It was a good thing McCormack couldn't see the wide grin on John W's face. It was like the fox guarding the henhouse. He took a deep breath to keep the excitement from showing in his voice. "Sure, Jack. How do you want to handle it?"

"Would it be all right with you if I sent a courier with a bank check and you could give him the release we agreed upon and the map to the mine? Of course, my courier will be an attorney I've used in the past. It's not that I don't trust you, John, but since I can't be there, I have to have someone who could read and understand a legal document."

"A courier's no problem, Jack. I wish I could offer you more help, but they tied my hands. At least you'll have the mine. Once you bring the gold out, the news should please your stockholders."

"Good, I knew you'd understand. My attorney is Neil Kaufman, and he'll be at your office within the hour."

McCormack was feeling better now that the Lost Four Peaks Gold Mine would soon be his, and he rubbed his hands together in anticipation, picturing all the gold he'd soon be bringing out of that mine. Now it was time to get rid of a few loose ends. He'd telephoned the two men the previous week, and he expected them to walk through his front door any minute. The two men were Erica Schroeder and John Burns, and an associate of Jack's recommended them. McCormack's lucrative money offer convinced them to drop everything and fly to Arizona for this job, to eliminate the competition. McCormack called them from a pay phone in Tucson, where they couldn't trace the conversation back to him.

Burns had remarked, "We wouldn't think of flying to the United States while we're in the middle of an assignment, unless you paid us serious money."

McCormack smiled. He was in his element, negotiating with men like these. "How about whatever your usual fee is? I'll double it, if you drop everything and can be here by tomorrow. I'll even cover your expenses here and back. Well? Can I expect to see you tomorrow, or do I call someone else?"

The two men looked at each other, and then nodded, agreeing to accept the deal and fly to America for this job. "We'll get our gear together and take the first flight out."

McCormack had given them his name as "Mr. Peaks," after the mine he just bought, then his phone number and his address in that order.

"We'll need certain equipment after we arrive. Can you handle that for us?"

"Sure, mining equipment is easy to get. I know what tools you need and you can rely on me to have them here for you when we meet."

"What do you want us to do, Mr. Peaks?"

McCormack studied the two men. He sat back in the chair and said, "Why, I want you to kill a few men for me. That's the reason I asked you to fly here."

The two men looked at each other, and an unspoken message passed between them. They both stood and, without saying a word, walked to either side of the desk, searching for a listening device. Satisfied that there was none hidden in the desk, they examined the rest of the room. It impressed McCormack with the professionalism of the two operatives. They knew how to look for bugs and they knew where to look. They themselves had bugged offices, hotel rooms, and private homes many times in the past. When it satisfied them that the room was clean, they sat back down.

"Very impressive, gentlemen. It looks like I hired the right men for this job."

Burns said, "Not so fast. We haven't said we'd accept the job yet. We still have the little matter of our fee to discuss, which will be much more than what you offered us. Killing people wasn't part of the deal."

McCormack knew that once these men heard there would be killings, their price would go up. He had expected no less, and he was prepared for it. Double the salary was just to get them here. He will pay much more to keep from going to jail. McCormack broke the ice and asked them. "What is your usual price?"

This time Schroeder spoke. "We get $50,000.00 each for a job, but for a killing we each get an extra $100,000.00 for each person we kill. But we draw the line with women and children. We won't kill them."

McCormack knew that as well, so he reassured them, "There are no women or children involved. Just three men. Two of the men are rather close, but the third is in a prison in Germany."

"Germany?" Burns said, a little louder than he meant to. The price just went way the hell up. "Are you crazy? You expect us to kill a guy in a German prison?"

"Calm down until you see what I have for you." McCormack opened a drawer and pulled out some photos. Most of them were telephoto shots, but two were aerial pictures. "This is Stadelheim Prison, in Munich's Giesing district. It's one of the largest prisons in Germany. The man that you're going to eliminate is a guest at this prison. I know you can't get in the prison to do the job, and I wouldn't expect you to, even if you could. The cramped cells the prisoners stay in are small rooms with little room to stand, let alone walk. The prisoners are let out at 1 p.m. and allowed one hour to stretch their legs and exercise in the prison yard. A high wall with electrified razor wire surrounds the prison. You will not concern yourselves with any of that. There are hills surrounding the prison and if a sniper with a high-powered rifle and his spotter were to position themselves, they would have a clear shot at the target. My corporation has offices all over the globe, so it will be no problem securing the proper sniper rifle for you to use. I suggest that once you find your firing position in the hills surrounding the prison, you dig a hole a little way from where your position will be. Dig the hole prior to the killing, then on the way out of the hills you'll drop the gun in the hole and bury it, then cover it with leaves. Use gloves so there'll be no paraffin residue on your hands, and bury the gloves with the gun. Then get out of Germany. Once you accomplish that, the rest will be easy."

CHAPTER THIRTY-EIGHT

The courier studied the claim filed by John Christo, and then the document, which gave McCormack all rights and title to the mine. Satisfied the documents were legal, and the mine was now McCormack's, the courier handed John the certified check. John waited until the courier left, then he motioned to his secretary, who took the check and electronically deposited it into his bank account. The moment the check cleared, John W called for a meeting, which included Lee Flowers, Angelo Muscano, Jason Sweeney, Jerry Sutphin, and three of Sweeney's best men, including Dan Harlbager.

When they were all seated in his office, waiting for what he had to say, John W looked at each man. "Glad you men are here. I asked you men to come to this meeting because I have a strong feeling someone will pay us a visit soon. Jack McCormack can't afford to have witnesses showing up at his trial. Jerry, did you find out where he's hiding?"

"Yes, as soon as he smelled trouble, he left his headquarters and headed to his place in the mountains, which very few people know about. He would have been safe if he would have stayed there, but he only stayed there a few days and then he moved to another location. I didn't know where, and I didn't know why. I tried to think of where he would go. He's still the president of a large company, so it made sense to put a tap on his phone lines at his corporate headquarters and hope that he called. I figured he'd show up at his office, but when that didn't happen, I got a little nervous. The phone calls that came in and out of the building were not suspicious. Then I got lucky, because one of the phone calls was from Tucson and it was him.

"I traced the number to a hotel and since nothing much was happening at his headquarters, I drove to Tucson and visited that hotel. My luck held, because as soon as I arrived at the hotel, I spotted McCormack having breakfast in the dining room. Now that I found where he was staying, it wasn't hard to set up a recorder and tap the line in his room. John, you were right. He's worried about witnesses showing up at his trial because, with their testimony, they'd send him to prison and he can't allow that to happen. Give me a second to set up the recorder, and you'll hear the conversations for yourself." Sutphin played the recording and paused it every so often to explain the veiled references to weapons, names, and places. "McCormack instructed the two hitters who arrived from South Africa to meet him at his hotel. It made sense that since he was making all of those phone calls from the hotel, then it was safe to assume that he would remain in the hotel for the meeting. I didn't think he'd hold the meeting in his room, which was small and uncomfortable. I thought the dining room would be the likely place he'd discuss business. He referenced a meeting in the dining room in one phone call, and when I heard that, I made sure I got there first. I entered the dining room and just looked at it for a moment. It's a sizeable room, and I tried to guess which table he'd choose for a private meeting. I said to myself, where would I want to sit if I didn't want anyone to hear what I was saying? I scanned the room and then I noticed a private table in a little alcove in the room's rear. That would be the table I would pick. It was perfect for them because it afforded them the privacy they needed. It was also perfect for me, because it was right by the window with part of the table facing the street.

"If they sat at this table, I could either set up a parabolic mike outside and bounce it off the window to record what they were saying, or I could sit in the dining room and do it from there. Outside was problematic when I thought about it, because my mic would be in the open where people could see it, so I chose inside instead. I was hoping my assumption of him choosing this table was correct. If he picked another table, it would have been harder for me to record their conversation, but it wouldn't have been impossible. I watched from a position by the door and I was right. McCormack led his two mercs to the table. I thought he would choose. They had never seen me before, so once they were all seated I carried my flight bag containing my electronic gear and sat at a table far enough away from them where they wouldn't be suspicious, but close enough to point a powerful miniature directional mic designed to look like a cell phone at them. Now listen to what he discussed with them."

Sutphin pushed a button on his recorder. When the conversation started, everyone in the room sat, transfixed at what was being discussed.

"Shee-it," Lee said. "This guy's gonna go after Rutgar Kleinst while he's in prison, and kill him."

"Yeah," Angelo said to Lee. "And after Rutgar's dead, he's gonna come looking for you and John Hardin, once they figure out where he's hiding."

John tapped his desk with his fingers, listening to what Angelo had just said. "We'll let them think we don't know they're coming for us. Let them become complacent and they'll take the bait. Don't worry; they'll come hunting for us after they return from Germany. And when they do, they'll walk into our trap. But under no circumstance can we underestimate these men. They are professional killers. You all heard what they said. They have no qualms about killing someone, and it's all about the money. It reminds me of the story of a guy who wanted this beautiful woman, so he asked her, 'Would you sleep with me for a million dollars?' Her eyes lit up, and she replied, 'For a million dollars… yes, I would sleep with you.' The guy mulled her answer over for a minute, then he asked her, 'Would you sleep with me for a dollar?' "He had insulted her. 'A dollar?' she said. 'What kind of woman do you think I am?'

"He replied, 'We've just determined that - now we're just haggling over the price.'" Everyone got the point and smiled. "Well, it's the same with these guys. We know what men they are. They're just haggling over the price for each person they'll kill."

Sweeney interrupted him. "Do you want me to alert the German authorities that they'll try to assassinate Kleinst at their prison?"

John W shook his head. "Negative. Let them do my work for me. He's getting what he deserves. Jerry, I want you to keep on top of what's happening at McCormack's hotel. When these men return from Germany, I want to be ready for them. Once they land in Phoenix, they'll head to McCormack's, giving him an update, and then they'll discuss how they're going to kill us. Jason, I want you to stay in touch with Jerry.

"Jerry, do you have any two-way radios?"

Jerry nodded, reached into his flight bag, and took out what appeared to be a set of six small, simple radios. "After I've explained a few facts about them, I'll give each of you a radio. Don't let the looks of these radios fool you. They're designed to look simple. These radios look like RadioShack specials, but in fact, they are sophisticated units of technology straight out of our government's experimental laboratories. I have a friend who works as an electronic systems design engineer for the government in a top-secret laboratory deep under the ground in Virginia. And, when he designed and built the first thousand units, all with serial numbers, he added another six units without serial numbers for me. Gentlemen, these are the units."

Sweeney, being a detective, was interested in how sophisticated they were and their capability. "Why are these simple-looking radios so special, Jerry?"

"Well, once you press the 'talk' button, this baby hooks up to a satellite that will relay the call on a unique frequency to a receiver with a corresponding frequency and your party will hear you, wherever you are in the world. Look at the unit and you'll see seven buttons. The first six are for designated users. For example, if Lee has Unit Two, then I'll press two to talk to him and he'll be the only one who can speak to me, or hear what I'm saying to him. If I want to talk to you, then I'll press the two buttons corresponding to the persons I want to talk to. If I want to talk to all of you, then I press seven, and then I'll be speaking to up to six of you or as many of you who are carrying an activated phone. Also, unlike other phones, this one's signal can transmit through three inches of steel. All calls from these phones are encrypted, so you don't have to worry about anyone listening in. And, if you don't have a weapon and you face someone with one, move the button A to the B position, which is to the right. Then point this innocent-looking antenna at the person and press the power button. My buddy figured out a way to tap into the power grid of the satellite and download a power pulse that acts similar to a laser beam. It will hit the bad guy like a lightning bolt. But that's not all. You can use it repeatedly or until the unit powers down. Tests have shown that you could incapacitate up to ten people with this little guy. But I caution you not to use it unless it's to save your life."

Lee interrupted him. "Why is using it to save your life the only time we can use it?"

"This unit has a built in warning system which will alert the government that one of their units is being used that they can't account for. They will know the unit you've just used is tapping into the satellite power grid and they'll come looking for it and if you don't destroy it, they'll find it because the unit itself will lead them to you."

"What good is it, then?" Angelo asked.

"Good question, Angelo. I didn't say you couldn't use it. Use it if you have to, but if you use it as a weapon, then destroy it as soon as you've finished using it. If you must make a phone call after using it as a weapon, do it and then destroy this sucker fast. Hit it with a hammer or a rock, or throw it in a furnace, or run it over with your car, but make sure it's no longer working, because the sooner you get rid of it, the safer you'll be. The guys that made these babies are rather protective of them and they will hurt anyone who shouldn't have them. Remember, this is the finest radio on Earth and it poses no threat to you unless you use the weapon part of it. If you do, then it's a bullet aimed right at your head and you must destroy it first chance you get. I'm asking you, though. Try hard not to use this as a weapon. Use it only if you have no other option because these little babies are irreplaceable. I'd have to charge Mr. Christo a small fortune if you destroy one or more of them. Does that answer your questions? Any further questions?" He looked around the room, but there were no raised hands. "One more thing. These six satellite radios and my master radio all have frequencies unique unto themselves. They made these radios as a package of seven and none of the other government radios has a similar frequency, which means they cannot listen to our conversations. I just wanted to make that clear to you. Only we can hear one another, so don't be afraid to use them." He wrote each man's name and the number of the phone on his pad as he handed him a radio. "It's all yours, Mr. Christo. I'll make copies of who has what number phone and hand the list out to you and the guys."

"Good job, Jerry. Jason, make sure you keep in touch with Jerry. We need to stay ahead of these guys. You don't want them to surprise you. You could end up dead if you let your guard down."

CHAPTER THIRTY-NINE

It was cold in the hills behind the prison but neither heat nor cold affected the two men when they were on a mission. It was part of their job. But it went far beyond that. The two men met when they were inducted into the Navy SEAL program and were assigned as partners, and they remained partners, even after being thrown unceremoniously out of the SEAL's after they were discovered buying and selling drugs. They took the name of an old western TV show *Have Gun Will Travel*, only they named their company Have Guns Will Travel. With the plural on GUNS, they formed their own company. They placed ads in *Soldier of Fortune* magazine and the EU version of the same magazine, as well as *Guns and Ammo,* the world's most widely read magazine on that subject. The jobs came in slowly at first, but they found that word of mouth was the best form of advertising, and they soon had plenty of that. As long as the price was right, they didn't care what the job entailed. Kidnapping, intimidation, murder - it didn't matter to them. Their only rule was, they wouldn't take a job that involved women or children, but everything else remained on the table.

McCormack was right. He told them not to worry; that he'd have the tools they needed delivered to their hotel room in Germany within an hour after they checked in. Sure enough, a courier, unaware of what the box contained, delivered the package to their hotel room. He was surprised but pleased at the generous tip he was given, and he thanked the two men, smiling as he left, thinking this was his lucky day.

Schroeder opened the box and discovered to his delight that it contained a German Mauser 86SR, which fired a 7.62x51mm NATO (.308 Win) .300 Win. This was an upgraded Mauser SP66 and it featured a new bolt, and a different stock, which was ventilated to help dissipate heat from the barrel. It had a detachable box magazine, which held nine rounds; a useful feature for rapid reloads, in which they weren't interested. One shot would do the trick for them. This weapon was fun to shoot and accurate as hell. Burt could put a grouping of 5 shots in a silver dollar at 400 yards anywhere, at any time.

They were in the hills since before daybreak. They had scouted the terrain the day before because they didn't want to chance running into hikers on the way up. They didn't need witnesses describing two men fitting their description at the scene of the shooting, so they left early and got to their killing spot while it was still dark. Burt set up the tripod and positioned the weapon, while Eric dug the small trench about 100 feet down from where Burt was setting up the rifle.

"Is the hole dug and ready for the rifle?" Burt asked. "Once I put this guy down, we don't want to waste a minute getting our asses out of here."

"I know. Don't worry. It's all set. I even have branches and leaves set up beside the dirt. All you have to do is drop the rifle where I show you and I'll shovel the dirt in and bury the rifle fast like. Then I'll cover it with leaves and no one in the world will ever find it. Then you and me, we'll walk out of here like two tourists on a vacation." They smiled, sat back, and waited.

At 1 p.m. sharp, the door to the prison yard opened and the prisoners began to amble out the door in two's and three's. Eric was the spotter and he had his long-range binoculars up to his eyes, scanning the prisoners as they came through the door. "There he is. Get ready," Eric whispered loud enough for Burt to hear.

"Got him." Burt waited a split second for one of the men to get out of his line of fire before his finger applied pressure on the trigger and he began to squeeze. The loud crack of the cartridge caused the lead projectile to blow Kleinst's head apart. Eric saw the pink mist spray out like a large red fan from behind Kleinst's head.

"Bingo! He's down. Let's get the hell out of here." Burt picked the lone shell up from the ground and pulled the rifle off of the tripod, while Eric picked up and folded the tripod. Both men turned and ran down the sloping tree-lined incline, stopping only to drop the weapon, shell, and tripod into the shallow trench. Burt pulled off his gloves and threw them into the hole while Eric quickly shoveled dirt into it. Then he bent down and helped push the dirt into the hole. It just took two or three minutes for the hole to be completely filled with dirt, and then they covered the area with leaves and branches. They brushed themselves off as they walked down the hill.

Burt put out his hand to signal to stop, and they looked behind them to see if they could tell where they buried the weapon. He smiled and slapped his partner on the back and laughed. "It's impossible to tell where we buried it. Hell, even we'd have a hard time finding it." They were feeling good as they walked down the incline, because even if they were stopped and questioned they had no weapon and no paraffin residue on their hands. They made it to their rental car and then to their hotel without incident. This kill was easier than they had expected it to be.

CHAPTER FORTY

John and his key men were at their corporate headquarters in New York planning moves, and talking about how they would handle the two mercs when they came calling. It was like a game of chess. You couldn't move your chess piece until you knew what your opponent's move was going to be. John looked at his watch. He had a phone call to make. "Okay, guys, time for a break. I have an important call to make. Stay here and I'll be back in a few minutes."

He walked out to the lunchroom, took out his cell phone, and called Howard Fineman, his stockbroker. "Howard, it's John Christo. Listen carefully; I have a company I want you to monitor for me. It's called McCormack Mining Company, Inc. I have inside information that the stock will drop shortly like an anchor. It's currently trading at $23.00 a share, but I expect very shortly for it to drop dramatically, probably in the next few days. Keep your eyes on it. It will hit a dollar, and when it does, buy all you can, because at the end of that day, I want to own the company."

Fineman interrupted him. "Excuse me, Mr. Christo, but what makes you so sure the stock will go down?"

"There's going to be an announcement concerning the company sometime this week and it's not going to be positive. When that happens, trust me, the stock will drop. You have your instructions and you know what to do. Be ready to buy all the stock you can once it hits $1.00 and remember: I said to buy all you can. That's all you need to know. Once I'm the majority owner, the stock will climb higher than it is now."

A week before, McCormack had ordered his team to start mining the gold in the Four Peaks Gold Mine. He couldn't wait for his shareholders to see the profits they'd make from all the gold that would be taken out of this new mine because when they did, they'd back him during these hard times. But, in order for him to have their support, he knew he had to get the mine producing. This was the 21st Century, so he didn't have to worry about the Tonto Apache Indians attacking and killing his men like in the old days. Even with all of his problems, he was a happy man. Life was good: his two mercenaries would take care of the witnesses and his new mine would make his shareholders happy.

News was broadcast every five minutes by all of the major television stations about the assassination of Rutgar Keisel, also known as Rutgar Kleinst, and how the assassins got away cleanly. *One down and two to go,* McCormack thought to himself. He was pacing the floor like an expectant father waiting for the good news from his latest addition to his family of gold mines, the lost Four Peaks Gold Mine. He stopped pacing, sat down at his desk chair, and stared out his window, seeing nothing while deep in thought. He thought that all he had to do was to wait for the good news from the mine.. Then, his private phone suddenly rang, jolting him out of his reverie. He spun around, banging his knee on the underside of his desk as he reached for the phone. *Damn*, he thought, as he rubbed his knee with his left hand, while he put the phone to his ear with his right hand.

His anticipation of good news faded as he sat in stunned silence, his heart pounding as he listened to the bad news. He slowly put the phone down but didn't remember doing it. He was lost in thought, thinking of what he could do to extricate himself from this nightmare. He couldn't say why he did it, but he picked up the phone and mechanically dialed John Christo.

John had been waiting for this phone call. "Yes, Jack. How are you doing?"

Hearing Christo's voice snapped McCormack out of his malaise, and his temper, which he never could control, flared. His voice raged as he spoke into the phone. "Did you know the mine that you sold me was played out? There was no gold in that god damned mine. I'm ruined and it's all your fault."

John smiled but he was careful not to let his voice betray him. "Why, Jack, how could there not be gold in the mine? Didn't you have your assessor check the gold nuggets you found there?"

McCormack was too upset to question how John knew about the nuggets being tested. "Yes. Yes. He checked the gold."

"And?" John W asked him.

"And it tested very good, better than that in fact."

"So where's the problem, then?"

"There is no other gold in that mine, just a few nuggets. Now what am I going to tell my stockholders?"

"I don't know, Jack. But why did you call me? What did you expect me to do about it? Business is a gamble, surely you of all people know that, and you know what?"

"No. what?"

"The what is . . . I'm glad I followed my hunch and didn't get involved in the gold mining business."

McCormack shook his head. "You knew something, didn't you?"

"Now what could I possibly have known, Jack? The old man left me what he believed to be a map to a valuable gold mine, but according to you, the mine is worthless."

As soon as John W hung up the phone, he called the *Wall Street Journal* and asked to speak to a reporter. When the reporter got on the line, John W told him who he was, and warned him that if he wanted this story, John would have to remain anonymous. Since this was John Christo, the reclusive billionaire, on the phone, the reporter agreed to keep him anonymous. "Do you have a recorder, or a pen and pad handy because I'm about to make your career, because I'm going to give you the story of the year."

The reporter couldn't believe his luck. "Hold on a minute. I have a recorder in my desk. Give me a minute to set it up. My name is Adam Wainright, by the way and I'm a reporter for this paper."

John laughed. "I figured that, Adam."

Adam's face flushed red. "Well, I just started and . . .okay, I'm all set - anytime you're ready, Mr. Christo."

"I'm going to start at the beginning, Adam, so make sure your recorder is on." Christo spent the next hour telling Wainright everything, except that he was the prisoner who was held in the Gila Bend prison. The young reporter knew he was recording the scoop of a lifetime. At the same time, John W knew that by giving Wainright the story, he was planting the seed of McCormack's demise. When tomorrow's edition of the *Wall Street Journal* reached the newsstands, all of the other media outlets would pounce on the story and they would take it to the next level. When the reclusive billionaire finished telling his story, Wainright couldn't wait to get off the phone to write the story.

CHAPTER FORTY-ONE

"Good work, boys," a weary Jack McCormack said. "Get the last two men and you'll make me a happy man. In return, I'll make the two of you happy. All you have to do is finish the job."

Burt scratched his chin and said, "Well, you've told us where this fellow Lee is working, but you haven't told us anything about the Hardin guy. Do you know where we can find him?"

"No I don't. But my best guess is that they're holding him at one of John Christo's two buildings. One is in New York City and the other is in Phoenix. I've had a bit of a setback, fellas, so the sooner you can complete your assignment, the better it will be for me. Tell you what. Finish the job fast. Get these last two guys and I'll see to it that you guys split a million dollars between you." The two men's eyes lit up. These men never showed emotion in front of strangers; it was a sign of weakness. The only time they showed emotion was when they were alone, but this caught them by surprise and it showed on their faces. McCormack couldn't help but notice their reactions. He loosened his tie and unbuttoned the top button of his shirt. Then he added, "There's a catch to earning the million, guys. To earn it, you have to complete your assignment within two weeks. If it's not completed by then, your fee will revert to our original agreement. I think that's only fair. Don't you?"

The men looked at each other then at McCormack. "It's fair, Mr. McCormack, and we'll do our best to earn the money."

CHAPTER FORTY-TWO

Jerry Sutphin caught it all on tape and the men sitting in the room heard everything.

Jason Sweeney shook his head. "Whew, one million dollars to kill Lee and John Hardin. Hell, Lee, for that kind of money, I'd kill you myself."

Angelo chimed in, "You'd have to get in line, Jason, because I think I'd get there first." The men laughed as they listened to the tape. It felt like they were at the meeting and were part of the hunt. Only in this hunt, the hunted would set the traps to catch the hunters.

"Lee!" Christo called.

Lee turned to him. "Yes, Mr. Christo?"

"How many security men do we have on staff?"

"Four, besides me, sir."

"Good. Call the men who aren't working and tell them to report to work. I'd like to have as many men as possible working until we neutralize the mercs. The men you hired. Are they competent?"

Lee smiled. "I hired ex-military. These men are tough, experienced soldiers. I must have interviewed one hundred men, and I narrowed the field down to seven. I hired four men with the best qualifications and told them to report here on Monday at 7:30 am. Times are tough now and these men needed a job. I would have liked to have hired all seven, but I couldn't. Not right now. I told them I'd put their names on the top of my hiring list and call them when openings became available."

"Do your men have carry permits?"

"Not yet. I've sent their applications to the state and I'm waiting for their licenses to arrive.?"

"How about you, Lee? Do you have your carry permit yet?"

Lee smiled. "I sure do, Mr. Christo."

"Don't keep me guessing, Lee. Do you have a weapon on

you?"

Lee pulled his jacket aside and in a holster on his belt was a new Beretta Px4 Storm pistol. He pulled it out and removed the clip, then pulled the barrel back to release a round from the chamber. He handed the empty weapon to John W. "This weapon is the most advanced expression of technological and aesthetic features in a semiautomatic sidearm," he said.

John W looked the weapon over, examining every part. "What makes this gun so special, Lee?"

"Well, for one, I think it's built around a modular concept that you can adopt a pistol to different needs and modes of operations, without compromising on the reliability and performance of the world famous Beretta reputation." Lee held the weapon for all to see. "The Px4 Storm emphasizes power, ease of handling, performance and reliability. It comes in three calibers, but the 40 caliber is my choice for this job. Look at the frame. It's light, durable and made of modern thermoplastic technology through the use of techno polymer reinforced fiberglass. There's a lot more to this gun, like the interchangeability of parts, but I'm not here to give you guys a lecture on why I chose this gun. This is my gun of choice. I will say this, though. The Px4 Storm is the ideal firearm for law-enforcement use, as well as personal defense."

John W looked at Lee. "That explained the merits of this gun. Order one for each man. If they have their own weapons, tell them to leave them at home. They'll carry this weapon as the weapon of choice for the men and women in the company's security division."

Jason asked to see the gun, and Lee handed it to him. After examining it, he told Lee, "I like it. Could you order one for me and my men and we'll pay for it out of the money due to us?"

"Sounds good, Jason. Lee, include Jason and his men when you order weapons for our security people. And call the other three men and ask them to come in for another interview. Tell them we may have a job for them. Then ask them if they're willing to move. If we can't use them here, we'll send them to our New York office. The only problem I see is gaining carry licenses for them in New York City. New York City is tough with guns and gun permits. I'll have to see what our lawyers can do to expedite carry permits for our men. What's hard about it is when Rudy Giuliani was mayor, New York had 600 persons with permits, when Bloomberg became mayor, people with carry permits dropped to 400, so getting our men carry permits will not be easy, but there has to be a way to get them. I'll have Sutter look into it for us."

Sweeney waited until John W finished talking, then he said, "Look, Mr. Christo, why don't we preempt those two mercenaries?"

"Explain what you mean by preempting them."

"Well, we know their plans - thanks to Jerry here. So why don't we nab them at their hotel?"

"Do we know where they're staying?"

Sweeney nodded. "Affirmative. I have one of my agents, Dan Harlbager, tailing them. He's been on them ever since they left McCormack's place. Dan checks in with me every hour." Sweeney opened his attaché case, pulled out an envelope, and handed it to John W. "Dan took these pictures of the two men."

John W looked at the pictures. "These are excellent pictures, Jason. It helps to know what they look like." John passed them to Lee and told him to pass them to the others. As they handed the pictures around, John W's intercom beeped. "Yes. What is it, Monica?"

"The security men you hired have arrived."

"Give me five minutes, then send them in." John turned to Lee. "Looks like the men you've hired are here. Is there anything you want to say to me before Monica brings the men in?"

"Yeah, there is. Do you want to use the new men with those two mercenaries coming for us?"

"They're security men, aren't they?"

"Yes?"

"Well, let's use them, even if it's just to watch over our staff. I don't want any of the girls getting hurt. They're innocent bystanders, for god's sake. Sure. Why not use them?"

There was a knock on the door and Monica escorted the three new security men into the room. Monica announced the men as they stood by the desk, facing John.

"Gentlemen, I'd like to introduce the newest members of

your security team. Steve Daley, Anthony Armetta, and Tic Doosy."

John W smiled at the men and shook their hands. "Welcome aboard, gentlemen." He said to Doosy, "How'd you wind up with a name like 'Tic'?"

Tic smiled shyly and said, "Got it when I was in SEAL training. I never realized it, but instead of being a chick magnet, I'm a tick magnet. Those damned ticks just love me. I think I kept them off every other trainee because it seemed like I attracted every tick in the jungle. They all loved me - even their relatives loved me. Before you knew it, all the guys were referring to me as Tic… and the name stuck - just like the ticks."

Everyone who was in the room couldn't help laughing at the amusing way he described to them how he got the name Tic. John W liked these guys and he thought that Tic and the other two would be a good fit in their organization. John turned to Lee. "Lee, why don't you take the new men to the conference room and tell them what they just signed up for?"

CHAPTER FORTY-THREE

Harlbager arrived early in order to be certain that he'd find a parking spot close to the hotel entrance, but far enough away not to be seen by the two very cautious men. Dan watched as the two men exited the hotel and entered the hotel garage. He waited until their car pulled out, then he followed them at a safe distance so they wouldn't spot him.

Being vigilant had kept them alive, and by force of habit, Burt, who was driving, checked his rear-view mirror every few minutes. One mistake and it was over for them and they knew it. Burt always checked for the anomaly, the one thing that appeared out of place, the thing that shouldn't be there, but was. "Eric, look behind us. See that Ford Escape about three cars behind us?"

Eric took a casual peek out the back window. "Yeah, I see him. You think he's following us?"

"Yeah, I think he is. But to make sure, I'm going to go around the block and let's see if he follows us."

Eric nodded in agreement. "Okay, do it. But if he's following us, it means that we blew our cover. They know about us and if they know that, then they know we're coming for them."

Burt agreed. "Yeah, but if that's true, then how did they find out?"

"I don't know. But for a million bucks, I'm not gonna let that stop us. If we can pull this off, we won't have to work any longer. With this million and what we've saved, we could retire and go to one of those islands that you read about in books and live like kings."

"Yeah, but let's get back to reality for a minute. What are we going to do about the guy following us, if he is following us? We don't know for sure that he is."

"We will in a moment." Burt swung his car to his right,

made a right turn, and pulled to the curb. The two men watched as the car they thought was following them passed right by them and kept going. The two men looked at each other and then they both broke into grins.

"Guess I'm just getting paranoid in my old age," Burt said.

"Yeah, well, better to be paranoid than dead," Eric chimed in.

Dan was watching their car for any sign that they spotted him, and when he saw the man look out the back window, he knew they had made him. They verified his suspicions when the car lurched to the right and made a quick right turn. He was nervous when he made a right turn and followed them. He realized his fears when he saw the car pull to the curb. Dan had his confirmation, and he drove right past them. Dan was a cool customer, but these guys were pros and he knew he couldn't tail them by himself. He needed a coordinated team effort to pull this off. Dan zigzagged his way out of the city, taking different routes to make sure *he* wasn't being followed. He pulled into a gas station. While he gassed up, he called Jason and explained the situation to him. "You fellas better be on your toes. These guys may be on their way there right now."

Sweeney agreed. "Come on in, Dan, and we'll plan something different. Maybe arrange a little surprise party for them if they decide to drop by."

Dan topped the gas tank off and then drove straight to the office without stopping for the cup of coffee he craved. The two mercenaries, if they were coming, hadn't arrived yet. He stepped into the security office before heading to Christo's office and poured himself a needed cup of coffee. "You don't know how good this taste," he said. "I looked forward to a cup of excellent coffee all morning and never got the chance to have it." He took a sip, and then, being careful not to stain the gleaming wood finish on the new mahogany desk, he placed his cup on a magazine. Just as Dan was about to pour a second cup, John W, Lee, and the rest of the security team walked in, saving him the trip upstairs.

John W didn't waste words. "Bring me up to date on what happened this morning."

Jason explained everything, including his feeling that he

blew his cover. "These guys are pros. I know they spotted me while I followed them. It's just a hunch, but I've learned to trust my hunches."

"I agree. We should have had two or three cars following with an unfamiliar car taking up where the other left off. No matter how professional you are, it's hard to spot a tail when you look in your rear-view mirror and you don't see the car you were sure was following. Well, that's all water under the bridge now. Lee, have one of your men watch each entrance to the building."

Lee shook his head. "Don't have to do that, Mr. Christo. I've assigned two men to watch the monitors. We can see every entrance and exit on our security monitors, so anyone entering or leaving will be on camera and recorded."

John smiled. He felt a little silly, not thinking of that himself. "Good work, Lee. I forgot about our security cameras. That sure as hell saves us a lot of wasted energy. We'll camp out on the top floor. There's no one else on the top floor now that I've moved there, except my office and my secretaries. Is your name and office number on the wall registry when you enter the building, Lee?"

"Yes it is, Mr. Christo. I had it put there this morning like you asked me to."

"Good. Don't alert anyone working that something dangerous might happen. I don't want them to show any sign of nervousness or fear if these two guys show up. Sweeney, you'll have to answer the phones for the time being, because I'm gonna send my secretary Monica down to the mail room for a few days to train our new mail room clerk. This'll keep her out of harm's way just in case something bad happens."

CHAPTER FORTY-FOUR

The following morning, two very well-dressed men walked over to the wall registry and looked under "F" for Lee Flowers's name. "It's on the top floor. Are you up for this?"

"Locked and loaded with a silencer."

"Good! Me too. When we get up there, we ask for Mr. Flowers's office. As soon as we enter his office, we cap him and then get out of Dodge in a hurry."

"They're here," Lee told the men in the room. They bought two very expensive decorative screens for this occasion and they placed one on either side of John W.'s office. The office had Lee Flowers's name on the door. The two mercenaries missed this one important clue that could have saved them from misfortune. Lee Flowers's name was on the wrong door on the wrong floor. Lee was in charge of security and should have been in his regular office on the main floor. That went unnoticed by the two men, who planned on killing one of the two men they hired him to kill. Greed placed a shadow over the part of their brain that signaled caution when something wasn't right. They always listened to that warning, but today visions of dollar bills, and topless girls wearing colorful thongs on a remote island paradise clouded their judgment. They approached the pretty receptionist, giving her their most ingratiating smiles, and asked her if they might have five minutes alone with Mr. Flowers. The receptionist was Mrs. Susan Slay, a very capable operative of Jason Sweeney's. When she asked them about their business, they handed her their card, showing that they were security consultants. The card wasn't their usual "Have Guns Will Travel" card. Instead, the one they handed her said, "Security Consultants Inc."

The receptionist picked up the phone. "Mr. Flowers. Two gentlemen here asked if they could have five minutes of your time. They're security consultants, Mr. Flowers, and they said they have something for this company that they're sure you would be interested in."

Lee knew that this was a ploy, and he went along with it. Behind each curtain were two of the new security men Lee had hired. He armed them with the new Px4 Storm 40 caliber Berettas Lee had handed out to his security team at yesterday's briefing. Lee and his team knew that as soon as the door closed behind the receptionist, the two men would start blasting away with silenced pistols. They also knew that these men didn't want to alert the entire building that they had just assassinated someone, and that by using silenced pistols, they solved that problem.

Susan Slay ushered the two men into the office. "Mr. Flowers, these two men would like to speak to you about security issues. I'll leave you alone to discuss it."

She looked at Lee, then she gazed at the screen on her left, which was in her line of sight, but she saw nothing. As soon as the door closed, Lee ducked as the two men whipped out their guns and were about to kill him, but they instead a fuselage of bullets greeted them from men emerging from behind both screens. Eric was still alive, but fading fast. He looked up at Lee without seeing him. Eric smiled as a beautiful girl in a colorful thong pranced in front of him, beckoning for him to follow her. He looked out at the clear blue water and tried to follow her, but his exhaustion wouldn't allow his body to comply. *The sun*, he thought. *I'll just rest here for a while, then I'll find that pretty girl. That's what I'll do. I'll just rest for a while.* Then his eyes closed and everything faded to black as his heart stopped beating.

John W pressed the intercom button. "Susan, will you call the police, please?"

Later that evening, a reporter for the local news channel reported the story.

"The police questioned everyone on the top floor of the Christo building and it satisfied them that this was a case of attempted murder. The security men noticed two men entering the building on their security monitors, and they surprised the attackers. They followed the men to the top floor and surprised them just as they drew their weapons. They licensed the security

team to carry firearms, and they fired on the two assassins, killing them just as they were about to shoot Mr. Flowers. The reason for the attempted murders is not yet clear. But a plausible reason is that Mr. Flowers is to be a witness in a very important trial in November. The police are investigating if his being a witness had anything to do with today's attempt on his life. We will keep you updated and report the facts as they occur."

The following morning at 9 a.m., on the top floor of the Christo Building, His security team was in session. John looked at the men assembled in his conference room. "We have to act fast now that McCormack's two killers are no longer with us. He'll hire more killers if he hasn't done so already. We have to stop him before he does that."

Jason was curious. "What do you intend to do, Mr. Christo? You always seem to have some sort of plan in mind."

"Funny you should ask, Jason. Only this morning I checked on McCormack Industries International's stock and it had dropped when they announced that there was no gold in his new mine. He spent over a half billion dollars of stockholders' money and has nothing to show for it. If there was gold in that mine, they would have considered him a hero, but since there's none, he'll become the goat. His stock is now at $3.00 a share. I placed an option to buy all the shares in his company when it hits a dollar. I expect that to happen today or tomorrow, at the latest. When that happens, I'll arrange a meeting at the mine with Jack McCormack and John W. Hardin. He'll come if he knows John will be there. Maybe he'll spill the beans and talk when he discovers I now own his company. I want everything set up before we get there. We'll have microphones spread out throughout the mine at spaced intervals. Jerry, you'll handle that. If we can get a camera hidden somewhere in the mine to videotape what he says, that'll help. Jason, I want you to leak a story to the *Wall Street Journal* that the attempt on Lee's life was because he's scheduled to be a witness as McCormack's trial and that John W. Hardin is in hiding because he fears there will be an attempt on his life. That should make the stock drop in a hurry. Is everyone clear on what their assignments are?"

"What about me?" Lee asked.

"You go with Jerry. Help him set up his equipment, then go hang out with Persistent. Stay with him until I get there."

Both Jerry and Lee nodded. Jerry asked. "Any idea how long we'll have to stay there?"

"It shouldn't be long. Once they announce McCormack was behind the attempt on Lee's life, his company stock should drop like a rock."

When the men left the room, John W picked up the phone, called Persistent, and told him he would have company for a few days. Then he explained his plan to him.

Persistent loved every bit. "Good. That rascal is going to get what he deserves. And, oh boy," he said, sounding like Gabby Hayes. "I can't wait," he said, rubbing his hands together.

The following day, John received a phone call from his broker. "Congratulations, John. You are now the principal shareholder of McCormack Industries International, Inc. I bought you sixty-five percent of the company when the stock hits $1.00 this morning." John thanked him and hung up the phone. He didn't allow himself to show any outward emotion, but he was ecstatic. McCormack did not know he had just lost his company, so John W put a call in to Jack McCormack, using Jack's private number. It surprised McCormack when he found his caller was none other than John Christo.

"Jack, I have something you may be interested in."

McCormack's senses were telling him to hang up, but he said, "Go ahead. I'm listening."

"I know where John W. Hardin will be." He added, "He wants to talk to you. If you're interested in talking to him."

"Of course, I'm interested," McCormack blustered. Then he realized he was acting the fool by bellowing. He spoke in a more moderate tone. "Do you know what he wants to speak to me about?"

John W said, "I believe he wants to talk to you about the property he thinks you stole from him."

McCormack paced the floor of his office. "Look, Christo. I stole nothing from him. He had a worthless piece of property and I did his mother a favor by buying it from her. I gave her $125,000.00 for it, plus a home and property in Flagstaff. That's what happened. I don't know why he has it in for me."

John W kept his simmering temper in check and spoke to McCormack in an even, controlled tone. “He’d like to know why they sent him to prison for all those years when he was innocent of the crimes, they accused him of, Jack. Can you explain that to me?”

“Well, I have to admit, his going to jail was unfortunate. I didn’t mean for it to go that far. If him and his mother would have just been reasonable and allowed me to buy their property at a fair price without a hassle, then none of this would have happened.”

“Well, what do I tell John Hardin? Will you meet with him or not? Either way, it means nothing to me.”

McCormack thought for a moment, then he asked, “Where and when, John? Where does he want to meet me?”

“He wants to meet you at the Four Peaks Gold Mine.”

“Why there? That mine was the worst mistake of my life. I hate even thinking of going to that place.”

“Don’t ask me, Jack. That’s where he said he wants to meet you if you’re interested.”

Jack McCormack let out a deep breath and sighed in resignation. “All right. I’ll meet him at the mine whenever he wants.”

“He said he’d be there tomorrow morning.”

“Tomorrow morning? It’ll take me a good 2 to 3 hours to get there.”

John W smiled and said, “Well, you’d better leave early then.”

“All right. Tell him I’ll meet him there at 11 tomorrow morning.”

“Okay, but he wants you to come alone. Do not bring anyone with you because he’ll be watching from a vantage point where you won’t be able to see him, but he’ll see you.”

CHAPTER FORTY-FIVE

When Jack McCormack arrived at the mine, he knew he was no longer the principal shareholder of his company. Someone had bought all the shares at $1.00 a share. That finished Jack and he knew it. But he had one more card to play before he checked out. John W. Hardin wanted to meet him here, eh? Well, this mine would be the last place the punk kid ever visited. Jack carried a hand grenade in his jacket pocket and when he left the mine, he knew Hardin wouldn't, because when the grenade he was planning on lobbing at Hardin exploded, it would bury him under a ton of dirt and rock when the mountain came down on top of him. McCormack smiled, thinking of Hardin dead. Right now, he didn't care if he lived or died. This finished him and he knew it. Once the trial began and all the dirt came out about all the years he cheated and robbed people of their property, they would bury him. Not bury in dirt and rock, but bury him in a cage of iron and steel, and that was something he couldn't allow to happen. He'd rather die than have it come to that.

McCormack made the trip by helicopter to the mine. He told the pilot to remain with the chopper and he went alone to the mine, just as they instructed him to. It took a while for him to navigate the mountain path and make his way through the hidden cleft in the mountain. Once through the slit, giving him access to the valley on the other side, he made much better time. Upon arriving at the mine, he could see no one waiting for him. Nor was there any activity going on. He was alone. He walked along the narrow ledge leading to the mine, stepped through the entrance, and then went into the mine itself. "Is anyone here?" he shouted.

"Back here," a voice answered.

Jack McCormack walked toward the second chamber and when he stepped into it, he saw a figure sitting at a table.

"Come in, Mr. McCormack. You and I have a lot to talk about, don't we?"

McCormack's eyes opened wide, displaying small pupils surrounded by the whites of his eyes. The man looked as if he had seen a ghost. John W was wearing chinos, a western shirt and cowboy boots, and the wig he wore made his hair look as long as it was when Jack last saw him.

"How did you escape the explosions? Where have you been hiding? I'd like to know how you made it out of the desert. It's impossible for anyone to survive in that god forsaken heat without water. How did you do it?"

John W. Hardin sat there at the table, facing opposite Jack McCormack, and he was smiling. "That's my little secret, Jack, and one I don't feel like sharing with you. Maybe someday I'll tell you, but not now, not at this moment. But first things first, Jack." John W got up from his chair, walked around the small table, and asked McCormack to stand and open his jacket. Jack did as he was told. "Do I have to pat you down, Jack? Are you carrying a weapon?"

"No, I'm not carrying a gun."

"Okay, then we can talk without worrying about one of us getting shot in the middle of our little talk. I'd like you to explain to me why you did what you did to my mother and me. You lied, and you cheated. Your lies put me in prison where I languished for seven years, so please explain it to me so that I can understand it."

Jack nodded his head. "I know, I know. It was Rutgar who set you up. We found that the played-out mine on your property held a large hidden vein of pure gold, and I wanted it. When you were gone, I made a deal with your mother. I gave her $125,000.00 and some land and a home for her property."

"What about me, Jack? Why did I have to remain in that hellhole of a prison for seven years when you got what you wanted? Can you explain that to me?"

"That was Holland Wilson's doing, not mine. I had nothing to do with you remaining in prison. Wilson wanted the old man's gold mine, so he set him up just like he had you set up. You went before his judge, his court, in his state. You didn't stand a chance. Yes! I cheated you and your mother out of the gold mine on your property. I even sent Tom Jenkins to Hayes Real Estate to see that we got rid of you. But that poor sap fell in love with Hayes's daughter. Can you believe that? The jerk goes and falls in love. Then I hired those two supposed experts. The two mercenaries I sent to take care of Kleinst and when they killed him, I sent them after you and Flowers. But Christo outsmarted everyone, even those two killers. Did you know I offered them a million dollars to kill the three of you? No! Of course, you wouldn't; how could you?" He sat in the chair with his head down cradled in his hands. After getting all of this off of his chest, McCormack sat down in his seat, a beaten man. Then he looked up at John W. Hardin and said, "I'm a ruined man. That bastard Christo owns my company now. He bought the controlling interest in my company. When the shares dropped to $1.00, he bought it all." Jack was confused. "The guy's one of the richest men in the world. Why would he want my company?"

John W smiled at him. "Why, to destroy you, of course. Why else would he want your company?"

McCormack looked at John W now. This wasn't the same ignorant, unschooled lout he had framed and had put in prison. This was someone with intelligence and cunning. "Tell me something. Are you John W. Hardin?"

John said, "That's who I used to be."

McCormack didn't like the direction this conversation was heading in. "Used to be? That's who you used to be?"

"Yes, that's right. That's who I used to be."

McCormack blinked. "If that's who you used to be, then who are you now?" Almost before the words left his tongue, he knew the answer. "Christo. Jesus Christ. John Christo. I should have seen this one coming. Of course, Christo and John W. Hardin are the same. You son of a bitch… you think you're gonna get away with this? Well, I have another surprise for you. I told you the truth when I said I wasn't carrying a gun. But I have this. He took the hand grenade from his jacket pocket and pulled the pin. "I'm gonna take care of you myself. Say goodbye, John Hardin."

As McCormack raised his hand to throw the hand grenade, two shots rang out, and the grenade dropped to the ground. John

W rushed over, picked up the grenade, and flung it as fast and as far as he could into the third chamber. Seconds later, there was a resounding explosion.

"Are you all right, Mr. Christo?" Lee asked.

"Man, it's a good thing you were there. He surprised me with the grenade because I didn't expect he'd have a grenade with him. A gun, yeah! But a grenade, never. Shows you how wrong a guy can be. Like I said, it's a good thing we planned this out before we came here."

It filled the chamber they were in with dust particles and they had trouble seeing where they were going.

"The grenade didn't block our way out, did it?"

"No. The entrance to the first chamber is clear. Let's look at the damage the grenade did to the third chamber."

The two men walked over stones and rubble and made their way into the third chamber. "Holy mother of god. Will you look at that wall?" John shined his flashlight on the wall and he couldn't believe what he was seeing. "That's a gold vein, and it's covering the entire wall. The explosion must have uncovered it. I guess tomorrow I'll be having a press release and a stockholders' meeting.

CHAPTER FORTY-SIX

On a quiet sunny Sunday morning, Priscilla Bluestone answered her front door. It surprised her to see a handsome, elegantly dressed young man standing in her doorway. A large, black limousine with a driver standing by the open car door looked in her direction. "Yes. How can I help you?"

"I didn't mean to intrude, but would you be Priscilla Bluestone, by any chance?"

"Why, yes, I'm she."

"Would it be all right if I came in for just a few minutes? I have something that I think you'll approve of."

Her curiosity got the better of her. She looked at him once again, then her eyes roved over to the limousine and the uniformed driver. There was no danger here, so she invited the elegant young man in.

"Can I bring you something cold to drink?"

"A glass of water would be fine. Thank you."

Priscilla left the room to get a glass of water. When they were sat, John opened his attaché case and took out an envelope. Priscilla's eyes never left the envelope, wondering what it contained.

"I know times have been difficult for you, Mrs. Bluestone, but I think from this moment forward, everything will be better for you." John handed her a cashier's check for one million dollars. Priscilla had to lean back for fear of passing out. When she regained her composure, she asked what the check was for. "You allowed an old man to read your grandfather's diary. You will never realize how much that meant to the old man. He struck it rich, and he asked me to see that you received this money. Do you have questions, Mrs. Bluestone?"

"Who are you?"

"My name is John Christo, ma'am."

"John Christo, the billionaire?"

"Yes ma'am, that would be me."

Priscilla threw propriety out the window and put her arms around the tall young man, crying with joy. "Sorry, I didn't mean to get my tears on your nice jacket."

He smiled a genuine smile at a good woman that hadn't had too many breaks in life. "That's okay, ma'am. Here's my card. If you ever need anything, call me. That's my private number, so you'll have no trouble getting through to me." He kissed her on the cheek and then drove out of her life… gone, but never forgotten.

McCormack Mining International Inc. Stock skyrocketed to $75.00 a share when the story of the monstrous new gold strike at the Lost Four Peaks Gold Mine broke and John now owned 85% of the stock in the company. He coaxed Persistent Sam out of retirement. It bore the old man out of his mind, and he was looking for something to do. John put him in charge of the investigation of new mining sites. This old man was the pre-eminent expert in evaluating potential mines, and he proved to be worth his weight in gold. He could sniff the gold or silver in a mine. The ones that he selected were the ones that produced, and the ones that he turned down, were barren of precious minerals. He was so successful that to his delight, John W. made him a partner in the company. John W called for a meeting and asked Lee, Angelo, Jerry Sutphin, Jason Sweeney, and agent Dan Harlbager to make sure they attended. He would brook no excuse for anyone not being there.

After everyone had coffee and sat down, he began the meeting. "Lee, you have done everything I've asked for and then some. This company will grow and so will your duties. I'm giving you a raise to compensate you for your growing duties. From this moment on, you'll be making $250,000.00 a year. Angelo, since you're now part of the team, you'll be making $150,000.00 from now on." He looked at Jerry. "Jerry, do you like working for me?"

Jerry, not knowing why he was at this meeting, didn't know what to expect. But he answered, "Yes, Mr. Christo, I have to admit that I have enjoyed working for you. You're a fair man and you're easy to get along with."

Christo smiled. "Good, because I want to buy your company

and have you work full time for me. Figure out what your company is worth and let Lee know and I'll cut you a check. Put together your tax returns from the last three years and I'll pay you whatever you made during those three years plus a 25% raise. That should satisfy you."

Jerry was beaming. "It sure does, Mr. Christo. When do you want me to start work?"

"Work that out with Lee. But I think Monday would work for both of us." Then John turned and faced Sweeney. "Jason, I like the way you handle yourself. I want to buy your company and make it an international enterprise. I intend to make it another Black Water company, only better. Tell your staff that they'll all be getting raises. I don't want anyone working for me to lack for anything. Dan, that includes you. I was pleased with the way you took care of Jenkins and protected the ladies, so whatever you're making with Jason here, we'll double it." Then John told Sweeney, "That pretty little girl who worked as the receptionist impressed me. Let everyone in your company know that since they'll be working for me from now on, they all can expect a raise in salary, especially Susan what's-her-name."

"Slay. Susan Slay," Jason answered.

"Yes. Especially Susan Slay. The girl acted like a profession under trying circumstances and that impressed me. Tell her she's getting a 25% increase in salary. Now let's talk about you, Jason. What do you make a year, if you don't mind me asking?"

"I take out about $100,000.00 in salary before taxes."

"Well, suppose we give you $200,000.00 after taxes? Would that work for you?"

Jason smiled like the Cheshire Cat. "It sounds great to me, but - er, well."

"Spit it out, Jason. What's on your mind?"

For the first time since John W met him, Sweeney appeared nervous. "Well, it's not that I don't trust you, Mr. Christo, but is an employment contract part of this deal?"

"Of course it is, you dolt. You don't think I'd take your company and hang you out to dry like McCormack would? After all, you worked hard to build the company I'm buying from you and I want you protected. You'll still be running the company. And that goes for you too, Jerry." John W looked around the room at the smiling faces of these men. “Look guys. I’m not an idiot. I don’t just go around handing out money to just anybody. You guys are now a big part of my inner circle. I trust you men. When the chips were down, you performed admirably.”

As he was giving his little speech, he noticed the two new security men sitting in the rear, near the door. “And you two,” he said, pointing to them. “You guys are new here, but since I’m in a generous mood, handing out raises to everyone, I’m including you two. Lee, what are you paying these men?”

Lee didn’t hesitate in answering. “They’re earning $55,000.00 a year, plus bennies.”

John W shook his head. “That’s not enough money for these men to live on. Give them $80,000.00 a year, plus benefits.”

The two men broke out into smiles, and one whispered to the other. “I had a good feeling about this place when I first came here.”

John motioned to Lee to get his attention as he was talking to the two men.

“Yes, Mr. Christo?”

“The other men you hired. You might as well increase their salaries as well. We’ll be growing fast as a company now and I’ll need their loyalties if I’m to do what I have planned. Assign one man as Persistent’s assistant. In reality, he’ll be his bodyguard. It’ll be an excellent opportunity for the young man to get to pick Persistent’s mind and to grow with the company. All of you people in this room can expect to get rich as the companies grow. But I insist on loyalty.” His face contorted into a mask of hatred, and his voice conveyed a sinister tone. They knew that whatever he was about to say to them would be chilling. He spoke slow and his words carried the inflection of his message. “If I ever discover that one of you has betrayed me, I’ll see that you rot in hell. I’ll destroy you. It will be as though you never existed.” It was as if his words sucked all the air out of the room and they were sitting in a vacuum. The benevolent good man that they knew as John Christo had become the personification of evil. Evil for just that one moment, but that moment was enough. The message got through to everyone in that room and the men had a newfound respect for their boss, John Christo. John had to do what he did. He had to let them know that while he was a generous man, he was also a man who would destroy anyone who betrayed him. He spent seven years in prison on a trumped up charge and he swore he would never let that happen again. These men had to know what would happen to them if they ever betrayed his trust, so he laid down the ground rules that these men had to follow.

"Gentlemen," he said. "With me, there is no grey area. It's only black or white. Either you're with me one hundred percent or you are my enemy. I can't put it any simpler than that. Be loyal and I'll make all of you rich. Betray me and I'll destroy you. Simple, isn't it?"

The sleek black limo pulled to the curb in front of the Hayes Real Estate Company.

"Do you want me to come in with you, Mr. Christo?"

"No, Angelo. I just want to have a few words with Mr. Hayes. It won't take me long." John W opened the door, asked the receptionist if Mr. Hayes was in, and handed her his card. As soon as she told Hayes who was asking for him, his door opened and Hayes came rushing out.

"Mr. Christo. Please come into my office with me."

When they sat, John looked at him and said. "There's something I have to confess to you, Mr. Hayes."

"You, Mr. Christo, have something to confess to me?"

"Yes. Please don't interrupt me while I tell you a story." John W. Hardin explained everything that happened to him from the time they put him in jail until this moment.

"My God, boy. You've changed so much, I never would have recognized you. Not in a million years would I have recognized you."

"I couldn't take the chance on telling you before this. I didn't want McCormack to know that Mr. Christo was, in fact, John W. Hardin… at least not until I was ready for him to know. Money changes a man, Mr. Hayes. With money, I found the confidence I lacked when I was penniless. When I was free, I took a year off and traveled through Europe, hired a tutor who taught me etiquette. The clothes I bought were the best I could find. I learned how rich men dressed and acted, and I emulated them. I transformed myself like a chameleon and became John

Christo. Mr. Hayes, you have always shown my mother and me kindness, and I would like to return it. You should move your corporate offices into my building. You will manage my properties for me, plus you can run your business from there. After all, I'm not asking you to leave the state. I'm asking you to move from here and into my building. I want to do something for you so that you will never have to worry about anything ever again."

Hayes looked at John W and saw the young man he gave the property to and the memory caused a tear to trickle down the right side of his face. He turned as he wiped it with his hanky.

John waited for Hayes to get his emotions under control, and then he asked him, "Is Virginia still staying with her aunt?"

"Why, no? Now that McCormack is no longer a threat, she's back home."

John's heart leaped with anticipation. "Is she at home now?"

Hayes was smiling now. "Yes. Do you want me to call her for you?"

"No. I'd rather go there and surprise her."

"Well, she's been pining away for that young rascal, John W. Hardin, for seven years now. So I guess she'll still be there waiting for him."

John's heart leaped a little higher. "Gee, thanks, Mr. Hayes."

Hayes shook his head and smiled. Here was this sophisticated young billionaire, acting just like the kid he used to be. Hayes was enjoying the change in the boy. John W no longer was he wary of danger or treachery. He was among friends here and he could let his guard down, at least for the moment. Hayes watched him bound out of the office and get into his limo. He was heading to the girl he never stopped loving and who still loved him. Hayes couldn't resist. He picked up the phone and dialed his daughter. It looked as if he would attend his daughter's wedding at last.

For more about the author, future novels, and events, please visit.
WWW.CORSOBOOKS.COM

IF YOU ENJOYED THIS STORY, PLEASE LEAVE A REVIEW ABOUT YOUR EXPERIENCE.

All of Joe Corso's books are available online.

Also by Joe Corso

The Comeback
The Time Portal
Lafitte's Treasure
The Last Gun-shark
Gunfight in Abilene
The Revenge of John W
Shootout in Cheyenne
The Lone Jack Kid series
The Time Traveler series
The Starlight Club series
The Old Man and the King
Engine 24 Fire Stories series
Tommy Topper and the Pixie Princess

www.ingramcontent.com/pod-product-compliance
Lightning Source LLC
LaVergne TN
LVHW091038080826
845145LV00002B/547

* 9 7 8 0 5 7 8 1 1 3 4 6 3 *